YOU DISCOVERED THE
ISLAND OF PLEASURE IN
THE BESTSELLING NOVEL

NOW MEET A NEW GENERATION IN

BURT HIRSCHFELD

writes of the young, rich, and
restless crowd. The glamor crowd
whose money and style make love easy . . .
and whose desires make it dangerous.

Other Avon Books by
Burt Hirschfeld

FIRE ISLAND

Return To Fire Island

BURT HIRSCHFELD

 AVON
PUBLISHERS OF BARD, CAMELOT, DISCUS AND FLARE BOOKS

AVON BOOKS
A division of
The Hearst Corporation
1790 Broadway
New York, New York 10019

Copyright © 1984 by Burt Hirschfeld
Published by arrangement with the author
Library of Congress Catalog Card Number: 84-91070
ISBN: 0-380-88088-1

First Avon Printing, July, 1984

AVON TRADEMARK REG. U. S. PAT. OFF. AND IN
OTHER COUNTRIES, MARCA REGISTRADA, HECHO EN
U. S. A.

Printed in the U. S. A.

WFH 10 9 8 7 6 5 4 3 2 1

"There are two tragedies in life. One is not to get your heart's desire. The other is to get it."

—George Bernard Shaw

Fire Island.

A sandbar thirty-odd miles long rising out of the Atlantic, a buffer for Long Island and separated from it by the Great South Bay.

At its highest only forty feet above sea level, the island is never more than a half-mile wide, squeezing down to less than two hundred yards at one point. Ocean Beach, Dunewood, Robin's Rest, Fair Harbor, Seaview, Cherry Grove, The Pines, Water Island, Lonelyville, Kismet; each community is as distinct in personality as it is in name.

Automobiles are prohibited, and at certain times in certain communities, so are bicycles. A child's express wagon serves as the main form of transportation, especially for groceries. Shoes are seldom seen on the island, and sex and love are talked about with the same frequency with which they are enjoyed. A party is called a Sixish and begins at seven, and the perfect gin and tonic is as elusive as the Golden Fleece; tanning oneself is a cosmetic duty as well as an existential art form.

Most islanders appear only on weekends, groupers sharing a house; others stay the summer, those with access to unlimited amounts of money, or those so poor that money ceases to matter, or those free-spirited enough to ignore career and future. Life on Fire Island advances from indolence to lethargy, vibrating with activity yet going nowhere. The beautiful people—clever, successful, clutching at a choice slice of life—in residence from Memorial Day to Labor Day in the eternal quest for a magical return on their season in the sun on Fire Island . . .

Return To Fire Island

MEMORIAL
DAY

One

Cindy

The Mexican cock crowed in the night, and the American woman sat straight up in bed, startled out of a deep and disturbing dream, a dream that left her coated with chilling sweat and shivering in the oppressive, humid air. She reached for a cigarette and listened to the cock crow again; his voice was strangulated and penetrating, a protest against his destiny. He had been bred and trained to do battle against other aggressive chickens, to kill and thus win money for his master, eventually to die. A violent, bloody death was his heritage, as certain as the sunrise.

The American woman wondered if human life was much different. Always a struggle, always a fight, always pain and suffering, until death put an end to the uncertainty, to the anguish. How morbid, she accused herself, how full of self-pity. Still, the cock was fortunate; though his demise was inevitable, he remained unaware of his own mortality. People always carried with them the burden of their own terrifying vulnerability.

She fell back on the pillow and smoked and waited for

1

the next cry of the cock, wishing she were somewhere else,
wishing that she were different, that her life were different.
Her name was Cynthia Ashe, and she'd been raised in the
concrete canyons of New York, a product of the city's nervous impulses, the quick, jittery changes of direction, pos-
sessing the polished veneer of an urban being.

What was she doing here?

To avoid the answer, she dressed. She pulled on jeans
and a red T-shirt with the words BLACK FLIES slashing
across the front, a souvenir of a skiing weekend in New
Hampshire with a muscular young man whose name had
long ago faded away. Her feet protected by Buffalo-hide
sandals, she walked along a narrow dirt track. Ahead, the
sun pushed up over the horizon, spreading its soft, early
light over the hilly landscape. A family of pigs fell into
step at her heels and followed her for a while, then they
disappeared into the thick underbrush that lined the road.
A tethered goat bleated at her, straining to break free. Another day of waiting had arrived, bringing with it the
sense of foreboding, of loneliness, of impending loss. Like
that fighting cock, she longed to protest against the inevi-
tability of life—and of death.

Beyond the meager wood huts of the workers, with their
corrugated plastic roofs, the hillsides were cultivated. Coffee plants were shaded from the oncoming subtropical rays
of the sun by strategically placed banana trees. Too much
sunlight, Francesca had informed her two days ago—was it
only two days since she had arrived?—could ruin the tender beans, spoil an entire crop, subvert the fragile economy
of the coffee plantation.

Francesca was a willowy woman with the delicate features of an aristocrat, born to a Mexican mother and an
American father. Pacho, as the plantation was called, was
part of her legacy. She owned not only all those hills and
valleys and all those coffee beans, there was also the land
in Acapulco and the two luxury hotels that had been constructed on it, the furniture factory in Oaxaca, the tile factory in Dolores Hidalgo, the ceramic factory in Puebla, the
Volkswagen dealership in the capital city, the television

assembly plant in Nuevo Laredo. All this was hers. It had been suggested there was still more.

But it was to Pacho—just outside of Jalapa—that Francesca was most attached. Here, she liked to say, "I feel most Mexican, closest to my people." And it was to Pacho that she had brought Roy Ashe, Cindy's father, to Pacho where he had learned to live in isolated splendor, cared for by servants, shielded by traditions of courtliness and class, protected by inherited wealth and status, removed from the temptations and the terrors of his former life.

"Now I got everything I want," Roy had once gloated to Cindy about Francesca, about Pacho. "I got a good-looking woman, all the money in the world, and an army of peasants who can't wait to snap shit when I tell them to."

Cindy wasn't buying. Roy's true habitat was among hordes of city people, caught up in constant activity, in competition, wheeling and dealing, proving himself over and over again, battling against the shifting loyalties and fortunes, never satisfied with his lot. Hungry always, that was Roy, caught up in the *game*, pitting himself against enemies, real and imagined.

Roy was the father she had come to know too well. And not at all. A skittery mass of contradictions and paradoxes, a man dancing on the fringes of whatever society he found himself in, never belonging anywhere, certainly never belonging to anyone.

Never intimacy, she reminded herself. Not with Roy. No loving exchanges. No gentle, compassionate moments. No lingering warmth. A widening gulf had separated Roy and Cindy from the time she was a toddler. She thought of him as Roy Ashe, a feisty bantam of a man, full of bluff and bluster, never as a loving father, which he had never, never been.

What was she doing here? She had come to preside over the death of her father.

Damn, damn, damn you, Roy Ashe.

She retraced her steps toward the big house. A wrinkled, brown woman crouched at the roadside in front of her shack; she was making tacos by hand, baking them in a

crude stone oven. She smiled shyly at Cindy, and Cindy
smiled back. It was a generous smile, asking nothing, expecting nothing.

Cindy paused, ran her fingers through the soft golden
curls that sprang out from around her finely shaped head.
She looked younger than her thirty years with the strong
well-formed body of an athlete. Her hazel eyes were wide
and observant, and under a mouth sculpted and sensual,
her chin was rounded and firm. She smiled again before
moving on, aware of how strange she must appear to the
small brown woman, like a creature from another world.

Back at Pacho she was served breakfast in the small din-
ing room, now warmed by a crackling blaze in the stone
fireplace. Freshly squeezed orange juice in a tall glass,
huevos rancheros and strong *café con leche* in a thick blue-
and-white ceramic mug. She concentrated on the food and
refused to consider life beyond this day. She remained in
place, lingering over a second cup of coffee, postponing
what lay ahead. Finally she left the table and went along
the covered gallery past the garden with its stunted trees
and bougainvillaea trailing up the pillars, the potted
plants still wet from their morning watering. In the eaves,
a hundred pigeons cooed and fluttered. At Roy's door, she
knocked and entered. The nurse, as if anticipating her arrival, was already standing, a subservient expression on
her bony face. "*Buenos días,* Senora Ashe."

"Senorita," Cindy corrected automatically. Her eyes
went to Roy, lying quietly in the double bed, a man who
hated to sleep alone, looking diminished, shrunken; even
in his sleep, it was clear he was a man who had always
yearned to be tall, to be a big man. Cindy stood at his side
and soon his eyes fluttered and opened.

"Hey, kiddo," he managed. "Looking good."

She kissed him lightly on the forehead. "You don't have
to talk."

"Ah," he breathed with satisfaction. "You smell fine."

She summoned up a bright smile. "Coconut soap and
water. You've got more color this morning."

"Yeah. Maybe. Inside I feel pale, damned pale. Rotten,
in fact."

Cindy glanced at the nurse, who shrugged and left the room. Cindy wanted to go after her, berate her, rail at her professional disinterest. "This is still a human being!" she longed to cry. "A man to be treated with respect and concern." Instead, she smiled down at her father and took his hand, withered and clawlike.

"Definitely more color," she said. "Looking much better, I'd say."

He grimaced. "Never kid a kidder, kiddo. This is it for me." He stiffened and set himself against the pain, the small body arching, his jaw clenched. His fingers closed tightly on her hand, and she was surprised at the strength he managed to exert. Then it passed and he fell back, breathing hard. The stench of death was heavy and foul.

Cindy wiped the sweat from his brow. "Shall I get the nurse?"

"Forget it. She's useless as tits on a boar."

"She'll give you something for the pain."

"Don't want anything. It's better when it hurts—that's how I know that I'm still alive."

"You're going to get better."

"Don't make book on it." Suddenly the feistiness was gone from his voice. "What are you here for? Go away."

"I'm your daughter and you're sick."

"Francesca called you. She wasn't supposed to do that."

"She was right to call."

"How long have you been here?"

"A couple of days."

He frowned. "Too damn long. Don't waste your time. Get out, go somewhere and have a good time. If it were you down here instead, I'd split in a minute, believe me."

"No, you wouldn't, Roy." Why couldn't she call him "Father"? Even now she couldn't hold him and tell him how much she loved him, in spite of everything. Why couldn't he . . . ?

"The hell you say. Nobody likes being around a dying man."

"Don't say that."

"It's okay, kiddo. I mean, what the hell, it's not that I want to die, but there you are. Nobody asked if I was ready,

not a damn soul asked me. They never do, do they? You believe in God, kiddo? In heaven and hell? I never have and I
don't now. I'm going out the way I lived, full of piss and
vinegar. The thing is, how'd I get here so quickly? I mean,
even when it was lousy, it was a great life. Not that I had
any plans for the future. I just wanted to repeat most of
what I'd already done."

"Hush, don't exert yourself."

"You know me, I'm no angel. Never have been. If there's
a heaven, I'm going to have a hell of a time talking my way
inside. But what the hell, they can't blame a man for trying, can they?" His eyes rolled in their sockets, located her
again, and grew brighter. "How's Maggie?"

"It's been a while since I saw her. She's all right."

"Would've been okay to see her again, not that I expected her to come."

Cindy made no reply.

"Not that I blame her," he said. "Hell, your mother's got
her own life to lead. How's she doing?"

"I haven't any idea. I've been living in California. Santa
Barbara."

"Santa Barbara, that's nice. On the water? I miss the
ocean. Funny, I never thought about it before—missing the
ocean, I mean. The smell of it, the sound of it, the way it
gets when a storm blows up. Those summers on Fire Island
were really great. They were the best. I loved those summers. What do you do with yourself in Santa Barbara,
kiddo?"

"Not much, Roy."

His hand tightened, suddenly strong. "Tell me."

"I work in a small art gallery. I manage it, sell a few
paintings. That's all."

"Sounds okay. What else?"

"Nothing else, Roy. Nothing else."

"Married yet?"

"No, not yet."

"Got a friend? A guy?"

"Nobody special, Roy."

"Just like me, playing the field. Never was good husband material. A bumblebee, that's what I was, taking

honey wherever I could find it." He laughed at that and
soon began to cough; it was a dry, racking, painful sound.
She helped him sip water through a straw until his coughing subsided. The light in his eyes dimmed, but he still
clung to her hand. "Francesca's been good to me. Worth a
fortune, that woman, a fortune. Took care of me when I
was down and out. After the trial, nobody in New York
would touch me. All my friends. Neil, Oscar Morrison, all
my pals—turned their backs. What the hell, look out for
yourself, I always said. Can't blame 'em for taking care of
number one." The coughing started again. "Oh, Jesus,
that hurts. There, it's better now.

"Tell me about Maggie. Never another woman like Maggie, not for me, anyway. Everything about her was custom-
made. The way she looked, the way she was built. If
Brooks Brothers made girls to order, Maggie would have
been top of the line. A button-down lady. I faked her out,
you know, made her believe I was better than I ever was or
could be. Should've been taller, that was my trouble. Just
a couple of inches. Oh, Jesus! God Almighty, the pain!"

"I'll get the nurse."

"No, don't leave me. Please, turn on the light. It gets
dark so quickly down here. Why does it get dark so soon?
Only thing I was ever sorry about . . ." His voice curled up
into a whisper, then ceased.

"Roy," she said. "Oh, Roy . . ." She called for the nurse,
and when the woman failed to appear, she screamed. The
nurse materialized, a disapproving expression on her face.
She took Roy's pulse, listened for his heartbeat, peered
into his eyes.

"Es muerte," she said to herself without emotion. To
Cindy, she spoke in English: "He is dead."

After the funeral, Francesca took Cindy to the airport.
They drove out of Pacho along a track made of crushed
yellow stone, advancing slowly past clusters of native
huts where smoke rose from the cooking fires, until they
reached the main road.

"I'm glad you could come," Francesca said. "He expected no one. He insisted that he had cut himself off from everybody, from his past."

"I suppose he did."

"But he missed it; his old life, that is."

"You were kind to him. He cared for you."

"We had a need for each other. A pragmatic arrangement. He wanted so much to be rich, to have power. I was able to supply the money, but the power never came. You do not mind, I hope, that I buried him at Pacho? It will be a comfort to me, having him near." A hint of anxiety could be detected in Francesca's aristocratic tone.

"Pacho was more of a home than he truly ever had before."

"Someday, perhaps you will come and visit?"

Cindy answered softly, "I couldn't let him die without some family near."

"I understand. You have your own life to pursue now. You will return to Santa Barbara?"

"I don't think so."

"Where will you go?"

"Back home," Cindy said, the words surprising her. "To where I belong."

Two

Neil

Neil Morgan stepped out of the shower in his suite at the Beverly Hills Hotel and vigorously toweled himself dry. His skin tingled, and he felt charged with energy and ambition, as if he were starting in all over again. Neil Morgan was a man who believed in keeping fit, in exercise, in proper diet, in keeping the poisons of contemporary life out of his system: no tobacco, no alcohol, no drugs.

He checked himself in the mirror. The morning's shave was holding; only a faint shadow lined his jaw, giving him a slightly threatening look. He appeared almost dangerous, a man liable to do something unexpected, even violent. Still, in the harsh light of the bathroom, there was a bit less color in his face than he would have liked, and a certain suggestion of slackness at his throat; in the mirror his eyes looked wet, he thought, somehow diffused. He shrugged it all away; other men showed the evidence of their years, not him. Other men allowed themselves to get fat and soft, not him. Other men lost the drive and power of their youth, not him.

He straightened up and lifted his chin. The image he

saw in the glass suited him. A tall man with a trim, firm chest and a flat—almost flat—belly. True, his hair was salted with gray, but he still possessed all his hair, a thick, lustrous growth, fashionably trimmed over his ears and at the back of his neck. Tennis, running, bicycling; no one he knew was in better physical condition. No one who didn't know better would believe he was past fifty. No one.

In the tiny kitchen, he swallowed five hundred milligrams of Vitamin E and a thousand of Vitamin C, washing them down with orange juice. Wearing only a long silk dressing robe, he went into the living room to relax. And to wait. He took much satisfaction in his cleanliness, his fine physique, who he was, and the way he looked.

Neil Morgan, independent motion picture producer with nine feature films under his belt. Admittedly, he had not achieved the eminence of Coppola or George Lucas, but he was successful and rich, having attained everything he'd ever wanted. Everything. Not that he intended to rest on his laurels, far from it. He was just coming into his prime in so many ways, *peaking,* and there was so much more he wanted to accomplish.

This trip to Los Angeles had been a good move. All the studios were in the market for new material, and he had come well prepared: a well-known novel, complete with a script and a preliminary budget, plus a personal track record of substance.

Any number of people had told him Tom Parson's new novel would translate into an exciting and popular movie. An adventure story with two of the most attractive characters since Scarlett O'Hara and Rhett Butler, it was a surefire hit project. He knew for a fact that Spielberg had tried to buy it and that Burt Reynolds was interested in it as a vehicle for himself. But he had gotten there first, buying it out from under all of them. That is, a one-year option. It had cost him twenty-five thousand dollars, more than he wanted to put up, but in this case, necessary. The book was a natural for film, loaded with action, conflict, and colorful, sexy characters. A can't-miss property.

Oh, sure, Universal and MGM and one or two other studios had turned him down. But he wasn't discouraged. The meeting with Larry MacDonald that afternoon had gone well. MacDonald owned his own studio, had his own distribution setup and access to unlimited funds. He was a man of taste and courage, a man with an appreciation for good literature who understood that Parson's book was a hot property. No committee decisions for MacDonald; he could make up his own mind and had promised to get back to Neil within twenty-four hours. This time tomorrow, the deal would be made. Neil could return to New York with financing and distribution set; he would be free to arrange for production facilities in the East; the Astoria Studios were his first choice. Maybe Sidney Lumet to direct and maybe Reynolds for the male lead. If Burt wasn't too unreasonable about his fee. With luck, shooting could commence in the fall.

That thought pleased him. It would allow him to get all the preproduction work out of the way over the summer, allow him to spend his weekends with Susan on Fire Island. Once again, things were going his way.

Neil took a great deal of pride in his accomplishments. And why not? After all, a man was measured by what he had done, and Neil Morgan had done more than most men. Much more. More than his own father, for example. He had earned more money, had transformed himself into a man of importance with a reputation to the makers and breakers on both coasts, advanced to a higher level of society. He had turned himself into someone to be envied and admired. Absolutely.

A knock drew him to the door. This would be Cookie. He straightened the dressing gown and admitted her, a welcoming smile splitting his craggy face.

She was a stunning woman, tall and shapely, with long dark hair that fell over her shoulders in gentle waves as she moved. She offered her cheek for a demure kiss and looped her arm in his, one full breast pressing against him.

"So good to see you again, Neil."

"I'm glad you could come."

"Are you having a successful visit?" She moved ahead of him, one long leg reaching after the other, her fine, round hips following in a slow, provocative swing.

"Better than I hoped for, Cookie. I'm about to close a big deal. A major picture with two top-name stars. What would you say to Reynolds and maybe Diane Keaton?"

"I love Burt, I really do. But Keaton"—she made a face—"a little too . . ." She reached for the right word. "Too refined, if you get my meaning."

"You think so? Well, maybe you're right. I'm considering Dyan Cannon also."

"Sounds like an exciting project, Neil." She removed her jacket and folded it carefully across the back of a chair. Very deliberately, she began to unbutton her blouse. "I prefer dark-haired women myself. Someone like Jackie Bisset, for example."

He felt his heart begin to race. "I'll consider it. You remind me of Bisset, Cookie. You should be in pictures; you're as beautiful as any of them."

"I gave up on that the year after I arrived in Los Angeles. Acting's such an uncertain way of life. I have always required security, steadiness of income, control over my own future."

"I understand." He sat back down on the couch and watched her. Her breasts were incredible, pale and large with large pink nipples, already erect. She smiled his way, a gentle smile, full of promise and affection. Very carefully, she stepped out of her skirt, put it aside. Without haste, she worked off her panty hose until she stood naked before him. The smile on her mouth now was a challenge, an invitation, a clear indication of her simmering sexuality.

"I hope you still approve, Neil."

"It's been so long—"

"Almost two years."

"I'd forgotten what you looked like."

She paraded before him with the same grace and haughty confidence a model on a runway would display. Her breasts swayed in counterpoint to every stride. She pivoted, displayed her rear to him, and came slowly about. "Any complaints?"

"Fantastic. Not a blemish, not a mark. You're so young."

"I'm only twenty-two."

"You could be my daughter."

"Shall I call you Daddy?" She advanced toward him, thighs rubbing smoothly against each other. "You like what you see?" She crouched in front of him, reaching out. "Oh, yes, you do like me, don't you? See how much you like me! How big and hard you are."

"You really think I'm big?"

"No one's bigger."

"No one?"

"Not *even* as big, Daddy."

"You've seen plenty of others, haven't you?"

She spread the dressing robe and bent over him.

"I'm not ready yet."

"I'm sure I can do something about that. What a lovely tool you have . . ." She bent lower. "Feels so good, tastes so fine . . ."

"Ah, that's good."

"We aim to please."

"Don't stop."

"I wouldn't do a nasty thing like that."

"Nobody's as good at this as you are."

"Thank you, sir."

"You must really enjoy doing it."

"Nothing could be finer," she crooned.

"It turns you on, sucking cock?"

"Your cock turns me on."

"More than someone else's cock?"

"Much more."

"Tell me why."

"Because it's yours."

"Go on."

"Because it's so hard, so big, so beautiful."

"You've done it a lot?"

She laughed softly, tongue working down to his testicles and back again. "Every chance I get."

"How many men?"

"All together? I don't know."

"Hundreds?"

"Thousands."

"That many?"

"More."

"And always good for you?"

"Always."

"Tell me what excites you most."

"Seeing a man's cock for the first time. Someone I've never done before."

"It makes you hot?"

"Wild."

"Tell me."

"I want it. I want it in my hands. I want to kiss it, to lick it, I want it in my mouth, to make it come, to fill up my mouth, to swallow him. The way I'm going to do you now."

"Oh, yes, please."

Then: "What's wrong?"

"I don't know."

"Is there something I can do?"

"Give me a little time."

"Sure, sweetie. Only I don't have all afternoon. You know how it is, time is money."

"Right. A minute or so. This never happened before."

"Never?"

"What do you mean? Of course not. What kind of a man do you think I am?"

"Let me try again."

"That's all right."

"I want you to get your money's worth."

"Forget it."

"It happens to everybody, you know."

"Not to me, not to Neil Morgan."

"Shall I try again?"

"Forget it. It's just that I've got too much on my mind."

"Sure, I understand." She stood up, expertly maneuvered her way into the panty hose. "You've been working too hard."

"Exactly, the press of business. There are millions involved."

"I understand." The skirt went on next, and then the blouse. She stepped into her shoes.

"Money's on the table."

"You're a very generous man. Say so and I'll hang around for another ten minutes, give it one last chance."

"That's very kind of you, but I've got some calls to make."

"Business, right?"

"Right."

At the door, he kissed her cheek. "Thanks for coming," he said.

"You'll call me? I so look forward to these little visits."

"First chance I get."

Alone, he swore silently at himself. Why had he wasted his time, his money? This shouldn't be happening, not to him. Tension, he told himself. He was under continuous stress from sea to shining sea. He laughed at the image. After all, tension came with his position, so much responsibility, so many people depending on him. A little time off for bad behavior and matters would return to normal. A brief vacation from women, from sex; he didn't need any more pressure. Forget about Cookie and all the others. Just forget . . .

Three

Nick

Nick Danning ran around the Central Park reservoir with the effortless ease of a professional athlete, which he had once been. His legs were lean, swelling at the thigh with long, heavy muscles. His arms were strong, his shoulders wide, his stomach flat, showing only the slightest beginnings of softness. He was a tall man with a faintly ironic expression on his angular face, a mischievous look in his hooded eyes as he glanced at the man alongside, trying so hard to keep up. He stepped up his pace one full notch and listened to Kolodny's harsh breathing.

In contrast to Danning, Kolodny appeared shorter than he was, and thicker through the torso. Although they were about the same age, Kolodny seemed younger, somehow vaguely immature, rather than boyish. He ran hard, struggling for breath.

"Come on," he gasped. "What've you got to lose?"

"The time of my life."

"Is the sporting goods business so good?"

"I've got something going with the networks."

"I know," Kolodny said, short legs pumping faster in or-

der to keep up. "You told me. Color man for the National
Football League. Okay, okay. I hope you get it, pal. I want
it for you, as much as you want it. But Fire Island isn't
Namibia or Katmandu. It's only a couple of hours away, a
phone call away. Have a good time."

"The entire summer? I never spent a summer in one
place before. When I played ball, summers were for training camp, exhibitions."

"Give yourself a break. Stay only weekends or all the
time."

Danning moved ahead. "I don't know," he said.

Kolodny exerted all his strength to catch up. "What's
not to know?" He puffed. "Sun, sand, sex, and swimming.
Did I say something bad yet?"

Danning grinned and led the way past two girls running
without effort. Kolodny worked his way around the girls,
determined not to look bad. The girls, he noticed, were
watching Danning with considerable admiration. He
pulled himself up to his friend's shoulder.

"Fun," he gasped. "You like to have fun, don't you?"

Danning made a reflexive pass at his thick shock of prematurely gray hair, a foxy smile on his long face. "It's the
ocean—"

"What about the ocean? You can swim, can't you?"

"Sure," Danning shot over his shoulder as he pulled
away, "but haven't you heard? Fish pee in the ocean."

They sat across from each other in the glassed-in street
café of Maloney's Eating and Drinking Establishment on
Columbus Avenue, not far from the Museum of Natural
History, and watched the pedestrian traffic. Every woman
drew an admiring remark from Kolodny.

"You're a dirty young man," Danning said.

"Practice, that's all it takes. You like women, don't
you?"

"Which one?"

"So I'm a lech. It's okay for you big, handsome football
stars to remain above the fray. But us ordinary mortals
have got to work hard for everything we get."

"I admire your single-mindedness."

Kolodny was working on his second Heineken; Danning drank iced tea. Wearing warmup suits over their running clothes, they were not out of place in New York City on a sunny afternoon in early spring.

"That's your trouble," Kolodny said. "You're not zeroed in. In this world, a man's got to specialize. Women, that's my speciality. Now, about the island, in or out? What's it gonna be?"

"Let me sleep on it."

"That's your trouble, Nick, you're too cautious. That's why you weren't all-pro every year. Too cautious. Throw restraint to the wind, man. Take chances."

Nick was shaking his head. "The reason I wasn't all-pro is because I couldn't cut sharply enough, I ran soft patterns, and my hands were made of stone. Otherwise, you got it right. Okay, let's hear it again. What's the deal?"

"A great house," Kolodny said with renewed enthusiasm. "Not big and barny, you understand, but ample. Ample. Three bedrooms, one guy in each room. None of that doubling up. Privacy is the watchword, right! What you do in your own room is your own business. Also who you do it with. I'm talking about three hot months of total debauchery, my friend. Party time from start to finish."

"It tires me just to listen."

Kolodny grinned lasciviously. "Ain't it grand?"

"Who is the third man?"

"I'll come up with someone, trust me."

"Sounds a little like a frat house. I'm too old for that."

"Man, stop putting yourself down. Forty is not too old for fun and games, for women. I am offering you the opportunity of a lifetime. Whataya say?"

"You want my answer now?"

"Exactly. Commit yourself."

"Here it is, then."

"Okay—you're in, right?"

"I'm giving you a definite—maybe."

Kolodny groaned and called for another beer.

"That's it, then?"

"Sorry, Nick. Broadcasting is a rough business; win

some, lose some." Dave Dempsey was one of three vice-presidents in charge of sports for Continental Broadcasting Company. He confronted Danning across his office desk with little interest and even less sympathy; his attention was clearly elsewhere. To Dempsey, Nick Danning was simply another onetime jock—dozens of them sat in that chair every month, all trying to get themselves hired as broadcasters, all dreaming of becoming another Frank Gifford or Don Meredith. Most of them, like Danning, Dempsey reminded himself, were used-up items, discarded by sports, of no further value to him or CBC. He stood up in dismissal, a neat man in a neat, five-hundred-dollar suit and a neat, thirty-five-dollar haircut. He offered Danning a neat hand. "Good of you to drop in, Nick."

"You told me my chances were good," Danning said.

Dempsey withdrew the hand. "They were. As good as anybody else, for the most part. But you're no Madden, Danning, no Merlin Olsen. Give it some thought; maybe you ought to try another line of work."

"I did college games for two years."

Dempsey seemed not to hear as he guided Danning to the door. "I appreciate your coming, Nick. We've got your résumé on file if anything breaks. If it were up to me alone . . . but it's not. Take care of yourself, Nick, and stay in touch."

Danning, oblivious to the admiring glances of the secretaries in the outer office, left. In the lobby of the building, he located the phone booths, dialed Gloria's number. She answered in a hushed, secretive voice.

"Oh, it's you," she began. "You were supposed to call earlier."

So often these days he heard criticism, actual or implied, in her voice. She reminded him of some of his former coaches. "Did you forget, I had a meeting?"

"How'd it turn out?"

"They're going for a big name, a bigger name. Out of sight, out of mind. It's almost ten years since I played ball."

"Oh, I'm sorry, Nick. I know how much you wanted it. Well, you can always go back to the college games."

"They needed a decision last week. I turned them down. I figured CBC was a sure thing. Gloria, can you get away?"

"Now?"

"Right now. Meet me at my place, say in twenty minutes."

"That's impossible."

"I have to see you. I need to see you."

Her voice grew soft, as if she didn't want to be overheard. "Nick, I *can't.*"

"Dammit, Gloria, I'm hurting."

"I'm not alone, Nick."

"You mean Alan's home?" Alan was Gloria's husband, an executive for a national food chain. "What's he doing home at this hour?"

"Not Alan, his sister. I can't talk anymore."

"When am I going to see you?"

"I'll call when I can."

"When?"

"When I get the chance."

"This is no good, Gloria. I hate sneaking around, stealing time. You're never there when I need you—"

"I'm a married woman, Nick."

"I know that."

"You knew it when we met. It didn't bother you then."

But it bothers me now, he wanted to say, and didn't. It bothers me that the woman I care about must be shared with another man, that our lives are separate and apparently on diverging paths. Intimacy, he had discovered, is shattered and left behind in adultery.

"Can you get away later, maybe for dinner?" he said.

"Alan and I are going to the theater."

"Damn."

"What can I do, Nick?"

"Leave your husband."

"Nick, please. We've been over that."

"I know. He's a big executive with millions in stock, and I hustle sporting goods. Not much of a life I'm offering. I don't blame you."

"It's not like that."

"How is it? Tell me how it is."

"This is not the time to talk."

"It seems to me it's never the time to talk."

"Nick, remember how it was between us in the beginning? You said you'd never intrude on my life, on my marriage, that you'd never make trouble."

"Sorry to cause you so much discomfort. I thought we loved each other."

"There are all kinds of love, Nick."

He detected a subtle alteration in her voice, a hardening of her tone, a clipped, angry quality in the way her words came out. And at once he understood.

"It's over, isn't it, Gloria?"

"It didn't have to be, if you would've played by the rules. We had our laughs, Nick."

"Laughs? Yes, I guess it has been a lot of laughs. But not for me. Good-bye, Gloria."

"Nick, what are you going to do, Nick?"

"Get drunk, I think."

"Oh, no, not after so long. Don't go back to the booze, Nick."

"Good-bye," he said again, and hung up. The craving for a drink was palpable in his mouth, the familiar desire to swallow drink after drink, to let the liquor ease the pangs of disappointment, the pain of a dissatisfied life, the anguish of past defeats. But for him to drink was dangerous. He was a compulsive drinker, an alcoholic, a falling-down, brawling barroom drunk when he got started. And all it took was that first drink to launch him on that terrible downward path. One drink—that's all he wanted. . . .

Danning lived in a studio apartment on Second Avenue. The view from his windows revealed a building that was the twin of the one in which he lived, made over into apartments similar to his, occupied by men or women very much like himself. Unmarried, upwardly mobile, and able to pay outrageous rents; people who had come to New York to build careers and have a good time along the way. The Upper East Side of Manhattan was, he had long ago decided, a massive concrete playpen in which children of all ages could indulge their favorite fantasies. Danning's fantasies were turning sour, becoming bad dreams that left him empty and unsatisfied even on those increasingly rare times when they were made into reality.

One morning, looking out his window, Danning saw a man staring back at him from an apartment across the way. The man was about his own age, trim, good to look at, with an intelligent glint in his eyes. For a fraction of a second, Danning imagined he was seeing himself reflected in a distant mirror. Then, swiftly, as if in flight, the man across the way disappeared behind closed blinds, never to be seen again. It was the last time Danning looked out the window.

There was a casual, comfortable style to the apartment. A deep couch covered in dark red corduroy and some soft club chairs. An oversize coffee table made of black wrought iron and glass. The obligatory stereo system and a library of tapes and recordings. A marble-topped buffet served as a bar, and books lined the shelves along one wall, overflowing and stacked on the floor. People were surprised to discover that Danning read that much, surprised to find out that a jock owned a brain and enjoyed putting it to use.

To Kolodny, the studio was a "pussy pad," a perfect place to bring compliant women who patronized the single bars along the avenues nearby. It was a game Danning had once played with considerable success. Until the names and faces of the women began to fade into each other and he could not summon up interest enough in any one of them to see her a second time. The game was transformed into a cold, calculated exercise in supply and demand that left him depressed and afraid, turning into the kind of man he disliked very much. Even before Gloria, he had stopped going to the bars.

Now, alone in the apartment, he became aware of a scurrying uneasiness under his skin, a vague desire that caused him to consider a return to his former haunts. This time of day, the bars would be crowded with pretty young girls anxious to make a connection, women aggressive and open about their sexual availability, women who, after a few drinks, were more than willing to pay a visit to a man's apartment. Sexual requirements were filled with no more emotion than it took to fill a prescription at the local pharmacy, and certainly no more intimacy. Danning longed for intimacy, for the deeper joy of loving and being loved, for the give-and-take of an ongoing relationship.

Gloria, he understood at last, was not for him. It wasn't her fault for being whatever it was that she had become. He should have known better than to get involved with a married woman again. How many had there been with husbands and children, with lives apart from him? How many, after an occasional afternoon of giggles and orgasms, had left him behind when they went home to their real lives? No more, he vowed. No more limited encounters. No more matinee lovers. An end to furtive meetings and partial friendships. From now on, he would insist on everything out in the open, all risks understood and taken, all possible rewards examined and reached for.

He checked his freezer for that night's dinner: Chinese vegetables with shrimp, or meatball stew. He sighed and sat down to watch "Live At Five."

Sue Simmons was interviewing a jazz pianist when the phone rang. "Kolodny calling. I'm thinking about a burger and fries, maybe a flick."

Danning was in no mood for Kolodny. "I've got plans," he lied.

"First-class material, I bet."

"The best," Danning said automatically.

"Made up your mind about F.I.?"

"F.I.?"

"Fire Island."

"Tell me something, Jack. Is there a difference between the island and all the bump-and-fuck bars on the East Side?"

Kolodny giggled. "On the island the ladies wear less clothing. Allows you to examine the merchandise in advance. So what's it to be?"

"I'm thinking about it," Danning said before he hung up and went back to "Live At Five." Chauncey Howell was interviewing an industrialist who collected teddy bears when the phone rang again. He recognized Tiffany's voice at once.

"Am I interrupting something, Nick?"

"I was thinking about calling you."

"Anything special?"

"I felt like talking to Jason."

"I'll put him on when we're finished talking. About this weekend, Nick; I've got a chance to get away for a few days."

"That's perfect. Jason will be with me and—"

"I thought I'd take him with me." ·

He made an effort to keep the resentment out of his voice. "I haven't seen Jason in nearly a month. After all, he is my son."

"Make that five weeks," she said dryly.

Again that implied criticism, so prevalent when they'd been married; nothing he'd ever done had pleased her; nothing he'd been was what she had truly wanted.

"I was looking forward to this weekend," he offered blandly.

"The point is, I want to take Jason with me. And he would like to go along."

"Where are you going?"

"Does it really matter?" she said with that quick flare of annoyance so familiar to him. "Oh, hell, Nick, Gary knows this inn in Massachusetts, in the Berkshires. We were lucky to get a reservation, and I can use the change."

Danning chose his words carefully. "Is that such a good idea, you spending the weekend with another man while Jason is there?"

"For God's sake, Nick! Are we children? Gary and I have been together nearly four months. Jason knows Gary, he likes Gary. Your son may be only ten years old, but that doesn't make him a fool. He understands about the birds and the bees."

"Does that mean if his mother is sleeping with someone, he has to be witness to it?"

"He isn't going to witness anything! He'll have his own room. What kind of person do you think I am?"

A long silence ensued. "I still don't like the idea."

"Jason *wants* to go."

"Let me talk to him."

"Nick," she said in warning.

"He's my son. I want to talk to him."

"Don't say anything to upset him. He's just a child."

"I thought you'd forgotten. Put him on." Soon Jason came on the phone.

"Hi, Dad," he said in a flat, almost disinterested voice.

"Jason, how are you, son? How are you doing?"

"Okay, I guess."

"What about school, is everything all right?"

"Oh, sure. School is good."

"How's baseball?"

"Okay. We won our first game."

"That's terrific. How'd you do?"

"I got a hit."

"That's great, just great."

"It was only a single. A little dribbler over second base."

"They all look like line drives in the box score."

"I guess so."

"Sure. Don't put yourself down. A positive attitude, that's what counts. That, and concentration. You've got the goods, Jason, I know that."

"Sure."

"What about your schoolwork?"

"It's okay."

"Doing your homework?"

"Don't worry, Dad, I'm on top of it."

"Sure you are. It's just that I'm interested. I am your father, right?"

"You bet."

"Look," Danning said, aware of his love for the boy, and the increasing strangeness he felt when they spoke, of a widening gulf between them. "About this weekend?"

"Mom wants me to go with her to Massachusetts."

"I hoped to see you myself."

"Oh."

"Don't misunderstand, whatever you want is okay. Make up your own mind."

"You mean it?"

"Sure."

"Your feelings won't be hurt if I go with Mom?"

"Whatever you do is okay with me."

"Well, I would like to go to Massachusetts. They've got horses, and Mom says I could learn to ride and—"

"It's settled, then."

"Maybe we can see each other next weekend?"

"Why not?"

"Thanks a lot, Dad. You want to talk to Mom again?"

"I don't think so. You have a good time."

"I will."

Danning replaced the phone and stared at the television. Frank Field was interviewing a physician about the benefits of exercise to the cardiovascular system. Danning picked up the phone and dialed Kolodny's number, and Kolodny's recorded voice came on.

"Hi, there. Kolodny speaking. I'm out having a good time, I hope. Leave the vital info and I'll catch you later. Do it at the beep, creep. . . ."

Danning hung up without speaking and went into the kitchen. Meatball stew . . .

Four

Susan

Ever since she could remember, Susan Morgan had been the object of men's admiring attention. As an adolescent, their frankly assessing stares, their open sexual ambitions, had disturbed and frightened her, made her wish she had been born plain and unattractive. Later, all that changed, and her beauty had brought her just about every man she'd ever wanted, most of whom had been desperate to please her and themselves. These days she sometimes wondered how many men there had actually been. And always she came up with the same answer: too damn many.

Even the best of them had left her feeling drained, without energy, asking herself why she had bothered. The doubts and the questions had been with her for a long time, and still she went on, victimized by the insistent cravings of her flesh, the searing need to be touched and loved by a man, to be held and caressed, to have the deadly tension that gripped her diminished. At least for a little while.

Not so long ago, the sight of a handsome man or a pretty boy roused her curiosity, her passion, made her ask, why not? More recently she asked only why. And infrequently found a good answer. Still, as always, men dominated her existence. There was always her husband, Neil, a distant satellite in orbit, adrift on a path that led nowhere. And BB, her son. In and out of her life as the alterations in his own dictated. A stranger to her in so many ways, flesh of her flesh, yet someone she seldom understood, nor even liked any longer.

Both of them still were connected by links clear and blurred, by remembered needs and affection and forgotten hurts exchanged over the years. Always part of her being, her family.

Other men came and went. Less demanding, less vital in her scheme of things, offering what they had to give— seldom more than their bodies, seldom less than painful disappointment—strong bodies so intent on spending their sexual capital inside her.

Lately, it all went past her. Noticed but without response. Let them flirt, suggest, let them plead; she had neither energy nor desire. Part of it was Turk, of course. Too much of it was Turk. His demands, his insistence on her attention, taking all she could offer and then extracting an extra portion, leaving her dry and empty when they parted, more defeated than gratified.

Turk Christie was different from all the others. More than any of them, and less. His appetites were greater, his passion more powerful, his cruelty more blatant and oppressive. He demanded she submit to his slightest whim on command, and when he abused her flesh, he abused not only her but Neil as well, and every other man she'd ever been with. He needed to be the best lover she'd ever had, the strongest, the fiercest, the most brutal. He pummeled her in body and mind until, weak and indifferent, she told him whatever he wanted to hear.

"Nobody like you, never. You're bigger, harder. Where others leave off, you begin. You are the greatest."

For so long she had submitted and had been afraid, allowed him to brutalize her flesh and her spirit. But no more. Not after today. It was over, and she intended to tell him so.

She was on West Sixty-seventh Street, walking rapidly with a long-legged stride. In a patterned skirt and a linen jacket that displayed a taut figure that would have done justice to a woman much younger. Her raven hair was cut into a thick, shining cap that set off features cleanly and sharply. Behind high cheekbones, Tartar-shaped eyes.

Men entering Café des Artistes for lunch paused to watch her passing, full of admiration and envy for the man in her life. She paid them no mind. Once inside Turk's building, she rode the elevator to his floor. Never thinking that she might not come, he'd left the door to his apartment open, another indication of her subservience. Turk was on the phone and failed to acknowledge her appearance.

"Gimme the Yanks over Cleveland, Reds over the Mets, and the Pirates over the Giants. I'll hold on the fight until Wednesday. Nope, the price is too jumpy. Where's that dough coming from? I'll get back to you in the morning." He hung up and gestured with one broad, fleshy paw. "Sit down."

"I'm not staying."

He glared her way. "What the hell's that supposed to mean? Sit down."

"I came to say good-bye, Turk. It's over between us."

His laughter contained no mirth, no pleasure or joy. He moved her way, stocky and glowering. He had the flat face of a boxer with scar tissue over one eye. Along the left side of his jaw, a long knife scar, a memento delivered by an unhappy loser. Turk Christie was a man who gambled for a living and made it a point seldom to lose.

"I don't believe in losing," he'd told her more than once. "At anything. When I lose I lose small. When I win I win big. It's what I do, it's what I am. Sooner or later, I always win."

"Always?"

"Always." It had been said heavily, loaded with threat as if even to think otherwise was a betrayal. That was the first time she felt his ominous power, the danger that he presented, and she had been afraid. But it was too late. By then she'd given herself to him, submitted to him, hooked on his muscular intensity, his refusal to accept no for an answer. She needed him.

Now he placed one hand on her chest and pushed. She fell back onto the couch. "I said sit down," he said in that thick, throaty voice of his. He took his place next to her, dropping his hand on her knee, squeezing hard. Pain shot into her thigh, and she struggled without success to free herself.

"You're hurting me."

He laughed. "Between us, it ain't over until I say it's over."

"Dammit, Turk, you don't own me!"

"The hell you say."

"You're not my master."

When he smiled and spoke quietly, the harsh street tones wiped away, he exuded a kind of rough charm that made him seem very attractive.

"Sure I am," he said softly. "You belong to me as long as I want you. I own you. And I still want you."

She shook her head and looked away. "I can't go on like this. Being ordered around. Being mistreated and hurt. This is no good for me anymore, and if it's no good for me, it can't be any good for you."

He rubbed her belly, and the power in his hand seemed to enter her flesh and radiate across her middle. She held herself still, her only defense against him. "Oh, it is good for me, Susan, very good. Never been anyone like you for me, never. That husband of yours, he is a very lucky man, having you."

"I didn't come to talk about Neil."

He took her face in one hand, immobilizing her, kissing her on the mouth, forcing his tongue between her teeth. She struggled briefly, but her strength quickly drained away, her muscles went slack. At that, his hand went under her blouse onto her bare breasts, fingers insistent on the tender flesh. When she moaned, he forced her over backward, tugging at her panties, then opening his trousers. He mounted her and pushed himself between her thighs until he penetrated, pounding at her until her arms went around his neck and she began to writhe under him.

"Wait!" she cried. "Please, wait."

As if in answer, he exploded, washing her insides with a monumental flood of hot semen, his spasms endless. Finally done, he stood up and adjusted his clothes.

"Fix yourself," he commanded, averting his eyes. "Sit up."

She did as she'd been told. "Bastard," she hissed.

"You love it."

"No, I don't. I don't love it. I'm weak, I give in, but I don't love it. I used to believe my husband was the worst lover I'd ever had. But you, Turk, you take the prize."

"Next time I see him, I'll tell him what you said."

"You would, I think."

"Bet on it."

"You were supposed to be friends."

"Friends, shit. Neil and me, we sit in on the same poker game now and then. I take his dough. Poor sucker, playing poker's another thing he can't do very good. The man's a loser."

"Compared to you, Neil's a prince." She hated herself for defending Neil, hated herself for betraying him.

"He's so terrific, why you been getting it on with so many guys for so long? Tell me that. Tell me why you been coming here so much, why you're here now."

"This is the last time."

"You keep saying that, like you're dumb or something. But you ain't dumb. You are one smart lady, so how come you haven't caught on yet? Why do you keep saying the same dumb thing over again?"

"I mean it, Turk. I won't deal with you anymore. It's over between us."

He grabbed his crotch. "As long as I say so, you'll deal with this whenever I want you to."

She met his gaze. "In the beginning, you were exciting. The way you are, hard, tough, so forceful. But there's no kindness in you, Turk, no affection, no love. We're finished."

Without warning, he slapped her, rocking her head back and forth. She sucked air noisily and swung back instinctively. He caught her wrist, holding her in place. "Bitch," he said between gritted teeth.

"You're an animal. I hate you."

"That's what I been to you, an animal. Only I ain't. I'm a man, just like your husband." That drew a caustic laugh from him. "Maybe not like him, not even a little bit like Neil."

She kicked out at him, and he avoided the blow, releasing her at the same time. "I thought we might act like civilized people. I was wrong, you don't know the meaning of the word."

"What is it, you found another stud?"

"You would think that."

"You're not screwing your husband, and I know you can't go without. So what's the story?"

"Can't you accept what I tell you? It's over. Your selfishness and your meanness, the brutal way you treat me, it's over. You mistake rage for passion, and brutality for lovemaking. You abuse me physically and emotionally, and I don't want that in my life any longer." She started for the door. "It's finished, Turk."

He caught up with her in three strides, surprisingly quick on his feet, spinning her around, taking her face between his massive hands.

"You're hurting me!" she cried.

"You go when I say to go. You come when I want you here. You take what I give until I call it quits. Nobody walks on Turk Christie, not even you." He increased the pressure on her cheeks. "That face of yours, Neil is right about your face. Best-looking dame I ever knew. Be a shame to mess up that face, to break it apart, to scar it, to splash acid all over it. You wouldn't like that very much and neither would your husband. Without that face, no more guys sniffing after you. Nothing anymore, just a lonely lady getting older and lonelier. That wouldn't make you happy, so smarten up." He released her, stepping back.

She measured him warily. "You wouldn't do that to me."

"You know better'n that. Now take off. And next time when I call, you get your ass down here quick as a bunny."

She left, convinced he meant what he said; he was capable of disfiguring her, of causing her great pain and anguish, or even worse. She left, determined never to go back, but in some small dark place in the back of her brain, she understood that he was right—he owned her.

BB

Her name was Julie; she was pert and pretty, and BB's shirt managed to enhance her full figure. She was padding out of the bedroom and along the long hallway toward the kitchen when the strange man appeared. She was startled but unafraid.

"Oh, hi," she said with a smile. "Who are you?"

He glared ferociously at her, a tall man with disapproving eyes and a mouth set firmly in distaste and anger. "I am Neil Morgan. This is my apartment. Who the hell are you?"

"Oh," she said, relieved. "BB's father. I'm Julie, BB's friend."

"Is my son here?"

She shrugged; some people didn't know how to be friendly, and she wasn't given to wasting time or energy on them. She hooked a thumb toward the room she had just left. "In there."

Neil found BB asleep in the double bed. He jostled him awake. BB groaned and opened one eye. Seeing Neil, he groaned again, shut the eye, and rolled over on his side, back to his father.

"There's a girl walking around out there half-naked," Neil said.

"Julie, her name's Julie."

"She introduced herself. At least she possesses some manners. Why are you here, BB?"

"Locked out of my own place. Damned landlord, owed him a little rent and he does that to me."

"How much do you owe him?"

"I don't know, maybe five months' rent. Maybe six."

"You're lucky he didn't evict you."

"Said he was going to if I didn't come up with the dough."

"So you show up here with that—your friend."

BB sat up. "How about it, Father? Can you come up with the rent? Six months at nine hundred per. What's that come to?"

"Fifty-four hundred dollars. You expect me to pay off that amount? Well—"

"Come on, Father, you've got the bread, you've always got it."

"What happened to that—photography business of yours? You were doing so well."

"Slow season. Things'll pick up. Jesus, I feel terrible."

"Where's your mother?"

BB yelled. "Julie, there's some beer in the fridge!"

"I want that girl out of here before your mother sees her. Have you no decency? What kind of a girl can she be?"

"Mother's not here." BB began to dress himself.

"Where is she? Aren't you going to shower?"

"Out on the island to get the house ready for summer. No." BB disappeared into the bathroom.

"What about the girl?" Neil called after him. A sound drew him around. Julie stood in the doorway, a can of beer in her hand. Neil frowned. "You have to understand. We live by certain moral standards in this house, and BB is expected to obey the rules."

She smiled. "I do understand. You and BB are a lot alike. He's got lots of rules, too."

"Does that mean you work for him?"

"On and off. A couple of nights a week. The rest of the time I'm a student."

"What kind of a student?"

"I attend New York Law. I'm studying to become a lawyer."

"A lawyer! I don't understand, how can you reconcile that—" He broke off suddenly. There was so much he didn't understand, he conceded to himself. About his son, about himself, about the swiftly changing world in which he lived. This girl, this attractive, pleasant, shining girl, about to practice law and still she worked for BB, not much better than a common streetwalker. No, he certainly did not understand, nor did he want to. "Excuse me," he said. "I have work to do."

"Oh, sure. I'll be out of your way in a second. Just let me get my things and I'm gone."

She stripped off the shirt and, naked, began prowling the room, on the hunt for her clothes. Neil, frozen in place, was unable to take his eyes off her. Another of those unspoiled young bodies he so desired. He watched the play of muscles under her taut skin as she moved about, reached, bent, lifted a leg to step into her panties. What a fine specimen. What, he wondered, would it be like to touch her, fondle her, abandon himself to that sweet young flesh? Too quickly, she was dressed in jeans and a tank top. She faced him cheerfully, ran her fingers through her hair.

"Hey, BB!" she called. "I'm on my way. Been fun, see you by 'n' by."

BB materialized in the doorway. "How about a coffee? We'll talk."

"Running late, lover. Take good care."

"You also."

Turning a demure smile in Neil's direction, Julie departed, leaving a void behind. Neil wanted to follow, bring her back. Instead, he turned to his son.

"Let's have some breakfast."

"Just coffee for me."

"It's important to eat something in the morning. Start the day right."

BB nodded aimlessly at the words he'd heard so many times and headed for the kitchen, Neil at his heels.

Neil had a tall glass of freshly squeezed orange juice, three eggs and toast, a glass of milk. BB drank his beer and hunched over a cup of steaming black coffee.

"I'm glad of this opportunity for us to be alone, son. For us to talk."

BB grunted softly.

"Sorry about your business."

"It'll pick up. About the rent money?"

"Very well, this time. I'll write you a check."

"Thanks."

"I wish you'd get out of that business, get into something more, well, suitable."

"Respectable is what you mean. Let's face it, we're in the same line of work, taking pictures."

"Not exactly the same." They sat without speaking for a few minutes. "That girl?"

"Julie."

"Yes, Julie. She works for you?"

"They come and go. Big turnover in help."

"She doesn't look like—I mean, she's so clean-cut, decent. Studying to be a lawyer, she said."

"She poses for pictures, Father. She's a model."

"I thought—"

"What the girls do on their own time is their own business, including Julie. It bothers you, the work I do? Well, that's too bad, it's what I'm into, running a photography shop. Maybe it's not worthy of Neil Morgan's only son, but there you are."

"You could be doing so much better. You have so much potential."

"Shit on that."

"Watch your mouth."

"Don't you ever swear, Father? Come on, say it. Say shit. Or maybe even the big F-word. Come on, Father, give it a shot."

Neil seemed oblivious to the boy's sarcasm. "In this house, I expect respect. If not for me, then for your mother."

"Mother's not even here."

Neil shook his head. Life had once seemed so simple to understand and to live. You played by certain rules, and if you played well and played hard, the results were positive. You were always rewarded in the end. And for the most part, it had gone that way for him. Until they began changing the rules. Unanticipated twists and turns, pitfalls, traps; he had suffered them all. The old ways, the old values and traditions, none of that seemed to matter anymore. A man built his life on a foundation handed down by his parents, by his grandparents, by everyone who had preceded him. And then they pulled out the rug. To hell with that; Neil Morgan had never approved of the changes, the new rules, the new ways of doing things. He was an old-fashioned man and intended to remain so, holding to the proven ways, the ways that worked. "What is it you're after?" he said.

BB lit a cigarette.

Neil waved the smoke away.

BB grinned maliciously; Neil disapproved of people who smoked, had preached against smoking over the years, hated the fact that his son and his wife refused to heed his demands that they give up the "filthy habit," as he called it. BB filled his lungs with smoke and exhaled deliberately. "Nothing," he said. "That's what I'm after, nothing. And anything I can get."

"I can help you, if you'll let me."

"How do you plan on doing that, Father?"

"Give up that cruddy business of yours. Work for me. Half the young people in the world would jump at a chance like this."

"To become the right hand of a big movie mogul, you mean?" A mocking smile curled BB's mouth, and his dark eyes glittered.

"You think I don't understand that you look down on me, on what I do? Well, let me tell you, I've made a place for myself, by myself. It wasn't easy. Nobody gave me anything. I scratched and schemed and fought my way up from an underpaid press agent into TV commercials until I was able to make my first feature. I never quit."

"Concentration and commitment, that's it, Father?"

"You find that amusing, to make fun of me. Well, go ahead, I don't mind. This is your chance. I'll teach you everything I know. Eventually you'll be able to write or direct or even produce on your own. I'm almost ready to start the new project."

"Congratulations. You made your deal on the Coast."

"Well, no. I've decided against going that route. I tie up with a studio and I surrender my independence. Besides,

Hollywood people are so superificial they'd ruin my concept. I'm going to raise the money myself, keep control, and make precisely the picture I want to make. Say the word, and you can come along."

BB went to the sink and rinsed out the coffee cup. He was a tall man, slender, with his father's high shoulders and his mother's coloring, smooth skin eternally tan, the same prominent cheekbones, the same black hair. "I don't think so," he said, coming back. "Making commercial movies is not what I want to do with my life."

Neil struggled against the rising resentment, the anger. "What do you want to do?"

"When I find out, I'll let you know."

Five

Billy

Henrietta was a screamer, Billy Grooms's first screamer. At least the first one to let go with a full-throated, open-mouthed shriek of such impressive duration and decibel count. Scared the life out of Billy, first time it happened.

Billy knew all the sounds women made during sex. Knew from firsthand experience. On-the-job training, he liked to say. There were the moaners, of course, the most commonplace, acting as if in acute anguish and about to expire. Others whimpered, pleaded, "Oh, please, please. Oh, please," whether for more or less, Billy never figured out. Some women gasped, some swore—a chain of obscenities that would put a truck driver to shame—and still others cried out, "Oh, my God!" demanding release from on high. There were the laughers and those who never uttered a sound, the biters, the scratchers, the ones who pounded the bed, those who dug their nails into Billy's back, leaving little red love marks behind.

But no one was quite like Henrietta. When Henrietta came, she screamed. A succession of lusty blasts capable of jarring the dead in their graves or at least waking the neighbors. Her voice climbed the scale, maintaining power and projection, a worthy challenge to the most penetrating wail of a fire engine siren.

Oh, yes, Henrietta gave Billy a jolt that first time. In his tiny room on West Eighty-fourth Street, her cry shattered his concentration, rocked his nervous system, almost made him lose his erection. Almost but not quite. Very little affected Billy *that* much. That was the nice thing about that machine of his; it was always ready, always operative, a proper marriage of design and function. A true work of art.

When Henrietta sounded off that first afternoon, Billy was sure someone would sound the alarm, dial 911, bring the cops down on him. He should've known better; city life being what it was, a scream or two never bothered anybody. If people heard, they paid no attention, going on about their own business. Screams in New York were an accepted part of the urban cacophony. A scream could signify a beating or a rape or a murder; nothing to warrant an uninvited intrusion.

So Henrietta had screamed her lungs out that day while Billy put her through her paces. First with his hand, then with his mouth, finally with that swollen cock of his until she begged for mercy and time to catch her breath.

"Nobody ever did me like that," she told him. "You're the best."

"Just getting warmed up."

"I'm through for the day."

He took her hand. "Feel this, I'm ready again."

"You're phenomenal. A human fucking wonder. And I thought I was doing you a favor."

"You liked it?"

"I loved it. You're the best," she said again.

"If I'm that good, maybe I ought to charge."

She came up on one elbow, smiling. "Name your price."

"Just a little joke."

"I'm serious."

"I can see that."

"Name your price."

"I'm not a hustler. I did you because I wanted to, for fun."

She glanced around the colorless little cell he lived in. "Is this the best you can afford?"

"My day will come. I'm going to be a star someday."

"I forgot, you're an actor."

"Loaded with talent."

"So I noticed. Will you let me give you a gift? A little envelope from time to time, to show how much I care."

Earlier, he'd made it clear that he was down on his luck, without funds, planting the seeds that had begun to bear fruit.

"I don't take money from women," he said.

"I've got lots of money. Frank's worth a lot."

Frank was husband Frank Caesar of Caesar Construction Inc., which translated into extensive real estate holdings, overseas building projects, hotel ownership, land development, and recreation areas all over the United States. That was Frank Caesar as in multimillionaire Frank Caesar. Billy knew all that, had fallen in love with Frank's money even before he met Henrietta. Billy had decided at once to deny Henrietta nothing, least of all the pleasures of his exquisitely defined body.

Two months had passed since their first meeting, and every few weeks Henrietta talked about rescuing Billy from the sump hole of poverty. Once in a while she passed over an envelope containing a few hundred dollars, insisting that Billy accept the gift. But the big money remained out of sight, tucked away in Swiss accounts, Billy was sure, beyond his reach. Billy decided on a radical step; he asked Henrietta to become his wife.

"You're kidding!"

"I mean it. I'm crazy about you. Don't you love me?"

She stared at him. "Best sex I ever had."

"There you are. So let's get married."

"What about Frank?"

"Dump him. Right after the divorce, we'll get married and live happily ever after."

"I don't think Frank would like that."

"It's a free country; there's nothing he can do."

A look of amazement crossed her face. "Oh, you don't know Frank, he can do a lot, a lot. Anyway, I've got a good

thing with Frank, why give it up? No, I'll stay married to
Frank and we keep on the way we are, sweetie."

Clearly, he needed another avenue to Frank Caesar's
wealth. He put his mind to it for a couple of weeks and
came up with the idea for a nightclub.

"A nightclub!" Henrietta said. They were in his little
room and she was working his zipper open. "What are you
going to do with a nightclub?"

"I've given enough of myself to the theater. Nobody
cares about art anymore, nobody appreciates real talent.
I'm thinking about a classy place, a restaurant on one
floor, a club on another, some private rooms for parties.
Nothing too flashy. A piano in the lounge. You know,
Gershwin, Cole Porter, Rodgers and Hart, like that. I
think it's a great idea."

"I agree." The zipper opened and she tugged at his
pants. "But where will you get the money?"

He pushed her away. "I thought you might put up some
dough, a lot of dough."

"Where would I get that kind of money?"

"There's Frank."

"Frank! Oh, he's not interested in show business. Only
in making big bucks with small risks." She fondled his
genitals; he removed her hand.

"Try him."

"What if he won't?"

"Give it your number-one best shot."

"I'd do anything for you, sweetie."

He replaced her hand. "Then do it. With me and with
Frank."

That had been a month ago and still no results. Desperate needs called for desperate measures, Billy decided, and
he refused to see her for a week. She kept calling until he
played his card in the hole.

"I've got a prospect, a backer for my club." He had already told her about a middle-aged woman whose husband
had inherited millions and who kept trying to get him into
the sack. "I don't want to prostitute myself, but you know
how it is."

She thought of that marvelous, fat, long, hard cock of his

in another woman, and it made her a little crazy. "I've been working on Frank," she said.

"Tell me."

"Come over here and I'll tell you everything."

"To your place?"

"Right now."

"What if Frank comes home?"

"He's in Washington, D.C., and won't be back until late tomorrow."

"I don't know. It sounds risky."

"Would I do anything to hurt my baby? I'm waiting . . ."

Grudgingly, he agreed to come. It was risky, but sometimes a man had to take chances. This could be it. He decided he'd ask for a million. A million had a substantial ring to it, it sounded right.

She met him at the door of the East Fifty-seventh Street apartment in a long black lace nightgown, a glass of champagne in each hand. He drank the champagne, thinking that she looked ridiculous, a dumpy broad playing at being Rita Hayworth; it was clear that she had once been pretty, but it didn't work anymore.

"Do you really have a backer?"

"Would I lie to you?"

She embraced him, standing in front of the fireplace. "I'm sure you wouldn't." She backed him against the wall, middle swinging up against him. She massaged his chest and unbuttoned his shirt.

"I can't wait much longer," he lied. "The building I've had my eye on, it'll be gone."

She led him to the couch. With Henrietta, making love was a geographical adventure, advancing from place to place, sort of a sexual Stations of the Cross.

She kissed his throat, she licked his ear, she nibbled his nipple. "I mentioned your project to Frank."

He straightened up. "And?"

She unbuckled his belt. "He's thinking about it."

"How long's he going to think?"

She reached under his undershorts. "Just long enough. He wants to meet you." She worked undershorts and pants down to his knees.

"Meet me?" He reached for a handful of her bleached strawberry blond hair and pulled her head up. He wanted to see the expression on her face. "You told him about me?"

"Not about this, silly. About the club. I said you were a good risk. I said you were very talented. I said you were very good."

"Did you tell him I sing?"

"I didn't know you could sing."

"And dance?"

"I didn't know you could dance."

"And play the guitar, the piano, and the saxophone."

"I love guitar music."

"Frank should know about all my talents. Jesus! Suppose he comes barging in and finds us like this. It'll ruin everything."

"You're not scared, a big strong stud like you."

"Bet your butt I'm scared. I'm an actor, not a fighter."

She laughed, pleased with herself. "Don't worry, I told him you were gay."

"That's a rotten thing to say."

"I didn't say you *were* gay, only that I told Frank you were gay. I know you're not gay."

"I still don't like it."

"Frank calls you the Fag Chorus Boy."

"Hey, where's he come off saying a thing like that?"

"I told him you were good company for me and safe, protection against other men." She slid to her knees onto the floor between his legs and pushed her face against him. "You smell terrific."

"When do I get to meet Frank?"

"Never mind Frank. See, baby's come alive. Baby likes to be loved."

She pulled him down on top of her onto the lush Bukhara rug. They kissed and he squeezed her great, soft breasts.

She moaned.

He pinched.

She groaned.

He touched her belly.

She shivered.

He reached between her thighs.

She writhed and squirmed and gasped.

"Ah," she muttered. "Now, now."

He aimed and thrust.

"To the left, left."

He made the adjustment.

"Lower, lower."

He took another run at it.

"You missed!" she whined, growing impatient. She grabbed and pulled. "There! Right there."

"Take it easy."

"Ah."

"You're hurting me!"

She tugged.

"You'll break the damn thing."

She sighed as he slid inside her. Seconds later, she screamed and screamed again until finally it ended in a whimper.

"Want to stay?" she said after they moved to the bedroom.

"You mean all night? What about Frank?"

"He's in Washington, I told you."

"What if—"

"Not until tomorrow."

"But what if—"

"You can always shoot him."

"Not funny."

"I mean it." Leaping out of bed, she went to the long, low, white dresser trimmed in gold leaf, and withdrew a small-caliber pistol from the top drawer.

"What's that?"

"A gun, silly. Frank gave it to me in case somebody broke in and tried to rape me." The idea amused her.

Billy shivered. "Is that thing loaded?"

She offered it to him. "Isn't it a pretty toy?"

"That's no toy. Guns frighten me."

She replaced it. "Rest, baby, and later we'll begin all over again."

He was unable to repress a despairing moan. She mistook it for anticipation and planted a heavy, wet kiss on his mouth. It was going to be, he concluded, a very long, tiring night.

Billy woke to the sounds of Henrietta providing mouth-to-genital resuscitation. No more, he wanted to protest wearily, until he began thinking about Frank Caesar's millions. He gave himself over to the moment, lying back with his eyes closed, uttering an occasional word of encouragement.

Neither of them were aware that Henrietta's husband had come home. He stood in the doorway of the bedroom, a square bull of a man, a man with no neck and thick muscular arms, his expressionless face resembling a granite outcropping. Snorting angrily, he trundled forward, hands made into lumpy fists.

"Tramp!" he said in a low, guttural voice.

Henrietta rolled one eye his way and scrambled to put distance between herself and her husband. "Frank," she said, "it's not what you think."

"I think you were sucking this creep's cock, is what I think."

Billy was instantly alert. His first thought was "There goes the nightclub." Then when he looked at Caesar he knew this was the stuff of his most frightening nightmare: a jealous husband intending to beat him to death. And Frank Caesar looked as though he could do it. Leaping off the bed, Billy ran for the door. Caesar cut him off, driving a forearm into Billy's chest. The blow sent him tumbling backward, fighting to suck enough air into his lungs to remain conscious. He feinted left and went right this time, making another dash for the door. Caesar swung a powerful left hook that caught Billy atop his head. He went to the floor, a terrible headache beginning between his ears.

Henrietta cheered her husband. "Give it to him, Frank! Ruin the bastard! The dirty little fag made me do all kinds of disgusting things. Kill him, Frank, kill him!"

It occurred to Billy that Frank intended to do just that. The irate spouse was advancing with chin lowered, those immense arms poised to strike. Caesar kicked out and Billy stumbled backward. Before he could get up, Frank was at him, both fists swinging.

Billy jerked backward too late; he felt his nose give way, the cartilage crushed. His eyes began to tear, and liquid began flowing out of his nose, across his chin and onto his chest. He was bleeding!

"Broken!" he screamed, remembering the nose that was. "You broke my nose!" He was mistaken; the abused feature was merely bruised and tender and after a certain amount of time would be as perfect and pretty as ever. But in his pain and fury, Billy lost his head. For a brief moment, he considered counterattacking, but one look at the oncoming Frank made evident what a futile exercise that would be. He was trapped, his back against the wall—finished. On impulse, he yanked open the top drawer of Henrietta's white-and-gold dresser and came out with the sweet little pistol. Frank broke off his advance at once.

"You ain't got the guts to use it."

Billy worked the hammer back. Click. Click.

"Don't let him scare you, Frank!" Henrietta cried enthusiastically.

"Oh, shit," Frank said.

"Exactly," Billy said. "Move aside."

Frank retreated to a spot along the back wall of the bedroom, naked Henrietta clinging to his arm. Billy commenced his withdrawal, pausing only long enough to gather up his clothes. In the elevator, going down, he dressed himself. By the time he reached the street, he'd made up his mind. It was time to get out of town. Take a holiday, a long holiday. The question was, where to go?

Maggie

Looking west past Robin's Rest toward Lonelyville, the beach was deserted. To the east, a single stroller was heading toward Seaview. On the hard-pack, sand terns skittered along in their eternal search for sustenance. A scattering of gulls circled above the ocean.

Maggie sighed and lowered herself back on the blanket, supporting herself on her elbows. Her features were still delicate, reminiscent of the pretty girl she had once been, her eyes pale and unblinking, her mouth pursed as if she were about to speak. She had a lush figure, only a pound or two heavier than she had been twenty years before, slightly fuller at the hip and the bust, a woman's body full of sensual promise.

"It's changed," she said, voice tinged with sadness.

Lying alongside on the blanket was Susan Morgan, eyes closed, face raised to catch the full impact of the late afternoon sun. "What has?"

"The beach. Its contours, the profile. When I first saw it years ago, it was much broader, a smooth, wide slope down to the ocean. All the years, the tide and the storms have damaged it, scarred it from one end to the other."

Susan forced her eyes open, pushed herself up into a sitting position, looking around. "It's skinnier," she agreed. "Eroded, the scars of time. Poor skinny beach." She lay back down again, hands clasped behind her head. "Time damages us all. The beach and me—we've both lost important parts of ourselves, washed out to sea. Just a jagged hint of what we used to be."

Maggie glanced down at her friend. In the long rays, Susan's skin looked smooth, untouched, a slender and lovely woman. "My," she drawled, "aren't we getting philosophical."

"I mean it, Maggie. I feel ugly and used-up. Diminished by everything I've ever done, as if nothing turned out right. I'm out of control. I've always been out of control—the way a child acts when he's being rambunctious and obnoxious, working himself into a tantrum, plunging headlong into some dark unknown and not knowing why the hell he can't stop. Heading right for disaster. Do you know what I'm talking about?"

"Unfortunately, I do."

She sat up again. "Yes. I used to believe I could do anything I wanted, get away with the most outrageous acts, as long as it made me feel good at the moment. But that's a mirage, a child's fantasy. There is an inevitable bar of justice, and it always extracts its due. Everybody pays for everything. Every day I pay more and more, and it hurts like hell."

"You really mean it, don't you?"

"The worst of it is, I am getting exactly what I deserve. All that freedom, all that pleasure, all those laughs and good feelings; those are the bars of my prison cell. What a waste my life has been! All that time and energy thrown away with virtually no return on my investment, as Neil might say. The dregs are all that's left, and they aren't worth a tinker's damn."

"Are you really in so much pain?"

"Aren't you? Every day is excrutiating, twenty-four hours worth of punishment. It gets worse all the time, and the ironic part is, I deserve everything I get. Everything."

"You're being too hard on yourself."

"Am I? I try not to think about myself anymore. The way I've lived, the way I'm still living. But I do think about myself, when I'm alone mostly, and the pain is most acute. No matter how I try to rearrange the facts, it still comes out badly. I come out badly."

"Come on, Susan. Look around. This is still one of the world's great beaches, and you're the most beautiful woman I've ever known."

"Fire Island and I, we're both long past our best days." Susan lowered herself back to the blanket, closing her eyes.

"Fire Island," Maggie mused. "By the end of every summer, I swear I've had my fill of it, that I'll never come back. But I always do, I always want to."

"I'm more at home out here than anywhere else, more at peace with myself. Not that I'm ever at peace with myself."

Maggie giggled. "If they gave medals for the time we spent here, you and I would have collected our share."

"Not to mention Purple Hearts for wounds suffered in action."

"It has been a war at times, and we're both veterans."

Susan sat up and glanced up at the empty dunes behind them. "That first summer, that was the best of them all."

"A beginning and an ending. Although I never knew it at the time."

"Life was never the same after that. The house was right there," Susan said, pointing. "Alongside the steps leading down to the beach. Neurotics Anonymous. Roy named it, I think, and it was an apt choice. What innocents we were. Poor Roy," Susan ended, mind reaching into the past. A storm had sent them all fleeing the island, a storm that struck land with hurricane force. Neurotics Anonymous had been ripped off its pilings and carried out to sea. When they returned, days later, the house was gone, with no sign it had ever existed. Thinking about it now, she missed that old house with its sharp angles and shadowed corners, missed the joy of that long-ago summer so filled with friendship and love and the promise of the rich life to follow. How had so much goodness been transformed into so much anguish and disappointment and degradation?

"Poor Roy," Maggie echoed presently. "Poor me. I think about him more and more these days. The Roy I loved, the young Roy, the cocky, happy Roy—he had a personal style, that Roy, a sense of the dramatic—that Roy died a very long time ago."

"I can still see him on the deck of Neurotics Anonymous, wearing his leather flight jacket and blowing his bugle, announcing it was cocktail time. Every day was a party, every weekend a suspension of reality. I used to believe Fire Island was pure fantasy and my life in New York was reality. Now, only the time I'm alone out here is real. All the rest is blurred and mythic."

"Roy loved to make Purple Jesuses for our parties. He insisted he invented the drink, but I don't think so."

"Purple Jesuses and gin and tonics—those were the drinks back when, the summer drinks." She smiled fondly at the memory. "It used to make Neil crazy, having to pay for all that gin when he didn't drink. Now most people drink white wine, but not my husband. Neil still is a teetotaler."

Maggie sat up and hugged her knees. A gull dived toward the surface of the ocean, making a small, neat splash, coming up with a wiggling fish in its beak. "Poor fish," Maggie remarked to herself. "Neil seems different somehow."

"It's an on-and-off thing. The old Neil is still presènt, but he's become softer, a little less convinced that he's right about everything."

"Life has a way of softening us all, forcing us to recognize our own humanity. Humbles us."

"Humble? Oh, no, not Neil. He can still be stiff-necked about a lot of things, but he's trying, I'll give him that. He tries."

"Still, you two stayed married, after so many years. That's more than I can say for most of us."

"An arrangement."

"As long as it works. I hate living alone, I hate being alone."

"The marriage works as long as I keep to the rules. Neil forgets them every now and then."

"All my husbands forgot the rules whenever it was convenient. Four marriages, I can't believe it. Not exactly what I had in mind when I married Roy. Love and marriage, to the grave and beyond. Now two of my husbands are dead, and the other two are long-gone. I used to believe in rose petals and pretty music, love songs always."

Susan pushed herself erect. "Those old songs, they're all sad songs now. Look ahead, that's what counts—this summer, this year's songs. Have you made up your mind, about renting the house, I mean?"

Maggie rose, and together they shook sand off the blanket, folded it neatly. "I don't need the money, and a summer in the sun may be just what the doctor ordered."

"Great! Like old times again, the two of us spending a summer together. Let's have a ball, Maggie, although I'm not quite sure what it is I mean by that anymore."

"Whatever, we can find out together."

"Skip down the yellow brick road hand in hand?"

"Why not?"

"Into the land of Oz."

"Sounds good to me."

"There's only one problem."

"And that is?"

"What if we get there and the Wizard turns out to be Neil Morgan? I don't think I'd like that at all."

They climbed over the dunes, holding hands, arms swinging, laughing all the way.

Kolodny

Kolodny's round face broke into a spiteful grin. "There's only one thing wrong."

Billy Grooms frowned. "What's that?"

"You may be too good-looking."

Billy took it straight. "You can't be too good-looking."

"Maybe you're right," Kolodny said quickly, anxious to take the edge off his words. "You'll certainly end up with all the women. Mind if I pick up on your leftovers?"

Billy shrugged. When he was through with a woman, it mattered little what she did or who she went to. "Be my guest," he said.

Kolodny couldn't be sure about the tall, blond man, yet could find no good reason for turning him down. What the hell, they needed another housemate, and the way he saw it, they would probably all go their separate ways. "Okay," he said, offering his hand. "You're in. You, me, and Nick Danning. It should be a great summer for us all."

"It will be for me," Billy declared forcefully. "I'll see to it."

Six

Cindy

Cindy woke to the rich aroma of freshly brewed coffee. Eyes still closed, she reached out, fingers grabbing.

"Gimme, gimme."

Her hand closed around the warm mug, and she swung up into a sitting position, passing the mug under her nose. "Best fix in the world," she said, forcing one eye open.

"I can remember when you would have said otherwise."

Rafe Giacomin sprawled gracefully in an overstuffed club chair, smiling approvingly at her. He was a lank man, unruly hair falling across an intelligent brow, his dark eyes glittering.

"You haven't changed a bit," she told him.

He made a face. "Middle age has cut me down to size, my dear. I have to rinse the gray out of my hair, and I've developed a paunch—"

"A cute paunch."

"Thank God for Harry. Nothing's sadder than an old queen cruising for young meat and knowing he's going to pay for it, one way or another. But you, my dear, you've never looked better."

55

She wrinkled her nose. "I'm picked-over goods, Rafe. A single lady with no prospects and a dubious past. I'm so grateful you're still my friend, Rafe."

"Always friends, always. If only I were straight, I'd marry you in a second and make you pregnant. We'd make deliciously beautiful children, you and I."

"Let's not talk about children," she said without expression.

"Sorry." Then with a sly grin, "Listen to me, the old queen catching up on his fantasy life. Not that I'd ever convert, you see. It's against my moral convictions. Still, a life with you is a delightful prospect. After all, you are my one true love, Cindy."

"Forever, Rafe."

"Was the couch all right for sleeping?"

"Perfect."

"Never been slept on before. Though Lord knows it has been submitted to just about every carnal activity known to man or beast. If I told you—"

"Don't."

"Coward."

"Absolutely. Oh, Rafe, it is so good to see you again."

"And you. I want you to consider this your home for as long as you like."

"I've got to find a job and a place to live."

"What about your mother? I'm sure she'd put you up, and it would be a lot more comfortable than that old couch."

"I don't think so," she said coldly.

"You're too hard on your mother, Cindy."

"I doubt it; there's a long history with Maggie, with my father."

"I know all about that. Your mother and Roy were apart for a long time. Roy's trial, the divorce, her other marriages. Cindy, all that was long ago. We're not flower children anymore, you and me. We're tall people now, grown-ups, or trying to be. We learned that life doesn't always follow the path we want it to take."

"Don't remind me."

His laugh was infectious. "Neither one of us is exactly

pluperfect. Certainly I'm not. Give Maggie the same freedom to fuck up her life that you always insisted on for
yourself."

"Go to hell, Rafe," she said lightly.

"I've already been there," he answered quietly.

"Haven't we all? You think I should get in touch with
Maggie?"

"She's the only family you've got left."

"I'll think about it."

"Meanwhile, about a job. I may be able to help you
there. Do you know Alex Stainback?"

"So you're a friend of Rafe's."

Alex Stainback was a man of medium height, stocky,
with dark hair falling off a long head to cover half his forehead. His eyes were quick, never resting anywhere for
long. His voice was thin, penetrating, with a taunting un-
dertone that made Cindy uneasy, as if he knew more about
her than she wanted him to know, as if he were laughing
at her. He got her seated, touching her more than she
wanted to be touched, hovering, until at last he went back
to the tall, black leather swivel chair behind his desk. He
made a steeple with his hands and gazed out at her across
the peak.

"He's told me a great deal about you."

That bothered her even more. Rafe was a good friend but
he had never learned to keep his mouth shut. He talked too
much about himself and his friends, spreading rumors and
gossip without restraint.

"Not too much, I hope," she said. "Have you known him
for a long time?"

The question seemed to make Stainback uneasy, and he
shifted around in the chair, looking elsewhere. "Rafe is
so—well, distinctly Rafe, if you know what I mean. He's
gay, you know. Of course you do. I don't mind, as long as
it's not catching." He laughed nervously. "In case Rafe
didn't mention it, I'm straight as they come."

Why tell her? She'd come for a job, not sexual revela-
tions. "Whatever suits you," she said.

"My feeling exactly. Now to business. Rafe said you worked in an art gallery somewhere on the Coast?"

"Santa Barbara," she offered. "I managed and sold and produced the shows and did some buying."

"I'm impressed." He allowed himself an openly measuring look at her, seated demurely opposite. She wore a simple skirt and a blouse; sedate, conservative, but unable to conceal the full heaviness of her breasts or the voluptuous curve of her hips. She was, he told himself, a spectacular-looking female. "I'm impressed with you, too," he added.

She chose to ignore the implication of the words. "About the job?"

"I operate a number of galleries. Nothing fancy. People want pictures, I sell pictures. If we don't have what they want in stock, we can get it for them in a hurry. I've got a roster of painters on call who can produce any subject in any style, any color. Want to match the living room carpet, my people can come through for the client."

"Sounds like an art supermarket."

"You got it. I operate seven places, two here in Manhattan. One in the Village, the other uptown. I need someone to run the uptown store if you're interested."

"I am," she said quickly. She was determined not to call on her mother for help, determined to make her own way.

"Well, good." He assessed her gravely. "The only problem is, can we work together? I mean, will we harmonize? Gel into a smoothly functioning team? Get along? Hand in glove, as the saying goes? You're an extremely beautiful woman. . . ." He let the words trail off.

She stiffened in her seat. Here it comes, she thought gloomily. Rafe should have warned me. "Thank you," she said evenly, giving him no encouragement.

"That's important to the business. A glamorous woman lends style to the business, a luster, if you know what I mean. Everybody responds better to an attractive woman. There'll be men, you see. You'll have to make sure they buy and at the same time keep them off."

"I can deal with that."

"You understand my concern. Can't have anything disrupting the normal flow of things. You strike me as a strong personality, an experienced woman. Rafe told me you had lots of experience." He grinned insinuatingly.

Damn Rafe, she thought, and his big mouth.

"We'd have to spend a great deal of time together," he was saying. "Evenings sometimes. I have a number of interests that keep me on the go days. I depend on my managers. You won't mind putting in overtime?"

"I'm used to working long hours."

"I certainly am impressed with you. There is one more thing, if you don't mind."

She braced herself. Here it comes; the kicker.

"Yes, Mr. Stainback?" she said sweetly.

"Once in a while I require an escort. A pretty woman on my arm. Someone who knows how to handle herself in public. That wouldn't bother you, would it? Rafe said you possessed all the social graces."

Damn, Rafe. Damn. An angry retort rose up in her throat, and she choked it off. She wanted the job desperately, she needed it. A chance to reestablish herself in New York, to take care of herself, to enjoy the freedom the job would provide.

"No," she said, with a long, slow smile. "It wouldn't bother me at all."

Nick

Danning and Kolodny boarded an early ferry out of Bay Shore for the last leg of their journey to Fire Island. Danning had anticipated a deserted vessel at that hour; instead, the ferry was already crowded with sleepy New Yorkers, early risers bound for their first weekend in the sun. Kolodny pointed out the error in Danning's logic.

"Memorial Day weekend is the official start of the season. Everybody figures to get a running start on a long weekend. Look at these women, will you? I can't wait to get out on the beach and check them out."

Danning had also been assessing his fellow passengers as the ferry moved away from the dock and into the Great

South Bay. In addition to the women in groups and pairs, there were an equal number of single men, men with the satisfied look of success about them, men in expensive resort clothes, carrying equally expensive luggage from Mark Cross, the kind of men who seemed to belong wherever they were. There were also family groupings, including children of all ages, and he found that reassuring. He would make plans to bring Jason out with him one weekend soon, spend some time with his son, get to know him better. Even if there were no horses on the island, there was the beach, the ocean, and other children to play with. Let Gary match that.

They stood near the open side door of the ferry, salt air washing their faces as they plowed along. Ahead, Fire Island lay low in the water, a blue blur at the horizon. The trip, Kolodny had told him, would take about twenty minutes, a pleasant transition from one world to another. He kept his eye on the approaching land mass, willing it to come faster, anxious to discover what it was he had committed himself to for the next three months.

He turned away to avoid a spume of water kicked up by a passing cabin cruiser, and his eyes met those of a cool, blond woman seated along the aisle. Her glance went over his face, and he dared a smile, only to be met by a look of disdain; she pulled her eyes away, and Danning gazed out at the island again. Perhaps coming had been a mistake after all. He felt boyish again, and uncertain, without confidence or belief in himself.

How odd it was, the contradiction between his fear of women and the way women were drawn to him. Since his junior year in high school, there had been women in his life. Many had been older, seductively aggressive, leading him into the mysteries of their bedrooms and their bodies, providing unimagined pleasures while discovering some rewards in his flesh. Always they had been the most attractive women, students and teachers, a friend's older sister, and later models and actresses. Yet it seemed to him that he had never won the affection of anyone he really wanted, the true prize always eluding his grasp.

Martha Luiz Antonio was the first of his lost loves. So

pretty and neat and clean with soft brown hair brushed to
a lustrous sheen, laughing eyes filled with the joy of living,
and a dazzling smile. Martha had been the love of his life
during his year in the second grade, though she had barely acknowledged his presence; the searing hurt had remained with him to this day, the emotional scar tissue a
reminder that he was so much less than he longed to be.

"Excuse me."

A man confronted Danning with hand outstretched and
a confident smile on his craggy face.

"Nick Danning, right? I saw you catch a lot of passes
when you were with the Giants. You made a lot of those
games fun. There was a time when you were the biggest
talent on the team."

Danning put on his public visage—a shy, appreciative
grin, what he called his Huck Finn face. He shook the
other man's hand.

"I'm Neil Morgan. You out for the weekend, Nick?"

"I'm sharing a house."

"That's great. Let's get together, talk football. I played
in high school. Nothing like you, Nick. I never had the gift,
but I loved the game. I'm a long-time Giants fan."

Danning kept his smile in place. You learned to do that
at all the football award banquets, while being interviewed
for television, and when strangers intruded on your privacy. Always a player, Danning had never become a football fan. Watching a game bored him, talking about it in
bars and at parties had always been a drag. Playing was
what it was all about; the competition, the contact, pitting
your body against the bodies on the other team, matching
wits, learning to use yourself to the utmost. Was that what
he lacked, he wondered, the fan's point of view? Was that
the reason he had missed out on the TV job for next season?

"I go all the way back to the Polo Grounds, to Mel Hein,
Tuffy Leemans, and Ward Cuff."

Danning didn't know any of the names. Players came,
had their moment in the sun, and faded into oblivion, their
accomplishments frozen in someone's memory, belonging
only in the past, even as he was part of a fading era.

"I'll see you," Neil Morgan was saying, "we'll kick it around."

"Be my pleasure," Danning lied.

Susan

On the dock, off to one side of the crowd waiting to greet the ferry, as if fearful of making contact with that swelling group of people, stood Susan Morgan. She wore white jeans and a black cotton sweater against the early morning chill. To one side, a child's red express wagon, loaded with food to take them through the weekend. Yesterday she had stocked up on liquor and mixers, six-packs of beer—all done before Neil's arrival so as not to remind him how much money they spent on booze that he never drank; it was still a sore point between them, even after all these years.

How many times had she stood and waited like this? How many ferries had she greeted over the years? Each docking was like each previous docking, a babble of greetings, kisses exchanged, information given hastily, plans made as people wandered off toward their houses, toward the bars, toward the beach.

So much of it was repetitive, empty, dull. Yet the thought of not being here, not being part of all this, made her heartbeat quicken. The island was vital to her existence; these summers were a necessary element in her life. How long ago her first ferry ride, how long ago that first summer, how distant those people and what they had encountered together.

Was it still the same, untouched by all those years, unchanged? Not really. Once Fire Islanders had stood apart from each other, individuals created in a variety of sizes, shapes, and shades of different materials, custom-made. They spoke in varying voices and accents, each marching to his own drummer. The men wore khakis and sports shirts; the women Bermuda shorts and shirts that didn't match.

Now there was a carefully contrived sameness to people as if they had been lifted complete out of *Vogue* or *Gentleman's Quarterly*. Hair was fixed in place by the same fashionable stylists, and bodies were shaped and honed by Nautilus or Jane Fonda, encased in tight jeans and branded on buttocks by Ralph Lauren or Calvin Klein. It was almost impossible to tell one of these beautiful and perfect people from another, and most of them bored Susan to tears.

Neil was approaching, one arm raised in silent salute, squinting against the glare of the sun. He kissed her on each cheek and assessed her in that intense, clinical way he had.

"You," he said, "look fantastic."

That made her smile. "How was the trip?"

He shook his head and reached for the handle of the express wagon. "Those Hollywood people don't want to make movies, only deals. Accountants and bookkeepers, that's who runs the studios nowadays. Louie Mayer, Harry Cohn, these men made moving pictures. They loved movies. Today, scared bunny rabbits."

"You'll work out something," she said as they moved through the shifting crowd.

"You can bet on it." That made her think of Turk. "Make book on it," he liked to say. Her husband and her lover had a great deal in common, and the discovery depressed her. "Those characters aren't going to get the best of Neil Morgan." He shot a glance her way. "That face," he said, "better-looking every day."

Her face was her fortune, he used to assure her. And her downfall, she had come to believe. For too long it had gotten her everything she wanted. Now, no longer the unmarked face of a young girl out of South Dakota, a girl naive and trusting and charged with unrealistic expectations. The face was that of a woman of experience, melancholy and somber, reluctant to show joy, wary, skeptical. She had traveled too far, had too many adventures, found out too much about herself, making her bitter about a life spent idly and in waste. She glanced up at her husband. Except for a splay of lines around his eyes and mouth, ex-

cept for the slow graying of his still full head of hair, he
seemed no different from the young ebullient soldier she
had met at a USO dance so many years before. That was
the trouble with Neil, with both of them; neither had
changed much or grown much or profited from the years
each had lived.

They were in front of the market when Neil saw Danning again. "Nick!" he called. "Come meet my wife." He
made the introductions.

"Nice to meet you," Susan said to Danning and then to
Kolodny.

"Don't forget our talk," Neil said on parting.

"I won't."

"Who is that?" Kolodny wanted to know.

"My last remaining fan."

"I mean the woman. What a beauty! A little long in the
tooth but prime material."

"Zip up your pants, Jack," Danning said with a touch of
annoyance. "Let's get to the house. I want to get out of
these clothes and onto the beach for a little sunlight. . . ."

Billy

Billy Grooms waited until Danning and Kolodny left the
house before he took off his clothes. He was in no hurry. A
couple of hours in the sun today and another session tomorrow would darken his tawny skin to a golden tan that
would enhance his sculpted, lean body. Billy approved of
his body in every perfect detail from his wide shoulders to
his strong ankles.

Under a cap of thick, curly golden hair, his face, too, was
a source of great satisfaction. His eyes were wide-set and
blue, pale almost to the point of being white, unsettling
eyes that never blinked, that seemed to penetrate to the
darkest, most secret corner of a person. His teeth were
evenly matched, his smile a quick white flash across a sensual mouth, a boyish insouciance.

Golden Boy. More than one woman had called him that,

said mostly in admiration, in envy occasionally, in denigration and dislike at other times. But as Billy liked to say, "It makes no never-mind to me." Nor did it. Not since he had discovered, when he was fourteen years old, that his appearance could get him almost anything he wanted. It supplied him with the prettiest of girls. It had provided him with a wardrobe of expensive clothes and flashy jewelry, had allowed him to dine in the best restaurants on either coast. But it had failed, so far, to put him where he wanted to be, to make him rich and independent of other people. Just a string of bad breaks, he told himself, some bad luck. All he had to do was keep trying until things began to come his way.

Just a matter of time. Keep pushing, keep his eye out for the main chance, the right woman who would help him get where he belonged. Too bad about Henrietta. She had owned all the necessary qualifications: an aging beauty, a pervasive loneliness, a sexual and emotional hunger that matched any he had ever encountered, and a rich husband who spent a great deal of his time away.

The mistake was his, Billy conceded. Staying overnight in her apartment was bad tactics. He had broken one of the cardinal rules; sleepovers took place only in his own bed, his own place, no matter how shabby that place might be. The fact was that the shabbiness added to his appeal, made the rich, middle-aged ladies understand the many ways in which they could help him, improve his physical comfort, put him in their financial debt, buy him.

But no one bought Billy Grooms. Rented him, yes. Gave him gifts, yes. But that was it. He remained his own man, going his own way, beholden to no human being. No time, nowhere.

He slipped into a black nylon bikini and examined himself in the mirror, liking what he saw. Black was a good color for him, contrasting dramatically with his smooth, young skin. The bikini outlined his cock, gave it a dark and menacing profile, let everybody know just how special he was. Being out here was a smart move. It was a good place to hide out until Frank Caesar calmed down. No neckless freak was going to vent his rage on Billy Groom's

pretty face. Henrietta had warned him about her husband's temper, and Billy had seen it in action at close
range. Better to stay away for a while.

He slipped on a black T-shirt, gathered up his belongings, and headed for the beach. Along the way, he examined the houses lining the narrow walk. Some were
insignificant while others were large and well cared for.
Each one was built close to its neighbors, space clearly at a
premium in Ocean Beach as it was elsewhere on the island. By the time he reached the steps leading over the
dunes, Billy made up his mind. Somewhere on the island
he would find a replacement for Henrietta Caesar. A compliant and generous woman, a woman willing and able to
make him happy, in return for which he would make her
happy. It was, he assured himself, simply a matter of time
until he located the mother lode.

At the top of the steps he paused, letting his eyes sweep
the beach. He picked them out, the women no longer young
but still handsome in face and form, the sort of women who
took care of themselves, who spent long hours in health
clubs and beauty salons, the kind who visited glitzy spas a
couple of times a year. Women of means, of wealth, some
with rich husbands, others with the fortunes of those men
they'd buried. Soon Billy would zero in on the right one
and *voilà!* Life would turn into the sweet thing he knew it
could be.

Billy was sure of it; he was in the right place at the right
time. He descended the steps, striding across the sand at a
leisurely pace, in no hurry to get where he was going. Let
them look, let them take a good look, let them see what he
had to offer.

Seven

Maggie

As the sun traveled the length of Fire Island, serious
sunbathers shifted around to gain the full impact of the
tanning rays, using oils, creams, lotions, and reflectors to
hasten the darkening of their skin. By late afternoon,
Susan and Maggie had positioned their striped canvas and
wood backrests so that they faced west, settling down for a
few more minutes of beach time.

"Look at that beauty," Maggie said in admiration.

Susan forced her eyes open. Thirty yards away, Billy
Grooms had just come out of the surf, was toweling himself
off. They watched the play of muscles in his trim body as
he moved.

"Very nice," Susan said.

"Better than nice, and hung like a bull."

Susan allowed her eyes to close again. "No, thanks.
There's been too many well-hung young men, much too
many."

"Old habits are hard to break."

"Have you ever figured out how many men you've
slept with? I tried adding them up once and lost count.

67

More than I can remember, more than I want to remember."

"Funny, isn't it? The way people change. When I met Roy, I was a virgin; he was my first lover. And I was faithful to him until that second summer out here."

"Eddie Stander," Susan said quietly.

"What a fool I was, another version of Roy, only taller. Otherwise, twins under the skin."

"What crazy times those were. Your marriage breaking up, you and Eddie tippy-toeing around. Mike Birns stayed with us that summer—didn't he meet his first wife out here? And I began fooling around with other men. Actually, it was that winter. Seems to me Neil and I have been existing in some kind of a garbage pit ever since."

Maggie brought her eyes around to her friend. "Life was a joyride. All of us were so beautiful, so smart, so full of promise. Fun and games was what it was supposed to be, Susan. What went wrong?"

"For me, too many men, too much booze, too many drugs. As I remember it, all I ever really wanted was to be a wife and a mother and live happily ever after. I used to believe I was a free spirit, capable of doing anything. The more the merrier, especially the men. Men—what a joke; and the joke's on me. Most of the men I've known—they were boys, playing children's games in this sandbox of ours. Emotionally stunted, all of us, rooting around in the mud. We never grew up."

"Peter Pan and Wendy," Maggie said.

"But Wendy went home, didn't she? To the life she was born and bred for. She grew up. Speaking for myself, I took a wrong turn."

"What the hell, Susan, if there aren't some laughs along the way, what's the use in living at all?"

"Once I would have agreed. Not anymore."

"You've changed."

"I want to be straight, at least with myself. Honest. All that time and energy spent on passing sensations with nothing left to show for it. My marriage is a mess, my son is a lost soul, and I don't have the foggiest notion of where I am or how I got here."

"Ocean Beach, Fire Island. Memorial Day weekend. The weather's good, and we've got a long summer in front of us. All those strong young bodies just waiting to make us feel good." She laughed in anticipation.

Susan didn't respond. "There's a man back in the city . . ."

"Isn't there always?"

"This time it's different. Most of the time I've been able to control the situation. I've been able to decide when it begins and when it ends."

"Not this one?"

"He frightens me, Maggie. He's threatened me and hurt me and refuses to let me break it off."

"Don't give credence to that macho crap. That's all it is, just crap."

"You don't know Turk."

"His name is Turk! I can't believe it."

"This is serious. When I tried to break it off, he hit me and threatened to throw acid in my face."

"That's ridiculous."

"That's Turk. He's that kind of a man. For a while it was exciting, but now I'm afraid, really afraid."

"He's not going to bother you out here. You've got the summer to let him cool off."

"I'd like to believe that."

"Maybe it's not so bad. I've forgotten what it's like to have a man want me that much. The men I meet act as if they're doing me a favor by being with me."

"Nonsense. You're beautiful and—"

"And an older woman. The last year or so, I've been frightened. Frightened of being alone, of living and dying alone. And when I come up against some beautiful young man, well, I can't keep my hands to myself. Oh, it isn't the sex I need so much, just the attention, just the idea that somebody wants me even a little bit, a warm body next to me during the night." A nervous laugh seeped out of her, and she changed position. "It's only an illusion, of course, self-deceit. The men I go with want only a quick and easy lay. I qualify on both counts."

"Don't speak that way about yourself."

"Look at that one." Maggie indicated Billy Grooms stretched out under the fading sun. "Lying still, he seems to be in motion. All cock and no brains. Sometimes I think I'm losing my grip on things, out of touch with reality. Look at them all, running up and down the beach—men and women—doing push-ups, sit-ups. Everybody's so trim and hard, struggling to stay young."

"It's the national health kick. Health food and exercise machines; don't smoke, don't drink. They're all beginning to look alike to me. When we first came out here, Maggie, everybody was different, distinctive. Look at them now— all lean and mean, boys and girls of all ages. So much beauty, so much perfection, so much damn emptiness. Once in a while I'd like a little imperfection, some flaw, some sign of human vulnerability. I suppose that's because I feel so vulnerable myself, so helpless and susceptible, victimized by my past and so terrified of what lies ahead."

"I don't want to think about that."

"But you do, don't you? We all do in those awful dark and quiet times when you're alone."

Maggie looked away. "What I'm most afraid of is growing old, having people feel sorry for me, pity me, afraid of turning into a pathetic old lady with nothing to hold on to, hating my life and too afraid to let go of it."

"Not you, Maggie, not either one of us."

"I want to be straight. To find a man who's right for me. A man of experience—quiet, gentle, and understanding. I don't expect my heart to go pitter-pat. Not anymore. Someone kind and friendly, that's all. Friendly would be so nice, Susan, so very nice."

Susan agreed without speaking, afraid for her friend suddenly, afraid for herself. When she lifted her head, she spied a young woman advancing down the slope of the beach in their direction, coming gradually into focus.

"Cindy!"

Maggie came to her feet, confronting her daughter tentatively, a confused expression on her oval face, hands fluttering. Mother and daughter were obviously cut from the same mold, of the same height with similar coloring and features. In an emerald green tank suit that outlined every detail of her superb figure, Cindy's youthfulness was apparent. Her body was firm, without excess flesh, the skin smooth and unmarked by time.

She accepted Maggie's embrace, stepping back quickly, then hugged Susan. The older women began to talk at once, asking questions, telling Cindy how well she looked, how glad they were to see her.

"You first," Susan said to Maggie.

"What are you doing here? You should have let me know you were coming. I—"

"Would you rather I hadn't come?" Cindy said softly.

"Oh, no. I mean, why didn't you call?"

"I did, but there was no answer. I called your apartment, Susan, and spoke to BB."

"Miracle of miracles, my son was at home."

"Said he planned on staying for a few days."

"Yes, I know. Neil came home to find BB entertaining a half-naked girl. That must have been a unique encounter, Neil being the kind of parent he is."

"BB told me you were out here, Mother," Cindy said. "I decided to visit, if it's not too inconvenient?"

"Don't be silly. I'd love to have you. You're looking wonderful, Cindy."

"Will you be staying long?" Susan asked.

"No, not long."

"You're welcome to stay as long as you like," Maggie said, anxious to get it in. "Whenever you like."

Susan excused herself. "You two must have a million things to talk about. I'll see you later."

"Drinks after dinner?" Maggie said quickly.

"At Leo's, okay?"

"Okay."

They watched her leave, tall and shapely, already browning from the sun, a remarkably handsome woman. Maggie forced her attention back to her daughter.

"You're looking wonderful," she said feeling foolish as she realized she'd said it before.

"You too, Mother," Cindy said, adding, "Younger than ever."

"The years add up. You still hate me, don't you?"

They were seated on the sand facing each other. Cindy stared into Maggie's eyes. "I never hated you, Mother."

"You were so angry all the time."

"I guess I was."

"You still are, I can sense it."

"Motherly instinct."

"Don't patronize me, Cindy. Whatever I am, whatever I've done, I'm a human being. I made my mistakes, I still make them, and I pay for them. Dearly."

"So did I, Mother. Pay for your mistakes, I mean, as well as my own."

"Can't we forget the past, start all over? Can't you forgive me?"

Cindy turned her gaze to the ocean. The tide was rolling in, the waves higher, the breakers spuming white spray. A few children were playing along the shoreline, challenging the waves, screaming in delight and mock fear when they were splashed or knocked down by a breaker. She could remember when she was their age, when she played as they were playing, when all her fears and hurts were soothed by—for a moment she had to think—not her mother, but a young woman employed for the summer to relieve Maggie of the burden of raising her own child. Mother's Helpers they were called, those girls, and every year another one appeared. Strangers who came and went, leaving young Cindy behind and alone. Tears welled up behind her eyes, and she blinked them back. Without turning, she spoke in a toneless voice. "Roy is dead, you know."

Maggie blanched and trembled, clutched her knees as if to keep from collapsing. "No. No, he can't be."

"He'd been sick for a long time, you knew that."

"His friend called me—"

"Francesca. She took care of him. She loved him. She was with him when he needed her most."

"And I wasn't? Is that what you're saying?"

Cindy ignored Maggie's words.

"I went to Mexico, to this coffee plantation way back in the country, a million miles from what Roy knew best, from the world he loved. He was safe with Francesca. He'd become afraid of the world he grew up in, afraid of being hurt again."

"Not Roy, he was never afraid of anything."

"We're all afraid, I've learned that much."

"Did he—mention me?"

"We spoke about you. You were important to Roy, you always were."

"Poor Roy."

"There was a great deal of pain, but he refused medication, refused to go to the hospital."

"Francesca said it was cancer."

Cindy nodded. "Even at the end, he was able to get off a few one-liners. Making people laugh always mattered to Roy. He made his mistakes, so many mistakes. But he paid. The trial, disgrace, and the way he died."

Painful images came rushing back at Maggie. Roy had been charged with killing a man—his bookmaker—and stealing his gambling profits. He had denied it, of course, and hired an expensive and flamboyant lawyer to defend him. The defense had been conducted skillfully in the press and on the airwaves before it ever reached the courtroom. Painting the dead bookie as little more than a hired killer for organized crime, the lawyer had created a groundswell of sympathy for Roy, and he was acquitted. Roy was a hero to his cronies and his girl friends, enjoying considerable notoriety for a brief period. But it had been a very bad time for Maggie, and for Cindy, and she had grown resentful and bitter, frightened for herself, her child, and for Roy.

"He did it, you know," Maggie said quietly.

Cindy nodded once. "I guess I always knew that." She glanced over at her mother. "Did he ever admit it to you?"

"Roy? Don't be silly. In Roy's world, people committed acts of aggression against him, not the other way around. Roy went on giving pain and injury and always getting away with it. If only he had been punished just once in his lifetime, made to obey the rules like the rest of us—but Roy laughed at rules. It was part of his charm."

"If there is a higher power—the way he died, that was punishment enough."

Maggie turned away. "I don't want to hear about it." Yet she felt so sorry for Roy, for the man she had once loved, still loved in some strange and vague way. "Damn!" she said. "That man is still a part of me, still in my life, and it still hurts."

Cindy reached out as if to take her mother's hand but thought better of it. "I know."

"You, too?"

"He was my father."

They sat without speaking for a long time, not looking at each other, each lost in her own thoughts until Maggie broke the silence. "What was she like?"

"Francesca? Tall, blond, and very wealthy. I think she loved Roy."

"He needed money. Roy always needed money."

"She took care of him, they took care of each other, and at the end, she was with him."

"And I wasn't, you're saying. Well, you're right, I couldn't bring myself to go to him. It's been a dozen years since I saw your father or talked to him. A dozen years and three other husbands. A lifetime separated us, made us strangers. Being married to Roy, he made my life miserable in a thousand different ways."

"You said it, Mother. That was a long time and three husbands ago."

Maggie fixed her eyes on Cindy, as if set on seeing inside her, of trying to plumb the dark, secret corners of her psyche, to know at last what made her feel and act as she did. "It's that, isn't it? That Roy and I couldn't stay together, that we got divorced? You still hold that against me."

"No, not that, not anything anymore. Hell, who am I to pass judgment on you, on anyone, the kind of life I've lived? But the history of our family, it exists, it's alive in my nerve endings, it's part of me, Mother, as it must be part of you. No, I don't hold anything you've done against you anymore. I didn't come here to do battle with you."

"Why did you come?"

"To see you. After all, you are my mother. To tell you about Roy."

"I'm glad you did."

"And to steal a few days in the sun, if you don't mind."

"The house is as much yours as it is mine. Roy bought it for me, you know; he paid for it, it's all I have left of him. Except for you. Stay as long as you like."

"I won't be going back to California. I've accepted a job in the city. I want to try and make a place for myself in the Big Apple, if I can."

"Use the apartment, there's plenty of room."

"Until I find a place of my own. I appreciate that."

"You are my daughter after all."

"Yes," Cindy replied thoughtfully. "I am."

Nick

A soft blue haze blanketed the island just before night set in. Already, lights began to come on in the houses that lined the beach. Here and there, smoke began to rise from chimneys, protection against the chill of the evening. Ice cubes clinked in glasses, and drinks were made as predinner partying began.

On the beach, wearing shorts and a T-shirt, Nick Danning ran along the water's edge toward the eastern tip of the island. One community flowed into the next, unmarked, with occasional stretches of unspoiled dunes covered by grass and stunted shrubbery. Underfoot, the sand packed and hardened, and each footfall jarred up into his powerful legs and torso. He ran without thinking for thirty minutes before turning back, his muscles warm and loose now, responding automatically, arms pumping to each stride. After all the years of football and basketball, from age eight on, he welcomed physical activity in which he competed with no one. Not even himself. He ran for the pure joy of running, for the simple sensation of putting his body into motion, of feeling the muscles and tendons stretch and retract, aware of the blood pumping in his veins, aware of the sweat covering his skin, of the sting of the salt air against his eyeballs. Nick no longer measured the miles he ran, nor the time it took to run them; he had long ago given up checking his pulse rate or counting the breaths he took each minute. The running was solely for Danning, for his flesh and his spirit, his mind, and he took immense pleasure in being by himself, losing himself in himself.

When he came close to where he had started out, he slowed to a walk, warming down for a hundred yards or so. He located his towel, dropped his T-shirt on top of it, and kicked off his running shoes before diving into the surf. He swam straight out for a hundred yards and rested on the swells, secure in the fast-closing darkness. Back on shore, he began toweling off. It was then that he noticed her for the first time, seated alone halfway up the beach, staring out to sea.

"Hi," he said, as he came abreast of her.

"Hi," she returned, without interest.

He paused. "You all right?"

"I like the beach at this time of day. So quiet with no-body on it."

"Sorry to interrupt your meditation."

"I saw you running. You move very well."

He held out his hand. "I'm Nick Danning. This is my first day on Fire Island." When she ignored the hand, he withdrew it. "You've been here before?"

She spoke as if to do so was an effort. "I feel as though I'd been born on the beach." There was no encouragement in the way she offered it, no reason for him to respond.

"Well, I'll leave you now," he said.

"Good-bye," she said, looking back at the water.

"See you again," he said automatically.

"I doubt it. This is just a visit, then I'm gone."

"Oh, that's too bad. Well, good-bye again."

He took two or three steps away when she called out to him. "Cindy," she said.

"What?"

"My name. Actually, Cynthia, but everyone calls me Cindy. In case we do see each other again." Then back to the water in clear dismissal.

Danning took the hint.

Eight

Neil

Neil Morgan had never taken much pleasure in bar-hopping. First of all, he didn't drink; secondly, as a non-smoker, he resented the smelly, polluted air; and finally, bars were always so crowded, so noisy, so full of empty talk.

From the first summer spent on Fire Island, Neil had avoided the bars when possible. The house parties with their forced, false gaiety, their noise and agitated, overactive bodies, were bad enough; the bars were out of the question. But the others had always enjoyed the bars at night, claiming they were the core of Ocean Beach's social life. Neil preferred to go to bed early, be fresh and vigorous in the morning, but his wife, his friends, insisted he accompany them on their rounds. So he did, mostly to keep a protective eye on his beautiful wife. At least, during those first couple of summers. Men found Susan as attractive as he did and were oblivious to her marriage, insensitive to Neil's feelings or Susan's innate good taste and fidelity. Later on, the situation changed, and Susan came to resent his presence, his intrusions, as she'd taken to calling them,

so he went his own way. He taught himself to ignore Susan
during those extended, often drunken, evenings, to consider his own interests and needs.

Since then, the bar scene had grown worse. More people,
more drinking, dope openly smoked. The blatant sexual
aggressiveness—particularly of the younger women—was
appalling, and on many such evenings he went back to the
house alone, trying to ignore the seamy path his life had
taken.

On this particular night, he went along.

"First big night of the season," Maggie said when she
appeared to collect Susan. They were a team, friends for so
many years, alike in many ways though so different in appearance.

"Are you coming with us?" Susan said, allowing him
room to make up his own mind.

"Why not?" he answered, surprising himself, as well as
the two women. "Sort of inaugurate the new summer."

First stop, MacCurdy's. A big sprawling restaurant and
bar, already crowded when they arrived. Neil fetched
drinks for Susan and Maggie and left them talking to some
people he knew slightly and didn't care for at all. For a
while he watched the players at the video games along the
wall where once there had been a bowling game played
with metal pucks instead of balls. Years before he had
spent more than one evening discussing sports or the future of the then young television industry or politics with
Eddie Stander or Roy Ashe or Mike Birns. How long ago
that had been. Roy was gone, Mike was still writing those
little mystery-thrillers of his, off in Maine, or was it
Vermont, and Eddie, the last he'd heard, was teaching English literature in a small land-grant college in western
Pennsylvania.

How different things were. The world he lived in, the
larger world outside. Nothing stayed the same, everything
changed, not necessarily for the better. How, he wondered,
had he gotten here, to this place and time in his life? How
had he become *this* Neil Morgan? Alone in a crowded sa-
loon watching strange young men pay for the privilege of
competing with a computer. Questions flashed through his

mind, and he sidestepped them all; introspection was useless. Life, he had long believed, required very little understanding; doing was all that counted. The here and now, and how a man dealt with it. Problems were to be confronted head-on and beaten into submission. Solved as quickly as possible. Neil Morgan was, if nothing else, a pragmatic man.

"How about that!" a voice said at his shoulder. "Meeting you here this way."

He made a square turn to the left. A girl in pink shorts and a tank top grinned up at him. She was pretty, sensual, with a frank, admiring expression in her round eyes.

"You don't remember me," she said cheerfully.

"I'm afraid not."

"Not that I blame you, the way we met and then only for a few minutes."

"You do look familiar."

"Ah, you're just trying to make me feel good. That's very nice of you, but it's all right. Julie. It's my name."

He repeated the name to himself, trying to attach it to a specific place, to an incident. He drew a blank. "I'm sorry."

"Ah, that's okay. BB's friend, Julie."

It came rushing back to him. The girl had come out of BB's bedroom that morning in New York. To return home and find his son entertaining a girl in his bedroom in his own parent's apartment—anger gathered in a moist knot behind his navel. His joints stiffened.

"I remember," he said.

She was oblivious to the change in his mood. "What a kick, running into you like this. You out for the weekend, Mr. Morgan?"

"I own a house in Ocean Beach. We've spent our summers here for thirty years." It was as if he had to establish proprietary rights.

Head cocked, tongue at the corner of her lush mouth, she assessed him. "Thirty years. Wow, you sure look terrific for your age. If I didn't know better, I'd never figure you for BB's father."

Though Neil took her words as a compliment, at the same time he was made uneasy by her directness. She was an immensely attractive girl and he remembered what she had looked like naked, with a spectacular body.

"Is BB around?"

"He doesn't come out here much anymore."

"Well, I sure will be. I'm grouping it up, must be twenty people in the house. What a mess." Neil had visions of chaos and disorder, of people competing for beds and for each other. Julie took a long pull on her drink, checked his empty hands. "You don't have a drink," she said. "Have some of mine."

"I don't drink."

She leaned his way. "I don't blame you. I prefer grass myself. There's a couple of joints in my pocket if you want a toke."

Drugs. Once it had been a dirty little secret, the sort of thing whispered about, conjectured about; years ago, Neil had known some musicians who referred to the "weed" they smoked. And there was that movie, "The Man With the Golden Arm." Sinatra had portrayed a man hooked on heroin; hopheads they were known as in those days. All very sleazy and disreputable, never done by nice people.

No more. Drugs of all kinds were openly talked about and used. Coke was blown at parties and grass was smoked in the streets and theaters and offices in Manhattan. Everybody used something these days, everybody but Neil Morgan. No, thank you. He was a man who had always treated his body well, and he had no intention of poisoning his system in return for a temporary jolt of pleasure.

"No, thank you," he said.

"If you change your mind, let me know. I'll be around." He watched her work her way through the press of bodies toward the back of the restaurant, then put her out of his mind, went looking for his wife. Instead, he saw Nick Danning standing by himself along one wall.

"What do you think of this scene?" Neil said for openers.

"I don't do too well with so many people in one place. I never have."

"I thought football players did a lot of partying."

"That's a long time ago."

Neil steered the conversation to football, doing most of

the talking himself. Danning's responses were brief and spare, as if he were reluctant to discuss his career in football. After a while he excused himself, saying he was tired.

"See you on the beach," Neil answered. "If you play volleyball, we have some pretty good games."

Alone, Neil tried to imagine what it would be like to be an athlete of professional caliber. Though he had participated in a variety of sports all his life, he had never possessed the necessary skills to be outstanding; no matter how hard he had tried, he always fell short of his athletic ambitions. He wondered if Danning knew how lucky he was.

Unable to locate Susan, he strolled over to Leo's, at the opposite end of Baywalk. Leo's was more intimate and, to Neil's way of thinking, more refined. Years ago, before Leo had sold the place, he used to play Broadway show tunes on the piano and occasionally some musical comedy performer would show up to sing Gershwin or Cole Porter or Irving Berlin. He was about to leave when Maggie, a young man at her side, appeared out of the crowd.

"Meet Billy Grooms," she said, teetering. "Neil Morgan is married to my very best friend, Susan, dear Susan."

"Neil Morgan, the movie producer?" Billy said with rising interest.

"Movie producer," she replied. "And prince among men, king of Ocean Beach, emperor of all he surveys."

"Maggie, you've been drinking too much."

"You've found me out. Billy, love, fetch me another, tall and strong, please." She watched him go. "What a pretty thing he is, so transparent and so young. What could he possibly want with a middle-aged lady like me?"

"What do you want with him might be a better question."

She made a face. "Climb down off your high horse. All these years and you're still going around with an iron rod up your ass. Loosen up, my friend."

"Listen to you, a woman of your background and breeding."

"I've disappointed you, poor baby. Well, don't take it personally. I disappoint everybody I know. My mother, my

father, my husbands, all of them, my child, and most of all
myself. So, you see, my friend, it isn't required that you remind me of my shortcomings." She grinned maliciously.
"Neil, baby, have I ever told you that I think you're a prig?
You have always been a prig, you will always be a prig."

"If it makes you feel better to kick me around, so be it. I
understand, you're upset."

"Upset about what?"

"About Roy."

"Don't you dare!" she cried. "Don't you dare talk about
my feelings about Roy. What I feel about Roy is mine
alone. Private. Secret. Something for me and no one else.
What Roy and I had once, it got away from us. Roy was my
first love, the love of my youth, the love of my life. That
Roy belongs to me, and I won't share him with anyone
else."

"I'm sorry."

"All of us are sorry. About Roy, about ourselves, about
the lives we've led, about the precious things we've lost, each
of us. Let it go at that. Please."

"Whatever you say, Maggie." Raw displays of emotion
bothered Neil, made him uncomfortable, always had. He
found it much easier to deal with anger rather than senti-
ment, with sarcasm rather than directness. Anyway, the
past was done with, irretrievably lost to them all. Regret
would change nothing; only the present and the future
mattered.

As if in agreement, Maggie's face broke open in a
pleased smile. "Here comes beautiful Billy Grooms with
my drink, ready to keep trying to talk his way into my
pants. You know something, Neil, I've already made up
my mind about him. He needn't try so hard or talk so fast.
Billy doesn't know that, of course, men never do. Women
are the ones who decide these things, and we make up our
minds long before a man gets wise to what's going on. You
don't know what I'm talking about, do you, Neil? That's all
right, too. No hard feelings, darling."

"No hard feelings," he said to her, retreating. He
watched her embrace Billy Grooms, pressing against him,

offering her mouth for a kiss. Neil decided it was time for him to go home.

Out on Bayberry, in no hurry to get where he was going, he kept on to the beach, not thinking, wanting to be near the ocean, to listen to the rhythmic pounding of the surf. The waves broke in a phosphorescent spray, dying at his feet, quickly absorbed into the sloping sand. He wondered, as he walked, how many waves had broken over this special strand over the years he had been coming to Fire Island? How much sand had been washed out to sea? The beach had changed, become narrower and irregular. At a point opposite the last street in Ocean Beach, he paused. Here was where they used to play softball on Saturday afternoons for a case of beer. Mike, Eddie, Roy, and he, all those others; an informal game that few of them took seriously. But Neil had taken it seriously, had always done his best, played to win; it was his way of doing things, it still was.

How long ago that had been. How young they all were. The years had twisted their lives out of shape, had rewarded some and destroyed others. It was ironic, Neil told himself, that he had achieved everything he'd ever wanted, and more, and yet some essential element still was missing.

Once, to be a successful press agent had been enough for him. To win good assignments, to meet interesting people, to extract a raise in pay. In those innocent days, Neil had dreamed of becoming an actor or a songwriter, possibly a singer; he had owned a pleasant baritone voice. Instead, a long, tortuous road had brought him to his present status—lofty status, he emphasized dryly; Neil Morgan was a famous movie producer. Even Maggie's blond beach boy recognized his name. Oh, yes, he was successful, wealthy, famous. And despite it all, an emptiness remained, part of him unfulfilled, the unsettling sense that he had run his best race and attained much less than he'd hoped for. How had it all come to this? That he, Neil Morgan, should find himself unable to raise money for a project he wanted desperately to do. . . . It was unthinkable. He hadn't had that many flops. But there's always someone behind you, he

thought, someone coming up fast, faster . . . He had no idea
how he was going to put this deal together, but he was determined to get it done. He didn't care where he had to go
for the money, he'd find it. "What went wrong?" he said
aloud.

"Nobody knows," replied a small, mischievous voice out
of the darkness.

He whirled around, resentful of the intrusion, ashamed
that he had allowed himself to speak out. A dark huddle on
the sand some twenty feet up the beach drew him closer.
Someone had been watching him.

"I didn't know you were there," he said.

"Do you always talk to yourself?" A tiny laugh followed.
"I do. Oh, not always, but plenty of times. When I'm alone,
naturally. It helps to work things out." The dark huddle
unfolded and stood up, took a step or two in his direction
and for a microsecond he was afraid. "Why, it's Mr. Morgan! Hi, Mr. Morgan, it's Julie."

He squinted, and her face came into focus. "Julie. You
shouldn't be out here by yourself at night. Never know
what kind of freaks are on the prowl."

"Why, Mr. Morgan, you care. How very nice."

Was she taunting him? So many people found his atti-
tudes old-fashioned, unyielding. What was it Maggie had
said, that he had an iron rod up his ass. He disapproved of
women talking that way, so free with their language these
days, using words his mother had never even known. Besides, it wasn't true; nobody made it in the business world
without being flexible, able to give and take as the situation demanded. "I'll leave you alone," he said to Julie.

"Don't go away. Keep me company." She sat and patted
the place next to her. On impulse, he sat down. "Want a
swig?" She offered a can of beer. "Oh, but you don't
drink." She finished the beer and tossed the can aside.
"Don't worry, I'll take it with me when I go. Save the environment, you know."

"Why are you out here all alone?" he asked. "A pretty
girl like you."

"I think you're kind of cute, too."

He decided not to respond, feeling awkward in her company, unsure of how he was supposed to act. "What do you do, Julie?"

She laughed. "I'm an actress, I really am. Actually, I want to become an actress. I've done a couple of months in summer stock and toured for six months with a bus-and-truck company. I decided to take the summer off, try to sort things out. I'm twenty-five years old, and my career is not exactly soaring." Again that laugh, joyful and open, as if she took pleasure in her own lack of success. But how could that be? Neil wondered. There was no joy in failure. "When BB told me about you, that you produced movies, I figured—wow!—here's my chance, maybe he could get me a part in one of your pictures. But I knew it would never work out. That stuff's for the fan magazines."

"How did you meet my son?"

"BB?" She glanced sidelong in his direction, as if checking the intent of the question. "I thought you knew, I worked for him."

"I forgot."

She grinned. "Rent a model, rent a camera, that's the idea. I used to put in some hours to make rent money, two, three nights a week."

"I see," he said, full of condemnation.

"You've got it all figured out? I take off my clothes and men take pictures of me, so I must be a hooker. That's what you think, right? I don't blame you, maybe that's what I am."

"I didn't say that."

"Well, maybe you've never gone without, Mr. Morgan. Without nice things, without rent money, without clothes, without hope. I have—and let me tell you, it's no fun. Maybe I did turn a trick or two to pick up extra bread. If I did, it was because I had to. Nobody's around to pay my bills, to take care of me. So if you want to put me down for the way I live, okay. But no apologies, to you or anybody. Unless, of course, you want to make me a movie star." She laughed again, her good humor returning.

He sat there listening to the waves, acutely aware of her presence next to him. "Do I impress you as a prig?" he said finally. "Someone said I was. Dammit, it's not the way I see myself, not the way I want to be."

"Well, you do seem to be a little square. Let's face it, Mr. Morgan, we are not living in the Victorian age."

"If you're talking about that morning at my apartment . . . If I had brought a girl to my father's house—my father, he would've come down on me hard."

"Mine, too. You're a lot like my father, only much better looking."

He shifted his position, and thinking he was about to leave, she dropped a restraining hand on his thigh. "Please don't go, not yet."

"All right."

"Are you making a movie now?"

"I'm working on a project."

She giggled. "Does it have a part for me?" She stroked his thigh.

He removed her hand. "That's not the way people get cast in my pictures."

"See how straight you are! I was only fooling around."

"What I mean is, I don't believe in permitting personal relationships to intrude on business."

"Does that mean you intend to have a relationship with me, Mr. Morgan?" she teased.

"That's not what I said."

"What are you saying?" She put her hand back on his thigh, fingers kneading the flesh. "If you kissed me, do you think the sky would fall?"

"You could be my daughter."

"That doesn't address the question, Mr. Morgan." She leaned closer, her breasts heavy against his arm, the mingled scent of beer and perfume drifting up into his nostrils. "Why don't you kiss me?"

He turned his face away, spoke out toward the ocean. "Is this some kind of game?"

"No game, I'm serious. I want you to kiss me."

"You're my son's girl friend."

"BB and I are not close. He's simply not as scrupulous regarding the hired help as you are."

"You slept with my son. You can't expect me to sleep with you, too."

"Why not? BB wasn't the first man for me. He won't be the last. We only did it that one time. I was curious, and he was cute and willing. It's not going to happen again."

"Is that what it is now, you're curious about me?"

"Curious, yes, and something more."

"That I'm a movie producer?"

Her grin was a quicksilver flash in the night. "I am not going to hold that against you, Mr. Morgan. Come on, what do you say, one little kiss?"

His laughter was choked. "Why do I get the notion that you're toying with me?"

Slowly, she lowered herself back on the sand, arms outstretched. "Come to baby, give us a kiss. A big wet kiss."

He hesitated before going down with her, mouth hard on hers, his tongue pushing between her teeth. Under him, her body grew tense and she broke away.

"Hey! Take it easy. Kissing is a loving act. Be gentle, be patient, let the feelings take over." Her fingers played across his mouth. "Make your lips soft, relax, let it happen." She kissed him lightly at the corners of his mouth, worked her way back and forth. "Bird kisses," she whispered. "Isn't that nice? Ah, see, you're a fast learner. That's good, Mr. Morgan, so good. I love the way you taste. . . ."

Her arms circled his neck, and her tongue danced across his lips, finding its way into his mouth. Soon she made small sounds back in her throat, and she guided his hand to her breast, the nipple already erect and firm. She rolled against him, murmuring wordlessly, reaching for him.

"Do me. Please do me."

"I can't, not here."

"What's wrong?"

"Nothing. Nothing's wrong." He sat up, leaning over his knees.

She measured him in the night. He was a fine-looking man, distinguished in a rugged, angular way. A little too tense, perhaps, too quick to posture and pose but still appealing. She spoke in a small, wistful voice.

"You're not gay, are you?"

"Gay!" A hard knot lodged in his gut, and his face twisted into a snarl. "Is that what you believe? Of course I'm not. Just because I don't want to make love . . ."

She touched him lightly. "Hey! Just kidding, that's all. I know you're not gay."

"I'm not obliged to have sex with every woman who comes along. It doesn't mean I'm gay."

"Just a joke, I told you. So many men are, you know."

He examined her closely, cooling down. She was so young, not much more than a child, yet she was experienced in ways he wasn't. "You know many gay men?"

She giggled. "Seems like every other man I meet prefers another man's body to mine. How boring it must be, all that sameness. That's what I love about men, they're not like me. They're everywhere, you know, the gays. Out here, I mean."

"Up at The Pines and Cherry Grove, I know."

"I mean *everywhere*. In Ocean Beach as well. A guy I know in town—fruity as they come, he's in a gay bar every chance he gets—he has a house over on Cottage Walk. Along with a wife and three kids. And a best friend . . ."

"You mean he's sleeping with his friend?"

"Right under his wife's nose, and she doesn't suspect a thing."

"That's disgusting."

"It's a changing world."

The world was changing, he agreed, and not for the better. Sexual liberation had become a euphemism for license. They lived at a time in which everything seemed to be accepted; only disapproval was disapproved of. All the old values were in discard, along with privacy and taste and discretion, and very few people remained to dare give them currency. He started to rise. "I should be going."

Her hand restrained him. "Look, I'm sorry. I really am. You're nervous, that's all. I understand."

Her fingers fluttered and stroked him, and he responded at once, the blood beginning to flow, bringing him to size, swollen and hard. The tips of her fingers beat a magical tattoo between his thighs. He groaned and pressed forward.

"Ah, darling, Mr. Morgan," she whispered against his mouth. "Let me get out of these clothes." Naked from the waist down, she arranged a place for herself in the sand, making herself available to him. "Here, Mr. Morgan, right here . . ."

He lowered himself upon her.

She tried to guide him into place, and he slumped forward on her body.

"What's wrong?"

"I don't know."

"It's me, isn't it? You don't like me."

"I think you're beautiful." He sat up, swallowing an angry reply. "I can't do it like this. I've outgrown this stage. I can't just turn it on and off on demand."

"Is that what I did, demand it? I'm sorry, I really like you. I thought you liked me, too."

"I do."

"Oh, I know. It's being outside this way. I should have listened to you. Well, that's easily fixed. Let's go someplace, to my room."

He climbed to his feet and adjusted his clothing. "Forget it."

"Don't be angry with me. I truly do believe you're some special kind of man. I'd be good for you, whatever you want me to be."

"Stop it, stop talking about it."

"Am I going to see you again?"

"Bound to. Ocean Beach is a small place." He left her sitting on the sand, looking after him. She called his name once, said "Good night," but he acted as if he hadn't heard.

Neil lay in his bed without moving, staring into the blackness, trying not to remember so many unpleasant events out of his past. Trying not to see the faces that had once peopled his life. Willing himself to sleep, a sleep that refused to come.

When the front door opened, he almost cried out in fear and relief. A murmuring of voices followed and then an ex-

tended, threatening silence. The door closed, and moments
later, Susan entered their bedroom. She moved deliberately in the darkened room, undressing, disappearing into
the bathroom. When she returned, she wore a long, filmy
nightgown and climbed quietly into bed, careful not to dis-
turb him.

"I've been waiting for you," he said.

"I thought you were asleep."

"My mind is so full."

"Shall I get you a pill?"

"I hate pills. Now that you're back, maybe I'll be able to
sleep."

"Is something troubling you?"

"I've been doing a lot of thinking."

"About the movie?"

"I don't understand it, they all turned me down. It's a
good story, a good project."

"I liked the book a lot. It will make a wonderful movie."

"Even Larry MacDonald rejected it. I was sure it was up
his alley."

"Someone will back you."

"And if no one does? What do I do then?"

She patted his arm. "All the success you've had, Neil,
and you still don't believe in yourself."

"Spare me the easy psychoanalysis, if you don't mind."

"Just trying to help."

"I'm a producer. What am I supposed to do if I can't produce?"

"If not this project, then another one. It's not as if you've
exhausted all the possibilities."

"I suppose you're right. There are still a few more avenues open." He wondered if that were true.

"There you are. You'll find a way. You're good at what
you do."

"Right," he said with more confidence than he felt. "I'll
find a way." He came up on one elbow. "You're always
here when I need you, Susan. I appreciate that."

"I'm your wife," she said flatly.

"Yes." He kissed her on the lips. When she didn't stop

him, he touched her breast. She didn't move. He brought her hand down to his cock. "Please . . ."

"Don't ask for that, Neil."

"You are my wife."

"We have an understanding."

"That was a long time ago. All these years, sleeping next to you and not being able to touch you."

"I wanted to set up a separate bedroom for myself."

"I won't have that. A man and his wife, they should share the same room, the same bed. Oh, Susan, what's to become of us?"

"We'll grow old together. We'll take care of each other. That's more than many people have."

"Couldn't we have a normal relationship? In bed, I mean. It needn't interfere with anything else—anything outside."

She put herself onto her side, her back facing him. "Go to sleep, Neil."

He sighed and settled down next to her. His arms went around her, holding her close. "Good night, my darling."

"Good night, Neil."

Nine

BB

Jill was the redhead, Laura Lee the one with short-cut brown hair. Otherwise, they were similar. Both pretty, in a brittle, flat-eyed way, with bodies full and blatantly presented. Insistent smiles creased their faces, as if each was intent on giving reassurance to anyone looking on, on building trust, a pair desperate to be believed and accepted for what they said they were.

Harvey believed. Harvey wanted to believe. Harvey's real name was Mason Peter Hendricks, of Cross Lake, Iowa, about forty miles outside of Des Moines. Harvey was a short, plump man with the pasty look of Silly Putty to him. His thinning hair was slicked back against a perfectly round skull, his eyes behind rimless glasses were pale and empty, and he was excessively neat and clean. Cleanliness was extremely important to Harvey, which is what he told Jill and Laura Lee his name was. Not that they cared; names were not their business.

To Harvey's concerned eye, Jill and Laura Lee seemed clean. Hardly any makeup—certainly no more than Karen Anderson, who was the hostess at Pearlie's Restaurant, wore. Each girl had nice white teeth and nails that were precisely trimmed and polished. Most importantly, their bodies were clean. There was that about the Snap Shop; you found out about a young lady's body right off. The Snap Shop was in a remodeled storefront on Eighth Avenue with signs in the painted-over windows that said:

> PICTURES! GIRLS! PICTURES! GIRLS!
>
> Cameras for Rent

It was that simple in the Snap Shop. You rented a girl and a camera for as long as you liked, in fifteen-minute increments, at fifty dollars a pop. Studio space came free with the girl. A Polaroid camera was supplied at the front desk—twenty dollars a session—and you retired to a studio. Each studio was a modest cell off the long, narrow corridor that ran from the front of the store to the back. Each contained a single bed and one flat, black wall, which served as a backdrop for those occasional customers who wanted only to take pictures. Most visitors to the Snap Shop wanted more.

Harvey, being forthright and honest, said straight out that he wanted more. "I want more," he said to Jill, as soon as she planted herself in front of the black wall. Without a word, she slipped off her bra, moving her shoulders and causing her large breasts to swing from side to side. She stood with her legs far apart, fingers hooked into the waistband of her panties, and gave Harvey her most fetching smile.

"You want to see more, you got to pay for it."

Harvey swallowed hard. "I'd like to do more than just look, if you don't mind."

Jill didn't mind at all, it's what she was there for, to service the johns. A few of them came just to take pictures of a girl in her panties and bra—the costume of the day in the front waiting room—and some insisted on getting a girl naked before snapping away on the Polaroid, asking for weird poses. Jill had one regular who always asked for the same pose: He insisted that Jill stand on one leg, the other drawn up, while he took a roll of pussy shots while lying flat on the floor. Some were tit men, shooting close-ups of her breasts from every conceivable angle; the ass men were the worst, demanding that she stand, head hanging, butt facing the sky, for long periods of time, all of which gave Jill a slight case of vertigo. But most of the men she did business with cared nothing about cameras and pictures, pursuing instead a more intimate form of action. Jill—and the other girls who worked the Snap Shop—were happy to oblige them, for a price.

A hand job in the studio was worth another fifty, 20 percent going to the house. Giving half-hand, half-head, was seventy-five. Fucking, regardless of position, was a flat hundred. Anything more, something freaky or requiring the services of more than one girl, was negotiable and was performed away from the cramped confines of the Snap Shop. Which is what brought Jill and Laura Lee to Harvey's hotel room.

Harvey waved them inside with a pudgy hand, which sported a heavy gold ring on the third finger, a ring studded with diamonds. On his other hand, another gold ring, this one built around a huge emerald. On Harvey's wrist, a thick gold ID bracelet, and on the other wrist, a gold Piaget watch. Harvey respected the lasting value of gold, the solid feel of it, and loved the way people's eyes widened at the sight of his rings, his bracelet, his watch, the way Jill's eyes had widened. Harvey enjoyed expensive objects, enjoyed letting people know that he could afford such baubles. Harvey could afford to buy just about anything he wanted.

Harvey owned a Datsun agency in Cross Lake. And four MacDonald's in the area, plus a pair of Dairy Queens. He operated a bowling alley, a video arcade, a steak house, three speciality shops for women in nearby towns, a men's clothing store, a travel agency, a barber shop, a beauty salon, and he held a strong position in a cable TV company setting up in Des Moines, as well as a small chain of motion pictures theaters.

"Ain't that wonderful!" he crowed to Jill and Laura Lee

as he fetched them drinks in his hotel suite. "A little old country boy getting rich and sassy off the land, so to speak. It's what makes America great, I always say." He studied them benevolently while they sipped their drinks. "We don't have a camera here, ladies, but I certainly am ready for some special poses from you girls. What do you say?"

Laura Lee asked to be excused. "Nature calls," she said demurely. "If you'll point me to the ladies'—"

"In the bedroom, sweetie. Through that door. In this place, everything good happens in the bedroom, ain't that a fact?"

"A fact we are going to prove to you over and over again," Laura Lee said, disappearing into the other room. She closed the door behind her, located the telephone, and dialed the number BB had given her. "Suite 1172," she said.

"I'll need about ten minutes," he said.

"You got it." She undressed without haste, laying each item of clothing on a chair in the order in which she would don it again: panties on top, bra, shirt, and slacks, shoes last. When she dressed again, she would be in a hurry. Naked now, she looked out into the living room. Jill and Harvey, on the couch, were locked in a passionate embrace. Jill's hand was between Harvey's plump thighs. "Hey!" Laura Lee cried in mock envy, "that's not fair, starting without me." She planted herself in the doorway. "Look what I've got for you, Harvey!"

He was on his feet at once, pulling Jill along. "Come on," he said, his voice suddenly husky and intense. "Come on."

"You get started," she said. "I want to get myself ready." Alone in the living room, Jill unlocked the front door, making sure it could be opened from the corridor. Only then did she join Laura Lee and Harvey in the bedroom.

When BB entered the suite, he locked the door and drew a pair of black leather gloves out of his pocket, fitting them to his hands with great care. He listened to the moist sounds coming from the bedroom, the labored exhalations, the muttered urgings. He knew what he was going to find.

Harvey was spread-eagle on the bed on his back, Jill working on one end of him, Laura Lee on the other. Harvey twisted and leaped about spasmodically, saying over and over in a thick guttural voice, "Jesus Christ. Jesus Christ. Jesus Christ."

He never noticed BB enter the bedroom, never saw him until it was too late. Without a word, BB shoved Laura Lee to one side, sending her rolling onto the floor. With no wasted motion, he drove his gloved fist into Harvey's face. The plump man grunted and tried to sit up. BB hit him again and Harvey fell back, not moving. BB hit him once more to make sure.

"That's enough!" Laura Lee cried.

"Shut up and get to work," BB said. He began stripping the jewelry off Harvey's hands. Jill searched for his wallet while Laura Lee went through his luggage and the chest along the wall. Satisfied they had located everything of value, the girls dressed and departed. BB waited for exactly sixty seconds before going after them, leaving Harvey unconscious on the bed.

Maggie

"You're all wrong for me," Maggie said.

He kissed her, licked her lips, stroked her neat breasts. "You're all right for me."

"For one thing, I'm old enough to be your mother."

In the shadows of the porch, he grinned with considerable satisfaction. He loved faking them out.

"How old do you think I am?" he said.

"Twenty-five," she answered without hesitation. "No more than that."

It paid to take care of yourself, Billy Grooms reminded himself. That boyish face under the carefully contrived, shaggy golden hair, the sleek, hard body; all contributed to the image he chose to project. Youth and sexiness. Naturally, he had to work at it. Exercise, the right kind of food, very little booze, and no hard drugs. He was tempted to tell her the truth, that he had only recently turned forty. How would she react? Shocked, certainly. Surprised and maybe disappointed. "You certainly don't look your age," she would say, as they all did when he told them. If he told them. But prudence dictated otherwise. Women like Maggie had a need for a young man's attention, living confirmation that they were not growing older, or at least not showing their age. It was Billy's place to strengthen the deception, keep them happy, and eventually get what he was after.

"Am I right?" she said.

"Almost. I'm—thirty," he conceded.

"You don't look it," she said. She hesitated before going on. "I have a daughter your age. She's staying with me for a few days."

"Is that why we're out here on the porch? You ashamed to let me meet her?"

"Ashamed! Seeing you with me wouldn't surprise Cindy at all. You aren't the first young man I've brought home."

"In that case, let's go inside and get it on."

"How subtle you are. How sensitive. How aware of my needs."

He kissed her and stroked the gentle rise of her stomach. For a woman her age, she was in remarkably good condition, he commented to himself. Firm and strong. "I find you extremely attractive," he said aloud. "Don't you want me?"

"You underestimate me, Billy, and you overestimate your charm."

"We've been together all evening," he protested.

"And you bought drinks for me and gazed into my eyes and now you expect to be paid off."

"Hey! What kind of a guy do you think I am? I'm here because I like you, a lot. You are one of the great-looking women of all time."

"Of all time," she echoed dryly.

"You mustn't give yourself the short end of the stick. Believe me, I could be with anybody I wanted."

"I believe you, Billy."

"What I'm trying to say is, I'm here because I want to

be." His voice was intimate, intense. "There's nothing I'd rather do than make love to you. There isn't anything I wouldn't do to you. Just name it." He kissed her again, and after a moment, she put her head back. He kissed the hollow at the base of her throat, moving up toward her ear, kissing and licking.

"That won't do it," she said in a still, soft voice.

"Then what? Any special places where it really gets to you? I aim to please."

"I can see that. You said you were an actor. Are you a good actor, Billy?"

"My looks are my talent."

"I never thought of appearance as being talent."

"Sure, what do you think? I've got a lot of ambition, a lot of good ideas. I've been thinking about opening my own nightclub. No sleaze joint, you understand, a first-class operation. Once I get that going, I'm going to produce big musicals on Broadway."

"My, you are ambitious."

"I told you. I've been raising money, talking to backers. I've only got room for one or two more sincere and solid people."

"You ought to talk to Neil."

"Neil?"

"Susan's husband, Neil Morgan. He's a movie producer."

"Oh, yeah," he said, making a mental note to work on Susan, to get her to talk him up to her husband. To hell with the nightclub. If only he could get his movie career started. He was a natural for movies, born to be a big star. But for now—"What about your husband? Is he in show business?"

"No present husband. Four priors, however."

"Four! That's pretty good. I'll bet you did okay."

He amused her. So hungry to make a big score, so obvious and crude that he was almost appealing.

"I'm not rich, Billy. Comfortable but not rich."

It was difficult to mask his disappointment, annoyed with himself for making the wrong choice. He might've spent the evening with Susan Morgan, made some Brown-

ie points. That husband of hers loomed larger in Billy's
plans; he was going to have to work on that.

"Well," he said, standing up. "It's pretty clear you're
not interested in me."

"Sorry things turned out badly for you, Billy."

"Oh, don't worry about me. I do okay, just fine, wherever
I am. See you around. . . ."

"I'm sure you will," she ended.

Cindy

Facing east toward the morning sun, willing it to oblit-
erate the year-long pallor, seeking health and beauty from
that distant orb as if fearful it might not shine again. Up
and down the beach in groups, in pairs, in solitary com-
munion with those tanning rays. They smeared Bain de
Soleil on their skins or iodine mixed into baby oil and a
hundred different lotions and creams that promised to
eliminate wrinkles, deliver a smooth and youthful skin,
increase vitality and sexual vigor. Many of them talked,
reliving last night's activities in alarming detail; they gos-
siped, they discussed the books they had read or were reading or the plays they had seen or a movie well reviewed in
the *Times* or the *New Yorker.* They were a chic group, edu-
cated, successful for the most part, and sophisticated, traveled, and hip. Some of them dozed to the rhythmic crash of
the morning surf, untroubled by the cries of children
racing up and down the beach. A few of them watched the
volleyball game.

It was the third straight victory for Neil's team, as he
liked to think of it. Thanks, he knew, to the extraordinary
athletic ability of Nick Danning. Danning was the best of
them all, his reflexes always putting him in the right position to make a return shot, his instincts leading him to
make the improbable kill. He was quick and strong, and
dominated each game.

But after three games, Danning had enough and went

for a cooling swim. When he came out of the water, Neil was waiting for him.

"You're good," he said."

"A little out of shape, I'm afraid."

"I wish I had your natural ability. I love to play, can't get enough."

"You did well."

"I always go for it," Neil said. "I hate losing." He gestured. "Come on, join us."

Danning agreed and followed Neil up the beach. Neil made the introductions. "This is my friend, Nick Danning. Nick used to play football for the Giants. You've met Susan, Nick. This is Maggie and Maggie's daughter, Cindy."

Danning seated himself, greeting each of them in turn. "We've met," he said lastly to Cindy.

"The runner," she said without interest, turning her face up to the sun.

Neil brought the conversation around to sports, to Danning's athletic career, recalling events Danning himself no longer remembered. Despite his best efforts to change the subject, to include the women, Danning found himself monopolized by Neil Morgan. Almost an hour passed and Cindy rose, gathering up her belongings.

"Enough sun for me," she announced. "I'm for a shower and a little lunch. See you all."

Danning stood up. "Nice to see you again."

She acknowledged him with a nod, saying nothing.

"I hope I see you again," he offered.

That drew a small, impersonal smile before she left. Neil continued to talk football, and Danning made an effort to pay attention, to seem interested, but he kept thinking about the woman who wasn't there.

Cindy, showered and cool, lay in her bed with a towel covering her nakedness, reading *The Name of the Rose*, when the phone rang. She tried to ignore it, but the ringing persisted. Wrapping the towel around herself, she went reluctantly into her mother's room and answered it.

"Yes?" she said.

"Maggie? Is that you, Maggie?"

"Maggie's not here. May I take a message?" And suddenly recognition came. "BB! Is that you, BB?"

"Who is this? Cindy, it's you, Cindy!"

"You son of a bitch," she said, a smile in her voice.

"Man, am I glad to hear your voice. How long have you been back? You should have called me."

"I shouldn't even talk to you."

"You don't mean it. Not anymore. That's all so long ago. What are you doing on the island? No one answered at my parents' apartment, so I called Maggie. How long will you be there?"

"I'm not sure," she answered warily.

"I have to see you."

"That's possible."

"When?"

"We'll have to arrange something."

"Suppose I drive out now?"

"The weekend's almost over."

"I want to see you. Call me when you get back to town."

"I may stay on for a few days. When the weekenders leave, I love it here."

"I'll be there in three hours. Meet me at the ferry."

She considered that. "I don't think I'll be able to do that, BB."

As if probing for a weak spot, he said, "I'm sorry about your father, Cindy."

"Thanks for saying so."

"I mean it. Cindy, are you involved with anyone?"

"There's no man, if that's what you mean."

"Good."

"BB, it's been a long time. People change. I've changed."

"I haven't, not about you. It's going to be like old times," he went on. "See you in a little while."

Back in bed, she let her mind drift backward in time to when she was young, very young, very trusting, and very much in love.

BB had been tall and lean with a hint of mockery turning one corner of his full mouth. His eyes were blue and observant, and his face, full of interesting angles, was turned brown by the sun. His black hair was thick and curled along the back of his neck, and to Cindy he had seemed almost mythic in his beauty. She would have done anything to please BB in those days.

She was eighteen with a look of hip innocence to her sultry features. A cheerful girl for the most part; optimistic, vulnerable. Her soft brown hair, bleached out by the sun, was worn in a ponytail that hung down past her shoulders. On that particular night, she had gone to the movies with BB, a war picture that was all sound and furious action, starring Jim Brown, the football player. Afterward, they strolled around town licking ice cream cones and stopping to chat with old friends. Killing time.

That night was vibrantly alive in her memory. Crickets had been chirping, and as they walked, voices from the nearby houses rose and fell. BB had urged her to go faster, and she had protested, begged him to reconsider, but he remained unmoved, insisted that she go through with it.

The house was on Surf Road, angular, shadowed, of no particular distinction, and a short round man in orange Bermuda shorts and a yellow golf shirt admitted them, layers of fat jiggling as he moved.

BB had left her with the fat man after accepting one hundred dollars from him. Left her to do the fat man's bidding, and she had. That was the kind of thing she used to do for BB back then, in order to earn money enough to feed BB's drug habit, to keep him content, happy, to ensure that he would continue to love her. But BB had never truly loved her, not in the way she craved love, not in any way that meant anything to her.

"It'll be like old times," BB had said on the telephone.

"Not if I can help it," she said aloud to the empty room in her mother's house.

Nick

Hunched over his knees up near the dunes, trying to sort out the conflicting impulses he felt. At age forty, Danning understood that he was no longer a man playing boy's games for glory and profit. Past triumphs no longer carried him. Doors once opened by his prowess as an athlete were closed to him now, and that easy way of life seemed lost in the mist of time.

A stab of terror sliced through him; what was he going to do with the rest of his life? He was without salable skills, without gifts special enough to carry him on to the end of his life; he was without a financial cushion to fall back on. For so long, he had believed the good times would never end. Always there had been another game to play. Another team to play for. Another salary check to pay his way. And he had spent the money as it came in, not extravagantly, perhaps, but steadily, without concern for his future. Abruptly, the future was upon him, and his football days belonged to the past, of no help to him anymore.

He pushed his fingers through the thick gray hair, moving it back off his forehead. These days he played in a league more demanding than any he had ever before experienced. The rules were often unclear and the path to the goal line was studded with cleverly concealed traps. Used to being part of a team, it occured to Danning that he had never before been so alone. Or so afraid.

He envied Kolodny. Never an athlete, ordinary in form and face, Kolodny had never been able to follow the easy way. Kolodny had worked hard to get through college, had worked hard since he'd graduated. At forty, Kolodny had carved out a place that belonged to him. For the first time, Danning understood that men like Kolodny had always known what they were doing, playing in the *real* game, preparing themselves for it.

Lost in his own thoughts, he barely noticed the woman walking along the water's edge across his line of sight. Gradually, he became aware of her presence, focusing on her. It was Cindy Ashe. She moved gracefully, buttocks swinging in counterpoint to each stride she took, going west toward Robin's Rest. Danning went after her.

When he caught up, she displayed no surprise, never slowing her pace. "You run," she said, "I walk."

"Mind if I join you?"

"I have some thinking to do."

"So do I. We needn't talk while we walk."

They went on for about fifty yards when she said, "Mr. Danning, isn't it?"

"Call me Nick."

"I am trying to avoid someone," she said.

"Not me, I hope."

"I don't know you well enough to want to avoid you."

"Exactly. I'll protect you from this dangerous person."

"I don't need protection, I need privacy."

"I'll see that you get it."

"By intruding on my privacy?"

"You have a point." They walked on. "Is that really what you want, for me to leave you alone?"

"It is."

"Unless you'd settle for a silent companion."

"Silence is not your strong suit, Mr. Danning."

"Nick," he said. "Starting right now." Twenty yards later, he said, "It's a man, isn't it?"

"See?"

"Your husband?"

"I don't have a husband."

"That's terrific. Lover?"

"Just someone I used to know a very long time ago."

"The way I see it, you require constant and vigilant protection, which I am equipped by nature and temperament to supply."

She stopped walking and faced him, hands on her hips. "Mr. Danning, you are a most persistent man—"

"Certainly a desirable quality in a bodyguard."

"I don't need a bodyguard." She began retracing her steps.

He fell into step beside her. "All this exercise, you must have worked up an immense thirst."

"I'm fine, thank you."

"Let me buy you a drink."

"You don't give up easily, do you?"

"Just trying to be friendly. This huge island and I don't know a soul. Except you, of course."

"You have your own house?"

"I share with a couple of guys."

"That's two people you know besides me. And my mother and Neil and Susan. You, sir, are a social butterfly."

"Nothing worse than to be lonely in a crowd."

She inspected him with a skeptical eye. "From the look of you, Mr. Danning, I'd say you've never been lonely for very long."

"I take that as a compliment. Let's have dinner."

"Impossible."

"Everybody has to eat."

She searched for an excuse. "It's my friend, he'll be along soon."

"If he truly cares, he'll wait. Learn to exercise patience, self-control, understanding. Have dinner with me, you'll actually be doing him a favor."

She had to laugh. "You do very well with the language, Mr. Danning."

"I'll tell you the entire, sad story of my life. Over dessert, that is. It doesn't take long."

"Promise?"

"Oh, oh, now I am in trouble."

"Or I am," she said cheerfully. "Where shall we dine, Mr. Danning?"

"Call me Nick," he said.

Ten

Neil

Later that same evening, Neil had dinner with Alex Kehoe at the back table at Mom Stone's. Kehoe ordered the veal parmigiana and a beer. Neil had a cheeseburger and a glass of milk.

Kehoe was a bulky man with a trim gray-and-white beard and small eyes that peered out at the world from behind puffy cheekbones. He stuffed great chunks of veal into his mouth around heavily buttered slabs of Italian bread. A third of the way through his meal, he called for another beer.

"And some more bread and butter," he commanded the waiter. "Never enough bread, you notice that. Like they're saving money. You asking for my opinion, Neil?"

"Nobody I know has your taste or talent, Alex. I trust your judgment. That's why I asked you to read Tom Parson's novel. With you on my team, how can I go wrong?"

Kehoe tore off another piece of bread, spread butter on it, and chewed vigorously. "Friendship is friendship, Neil, a job is a job. My loyalties are to the network, I needn't tell you."

"Would I have it any other way?"

"As long as you understand."

"Would I ask you to go against your principles? Never. I am an honorable man, Alex, I do business in an honorable way. Besides, the book speaks for itself. A distinguished literary effort, and more. There is a real story here, a compelling adventure, distinct and compelling characters. I am giving you my honest professional opinion as a producer, Alex, and you know my track record."

"I certainly do."

"This book is going to make a marvelous miniseries. Certainly I could go Hollywood, make a feature first, and sell the TV rights afterward. But it isn't only money we're talking about here. This book deserves special treatment from the start, the kind of detailed and loving attention *Roots* received. Or *Winds of War*. Seven parts is the way I see it, shown on seven consecutive nights. Kicking off with a three-hour premiere, then two hours a night for the next five nights and finishing up with another three-hour session. Sunday through Saturday. The entire viewing audience will be locked up, we'll blow the ratings through the sky. You see where I'm going, Alex?"

"Nobody thinks bigger than you do, Neil."

"Big dreams, big accomplishments."

"I can't argue with that."

"To reach for the sun, that's what a man is meant to do."

"You certainly do come up with the ideas."

"My brain is never still, Alex. Sometimes I wake in the middle of the night with a full-blown idea. All the elements in place. Do your homework, and the unconscious never stops working, always makes a contribution."

"Genius," Kehoe said, finishing up his veal. "Undeniable genius." He gulped the last of his beer. "True is true, Neil. I want you to know I read the book myself. Also Sylvia, my secretary, read the book."

"Sylvia has a visual imagination, Alex, I realize that. She reads and sees the pictures. The woman is fantastic."

"My reader read the book."

"Charlotte is brilliant, a fine mind, perceptive."

"Noel Finklestein, who teaches English literature at NYU read the book."

"Noel, a literary maven. I love him like a brother."

"Nobody likes it, Neil."

Neil swallowed hard. "That's not funny, Alex."

"Not Sylvia—"

"What does a secretary know?"

"Not Charlotte."

"Readers are notoriously unreliable."

"Not Noel."

"The man is a prisoner in the academic clouds. Nobody listens to Finklestein."

"It lacks scope, Neil."

"Release your imagination, Alex. Let your vision be free; it is the stuff all our dreams are made of."

"The characters internalize everything."

"We'll dramatize for the series. We'll—"

"I can't identify with the environment."

"Listen to me, Alex. They'll lionize you at the network. Opportunity is at hand. Your future stares you right in the eye. Don't blink, Alex."

"What can I tell you?"

"A chance like this comes along only once every decade."

"Follow your instincts, Neil. Demonstrably, I am not the man for the job. Go elsewhere, Neil. You're undoubtedly right and I'm undoubtedly wrong."

"Alex, I can't let you do this to yourself. It's professional suicide. You'll become a laughingstock."

"I know, I know."

Neil smothered a belch. His eyes teared, his nose ran, a pain flashed across his chest, and his bowels went into spasm. He gasped, he choked, he fought for breath. He lurched to his feet, staggering toward the exit. His knees gave way, and he went sprawling to the floor.

Hands raised him up and deposited him in a chair. Blurred faces encircled him, and concerned voices murmured from afar. One face drifted into focus, gentle, kind, reminding him of his mother.

"Are you all right?"

"Mother—"

"I'm Debra Spangler. Are you going to be all right?"

He coughed, cleared his throat, managed to nod. She handed him a handkerchief.

"Blow your nose."

He obeyed.

"Drink this." She gave him a glass of water. He drank. "There, that's better."

He tried to stand but fell back in the chair.

"Any pain?" she said.

He shook his head.

"Heart trouble?"

"Never," he said, resenting the question.

"Blood pressure."

"Are you a doctor?"

"You should see a physician."

"I'm all right now," he said, embarrassed at the display he'd made. "I'll be all right."

"The color's coming back into your face."

He made it up to his feet, legs reasonably steady.

"Where are you going?"

"Home."

"If you like, I'll walk with you."

"That's not necessary."

"If you're sure?"

"Oh, I am, I am sure."

Neil stumbled and almost fell. Faint, his joints loose, his limbs out of control, he felt suddenly old and enfeebled. He swore at the world he inhabited for ignoring him, for failing him, for its repeated betrayals.

For so long his work life had gone the way he wanted it to go; he operated with skill and dispatch when assembling a production, turning a novel or a story or merely an idea into a shooting script, casting actors, hiring a crew, raising the necessary funds. Until, abruptly, that world had shifted on its axis, and all bets were off; the movie business was being run by conglomerates, decisions made by accountants in silk suits who cared nothing about making pictures. Deals interested them, and inflated profits. They produced movies about robots or cartoon characters and ignored the drama in the lives of real men and women. Storytelling, once at the heart of the motion picture business, was a lost art. Special effects and comic strips had taken over.

This project was vital to Neil Morgan. So much of himself was invested in it; his time and energy, more of his personal fortune than he was prepared to admit. Susan had made light of the possibility of failure. He could do something else, she had assured him, come up with another film project. Neil no longer believed that.

Making films had become too complex, too much of a strain on his resources: financial, artistic, and personal. Distribution, funds, production facilities; all had become increasingly remote. His recent track record included too many movies that hadn't shown a profit, and now the men who controlled the money and the studios were less forthcoming, less willing to take a chance on him. Frustrated and increasingly desperate, Neil grew afraid in ways he had never before been afraid.

After all, he was no longer young. Lucas, Spielberg, DePalma, some of the others; they were nearly half his age. Had he run dry? Was he indeed finished as a producer? Written off by the powers-that-were? A chill twisted his body and he walked faster. He refused to believe that. There had to be someone who still was willing to take a chance on Neil Morgan. Someone who believed in him. Someone with a good deal of venture capital.

Make yourself known, he cried in silent challenge. He needed help and he needed it soon. Given the chance, he was ready to make a deal with the devil himself. Whatever it might take, he was willing to pay the price. Trouble was, nobody was interested, not even the devil. Not in him.

Not at all.

Kolodny

She wore a flaming red jump suit that clung to her like a second skin. The oversize industrial zipper had been care-

fully worked down so that her impressive white breasts
swelled and receded in tantalizing fashion each time she
changed positions. Kolodny's eyes went swiftly from her
cleavage to her mouth and back again.

"You're too obvious," she said.

"If they gave Brownie points—"

"Forget it."

"I'm insanely in love with you."

"All you want is my body."

"It's a place to start."

"You just want to screw me."

"No, no, there's lots more I want to do."

"You've got a dirty mind."

"Let me share it with you."

"Oh, boy!" she said, slinking away. "Oh, boy!"

He watched her go with a deepening sense of loss. "Oh,
boy . . ."

BB

In the midst of all that sound and fury, BB was an island
of icy calm. Or so he assured himself. Billy Idol sounded
out his anger over MacCurdy's stereo system, and dancers
jerked and humped in sullen focus on the driving beat of
"Dancing with Myself." At the bar, BB finished off his
third Rob Roy of the evening. Around him, the babble of
voices blended into a single, oppressive sound, the jostling
bodies transformed into a single, mindless body, a strange
and hostile creature that became a threat to his safety.
The air was blue with smoke and the distinctive scent of
burned marijuana. He yearned for a joint, a long, satisfy-
ing toke, the familiar comfort of an easy float toward
never-never land.

A painted blond in red shorts and a tank top worked her
way against him at his place at the bar, cheap perfume of-
fensive in his nostrils, intrusive, breaking the spatial
rules according to which he existed. He tried to pull back.

"You alone, honey?"

"In this crowd?"

She giggled, breasts touching his chest. "Wanna dance?"

Chintzy and obvious, she looked more like a hooker than the girls in his employ at the Snap Shop.

"I could be very good for you," she offered. "Name it, I do it."

He swallowed the last of the Rob Roy and shoved his way through the crowd, away from the overflow out in the street. He retraced his steps to Mom Stone's and to Leo's, still searching for her. She was not to be found.

He swore at his bad luck. Coming all the way out to Ocean Beach to be with Cindy and she'd skipped out on him. Not at her mother's house, not in any of the bars, gone; he imagined her out partying, getting it on with some strange stud, crying out in ecstasy. *Cunt!* A cold fury seeped through his guts.

Damn her.

Damn all of them, all the cunts, the whores. An earlier fleeting glimpse of his mother dancing with a tall, slim young man had enraged him, recalled all the things he loathed about his life, past and present, about his parents, about the way they and he had lived. All the bourgeois glitz and glitter, all the lies that existed behind the respectable veneer.

In Mom Stone's, the first time around, Neil, head-to-head with another man, obviously talking business. Making money was his father's solitary concern in life, becoming rich and famous, looking good, collecting *things*— expensive cars, jewelry, valuable works of art, a ritzy address on Park Avenue. BB had avoided Neil, had fled without making his presence known.

Fuck 'em all.

He picked his way past the tennis courts to the ferry dock, deserted now, peaceful in the darkness. He sat, feet dangling over the water, peering out at the bay and the lights of Long Island beyond. The lights of proper homes and proper families, smug little people leading smug little lives.

Fuck 'em all.

He smashed his fist into his own hand, resentful and furious at a world that refused to understand, a world that refused to change according to his lights, a world that insisted on doing things its own way.

"Smoke?" a voice said behind him.

Without turning, he growled his answer. "Beat it."

"Now I ask you, is that friendly?"

A figure in white materialized: white slacks, white loafers, a filmy white shirt. A man with a neat beard, gray at the temples, with still, searching eyes and an enigmatic smile. "May I?" he said, and seated himself an arm's length away.

"You looking for company," BB snapped out, "the bars are loaded with people."

"I noticed you in MacCurdy's. You seemed very antisocial."

BB glared at the man in white. "You been following me?"

A short shrug, and a gold cigarette case appeared in his hand, opening magically. He placed a thin brown tube between his crimson lips. "Mexican Gold," he said, a hint of sibilance to his speech now. "Help yourself."

BB hesitated before accepting one of the joints. The man in white produced a gold lighter, and they smoked in silence for a long time.

"Good stuff," BB said finally.

"Henry, my name is Henry."

"They call me BB."

The man in white held out the joint as if in offering. "There's more where this came from."

"You're not a pusher."

Henry shook his head, a slow movement charged with mystery and repressed excitement. "A user of this and that. Chemicals for pleasure, that's my motto. For relief of tension. For fun and games."

A long, long beat, BB staring until he laughed, a series of breathy gasps. "You remind me of Professor Hailey."

"Ah?"

"Professor Hailey used to keep his goods tucked away in his refrigerator. He turned me on to LSD."

"Acid's not my style. Grass, yes. And some excellent coke recently brought in from Colombia."

"There's one more thing, isn't there?"

"I'm afraid I don't understand."

BB grinned mirthlessly. "Come on, Henry, admit it, you're still in the closet, aren't you?"

Henry's lips tightened. "I see the way your mind is working." He made a move as if to rise.

"Sit down," BB commanded. "There, that's better."

Henry looked out at the bay. "I'm just trying to be friendly is all."

"The hell you say." BB took the other man's hand, placed it on his crotch. "That's what you want, isn't it?"

"You're so angry. Why are you so angry? I mean you no harm."

"Professor Hailey was like you. All he wanted to do was go down on me. Couldn't get enough of it. Said I had the prettiest cock east of the Mississippi. Professor Hailey was from St. Louis, Missouri. Is that what you want, Henry, to suck on my cock?"

"You have no right to talk to me this way."

"Go ahead, do it. Right now, right here."

"I'm not like that."

"Sure you are. Pick up strangers in men's rooms and blow them in the stalls, isn't that your way?"

"Oh, my God, no." Henry held his face in his hands. "I can't help what I am, what I've become. You're such an attractive young man. I only wanted to talk to you, to get to know you."

"You have a house?"

"On the bay, in Seaview. Would you like to see it? It's very lovely, comfortable, and we can be alone there, if you like." His eyes traveled down to his hand, still at rest on BB. "You do like me, don't you?"

"Coke, you said?"

"The best stuff."

BB stood up, and Henry did the same. "Just one thing . . ."

"Yes, anything."

"I don't give head."

"It's all right. It's—"

"I'm not a queer."

Henry grimaced. "You're so judgmental."

"Maybe," BB said harshly. "Maybe if you're nice, I'll let you suck me off, maybe. And you know what I'll be doing then? Thinking about a woman is what. I'm no faggot, you understand. I'm not."

Henry smiled softly, eyes steady again. "Oh, I understand very well. I certainly do. Shall we go now? The night is young and there's so much I have to show you, dear boy. . . ."

Susan

By Wednesday, Susan felt as if she'd been on the island forever, in harmony with the tempo of life at Ocean Beach. She spent a great deal of time alone, rising when it suited her, going to bed when it suited her. For the most part, she remained in the house reading, thinking, sunning herself on the back deck. She had an early dinner with Maggie one evening at Leo's: a small steak and buttered green beans, salad, coffee, along with a bottle of soave. She began to feel rested, at peace, isolated and safe from the world beyond Fire Island. Until late the next afternoon when Turk Christie phoned.

"When are you going to be in town?" he said, that rough voice sending shivers along her spine.

"I won't be."

"The hell you say. I'm horny as hell. Come in now. We can have a little dinner and spend the night at my place. In the morning, you can go back, if you want."

"You didn't believe me, Turk, it's over between us."

"Christ, you're a hard-assed dame. Will it make you feel better if I come out there?"

"It won't do you any good."

"Don't bet on it," he said, and hung up.

She stared at the dead phone for a long time, wondering if he meant it. She kept hearing the threat in his raspy voice, the danger. Suppose he did show up, how would she handle it? She found no suitable answer and put him out of her mind. After all, there were much better things to do with her time than to worry about Turk Christie. She began to get herself ready for the evening and the good time she intended to have.

Billy Grooms, drink in hand, positioned himself against the wall in MacCurdy's, watching the dancers in the center of the big room. The contrast with the weekend was pronounced; there were fewer people, for one thing, and most of them seemed to belong together. Matched pairs, young married couples or lovers with eyes only for each other. All that would eventually change, he assured himself. The marriages would grow dull, the lovers would fight; everyone would look around for new adventures, new excitement. That's where Billy came in.

Here and there a white-haired man with a young girl; or middle-aged women clutching at equally young men, boys almost, some of whom he recognized as lifeguards. The time between weekends, Billy decided, was a good time on Fire Island for a dude with a hankering for older women. Married women, mostly, left to their own devices by successful, work-driven husbands. Not that Billy cared one way or another; he had plans of his own, and they included Susan Morgan. He watched her dance.

What a beauty.

She seemed to have it all. Tall and slender with tawny skin stretched tight over delicate cheekbones and clear, focused eyes and a mouth quick to smile, all framed by shining black hair that bounced provocatively as she danced. He enjoyed watching her move—smooth, a natural flow, using her body freely.

Billy made her partner out to be no more than eighteen or nineteen, callow, unformed, eager. He was disappointed in her; after all, good taste dictated a certain limit to these arrangements. When the music stopped, Susan made her way to the bar. Alone. Billy wasted no time making his move, positioning himself an arm's length away, studying that finely etched profile.

"Anyone ever tell you that you have a fantastic face?"
he began.

She brought her eyes around slowly, inspecting him
openly. "Yes," she said, after a moment, "someone has."

Her answer threw him off stride, but he recovered
quickly. "It's special," he said. "Unique." He held out his
hand. "I'm Billy Grooms."

"I know you," was her answer.

"You do?"

"I know *about* you," she added.

He didn't like that. He didn't want anyone knowing too
much about him, least of all a woman he had never talked
to before. "What do you know?" he probed.

"You ask a lot of questions. About husbands and about
money. The word is out on you, Billy Grooms. You are a
hustler."

"Listen, you got it all wrong."

"Most young studs around here are content to get some
easy sex, not your kind."

"Listen, you don't know anything about me. Whatever
you heard, it's not true."

"Considering your line of work, you're too touchy, Billy.
That just won't do."

He grew sullen and silent, but after a while, he decided
to give it another shot. "Who you been talking to?"

"I'll never tell," she said lightly.

"It's that Maggie, she's a friend of ours. That's who it
was."

"It's true, though, you are looking to make a score?"

He decided to change his approach, shift gears. She was
too smart to fool, too experienced in this game. He gave her
his most sheepish smile, a helpless confession, acknowl-
edging that he'd been found out. "Okay, I did give it a try,
but it's not my way. I can't be comfortable around anyone I
don't really like."

She eyed him at length. "You're cute, Billy, and you're
good. What happened, did your last keeper throw you
out?"

"Nobody throws me out!" he flared; he checked his anger, went on in a more conciliatory tone: "There was some-

body, somebody I cared for very much. Hey, what am I doing?" he said with a shining grin. "You don't want to listen to my sad tale of woe."

"But I do. I'm fascinated." She beckoned to the bartender, who brought her another drink. "Give beauty here one, too. Everybody works better with a full glass."

"I don't think so." He straightened up. "You make me out to be just another stud coming on to you, another bullshit artist. So be it, lady. Only I don't have to go along."

She watched him leave, straight and incredibly handsome in a white shirt and tight white jeans. He had a fine, round bottom that matched the rest of him. He was, she decided, the best-looking man she'd ever met.

The next morning, Susan and Maggie were on the beach as he walked along the shore. They were watching him, he decided, talking about him, comparing notes. Let them talk, let them look; it was the last that mattered most. He was trim and muscular and as pretty as any man on the island. Let her take that image to bed with her for a couple of nights.

That night, in MacCurdy's, their eyes met, and for a split second he thought she was going to approach him. He didn't give her the chance; he left at once.

Two hours later, in Leo's. Seated at a table with Maggie and two other women. She spotted him, he was sure of that, and once she did, he made his exit.

The next morning he went for an early swim. When he came out of the water, she was by herself halfway up the beach, eyes fixed on him. He began talking to a pretty girl in a string bikini. When he looked again, Susan was gone.

He spent the entire afternoon on the deck of the house, making sure she didn't see him. Let her believe he was with the girl in the string bikini. Let her imagine him making it with the girl. Let her do his work for him. . . .

It was nearly eleven o'clock that night when he saw her come out of Mom Stone's alone. She turned toward the ocean, and he trailed after her. On the beach, she strolled westward along the water's edge, and Billy kept his distance. When she sat down, he approached her.

"Hi," he said.

She was neither alarmed nor surprised.

"It's Billy Grooms," he said. "I see you like the beach at night, too. May I join you?"

"Suit yourself."

He lowered himself to the sand, and for a long interval neither of them said anything. "There's something eternal about the ocean," he offered finally. "It's always there, always changing, always the same. These same waves, this same water, might have washed ashore somewhere in the time of Jesus, or even earlier."

She glanced over at him. "Do you store them up? These clever little surprises, bits of exotic information or philosophical insights or historical references? The way a squirrel stores nuts, for use at an appropriate moment? Perhaps there's more to you than meets the eye, young Billy."

He grinned in the darkness. "Quit picking on me." He said it without animosity, without resentment. "I'm too young and innocent."

She measured him thoughtfully. "I think you're not so young as you seem and certainly not innocent."

"Maggie's been telling you things."

"Not so much."

"I told her I was thirty."

"But you're not?"

"Does that surprise you?"

"I'm beginning to think nothing about you will surprise me."

A powerful impulse to tell her the truth, to tell her that he'd passed his fortieth birthday a couple of months ago took hold of him. He wanted to explain how troubled he was, so afraid that his best time was over, that he was on the down side of life. Instead, as always, he lied.

"I'm thirty-five." She made no reply. "Don't you believe me?"

"I believe whatever you tell me to believe."

That brought him up short. "What if I'm lying to you?"

"It doesn't matter anymore."

He wondered what she meant by that and, wondering, was afraid to ask. Once again, he called on tried and trusted ways. "You truly are beautiful . . ."

She laughed and leaned back on her elbows. "I'm listening."

At the front door of the house, she faced him squarely, saying softly, "Good night, Billy."

"Ask me in."

"Oh, no, not yet. Not nearly yet."

"I thought you liked me."

"Like you! I'm not so sure about that, Billy. Attracted to you, yes, but that's something entirely different."

"In that case, let's definitely go inside."

"Not so fast. I'm not ready for you, or anybody like you."

He experienced a strong surge of desire, and he embraced her, pressed himself close, and bent to kiss her. She turned away, and his lips came down on her cheek. He reminded himself that he was playing for big stakes, had long-range goals that went beyond a one-night stand. He released her and stepped back.

"You set the pace, Susan. Whatever you want, whenever you want it."

"And what if I decide that you aren't what I want?"

"Then that's how it will have to be." He kissed her other cheek. "I have very strong feelings toward you, Susan."

She searched his face for a hint of insincerity or deviousness and found nothing. "Good night, Billy."

"Will I see you tomorrow?"

"I'll be around."

Turk Christie was in the kitchen, noisily eating some cold chicken he'd found in the fridge. He kept eating when she appeared, washing it down with a long pull on a can of beer.

"You eat like a pig," she said, dismayed and frightened by his presence.

"My manners are not so good, right? It goes with the neighborhood where I was born." He put the chicken aside, wiped his mouth with the back of his hand, and leered at her.

"You're not welcome here," she said. "I want you to leave."

He rubbed his hands on his trouser legs. "Good chicken." He belched loudly and grinned again. "You cook it, baby? Sure you did, everything you do is first-rate. First-class lady, first-class cook, first-class piece of ass."

"If Neil finds you here—"

"Neil is back in the city sucking after some picture deal."

"You're wrong, he's—"

"Don't shit me. I checked him out before I left. He ain't coming out until late Friday, so we got lots of time, baby. All the time I want." He started forward and she backed away.

"It's over between us, Turk. Can't you get that through your skull?"

"Whataya expect from a pig, I'm dumb."

"You're not dumb, just uncaring, without concern for another human being."

"That's me, okay. Just remember what I told you, you belong to me."

"I'm not your property."

"The fuck you say. My car, my stereo, you. It's all the same to me."

"Go to hell." She made a move toward the door, but he was too quick, jerking her around and flinging her to the floor. He positioned himself astride her, opening his pants, already hard and quivering. He began to tear at her clothes.

She kicked out and caught him on the thigh. In response, he smashed one big hand across her cheek. She cried out and turned away. He hit her twice, rocking her head back and forth. She protested weakly and tried to roll away. He planted one heavy foot on her stomach, pressing down, emptying her lungs of air. She tried to scream, but no sound came forth. He bent over her and worked her slacks and panties off. He positioned himself between her legs, despite her feeble attempt to resist.

"You," he muttered, "belong to me."

He lowered himself on top of her, and she mustered up all her remaining strength, driving her fist up against his nose. He grunted and rolled away, holding himself.

"Cunt!" he growled.

She tried crawling away; he yanked her back, punching her behind the kidneys. A silent cry of anguish broke out of her. He picked her up as if she were a toy, and slammed her back down onto the floor. When she tried to knee him, he powered his fist into her middle, doubling her over. Retching, unable to breath, she was helpless. He shoved two thick fingers into her crotch, scraping, tearing at the tender flesh, entering her and unloosing a series of sharp pains up into her belly.

"It's mine," he muttered. "Every part of you belongs to me. I can do anything I want with you." He turned her again, facedown, and mounted her from the rear, entering her with all his strength. An anguished cry broke out of her, fading quickly to a low, sad moan. She lay under him, trying not to move, not to feel, waiting for it all to be over.

SUMMERTIME

Eleven

Nick

Nick Danning felt tan. Inside and out. Six weeks of Fire Island sunshine had done it. Six weekends plus the last three full weeks out in the sun. Swimming, sunning, volleyball; even the ceaseless partying. Kolodny had been right; it was fun. And a seemingly endless supply of women who were more than willing to cater to him. Not that it had been any different in the recent past; there had always been women. That faintly ironic expression, the hooded eyes that provided a vaguely dangerous look, the prematurely gray hair; that, and a fair amount of football talent, was all it ever took. Danning had come to believe that football players stirred the feminine libido more than most men. Perhaps it was the violence of the game, the brutal contact, the ever-present threat of danger and pain, even blood. Whatever the cause, women were drawn to football players in great numbers, anxious to share their beds.

Football, it seemed to Danning, had given him a lock on life. From the Pop Warner leagues on, he was a natural. So many of his friends had lost it in high school, had failed to develop as players. Not Danning. He was a legitimate high school hero. Recruiters by the dozen gathered around: trips to this football factory and that one, flashy cars to drive, vows of an easy academic ride, no-show jobs, money under the table, all manner of pleasant extras were promised. And with it came the parties and the girls. Always the prettiest girls, the most compliant, desperate for the chance to please him.

You've got to be a football hero . . .

When he advanced to the pros, it was no different. Women competed for his attention, men deferred to his opinions. Until things began sliding downhill. During his second year, there was some severe damage to his left knee. He missed the last three games of the season and spent the off-season rehabilitating the tendons. But the knee never made it all the way back, and in the second pre-season game, down he went again. The following year he played with a brace on the knee, but his speed was diminished and so was his ability to make those sharp cuts that allowed him to run the best routes in the league.

During his fifth season, a cutback block took out the same knee again, and he understood he was on his way out. He managed to squeeze out another two and a half seasons after that, until the Giants put him on waivers. The Packers picked him up, using him on special teams for a couple of games, which was not his idea of the Good Life. After Green Bay, Houston for three games, and that was the end of it. The paychecks stopped coming, the glory faded, and the struggle to create a new life for himself began.

"Always before," he explained to Cindy Ashe over lunch at Flynn's in Ocean Bay Park, "there were people around to do things for me. That's the way it is with a jock in the big time. Someone to book you on a plane, to take care of the luggage, to see that you eat right, that your medical needs are looked after. Even your social life revolves around the team. . . ."

"All those parties," she said.

"When I stopped playing, I had to learn how to take care of myself all over again. Cradle to grave, the football player's road, and when your career gets cut short, you die a little."

"Maybe more than a little?" she said.

"More than a little. A lot of guys never do grow up."

"Did you?"

"I'm working on it."

"Keep working, it's the American ethic."

"You're not taking me seriously," he said.

She ignored the comment. "And now you sell sporting goods?"

"I'm taking the summer off. My boss didn't like it much, but I need time to think."

"You don't like what you do?"

"Not much."

"Then why do it? Is it the money?"

He avoided her still, unsettling eyes. This was the third time they'd been alone—and always during the day. She kept away from him at night, as if the dark presented a threat she chose to avoid. Of all the women he'd known, she was the most opaque, the most impenetrable, the most mysterious, as if she knew secrets no one else could share, as if she owned answers lesser beings couldn't hope to share.

"I need money," he said. "I went through all the football money I earned."

"Too many women," she said in a mild taunt.

"Too many plus one," he answered. "My wife."

"You're married?" The idea startled her, made her see him differently. A man this desirable, of course he'd have a wife.

"Divorced."

She nodded and looked away, afraid of what he might see in her eyes.

"I have a son. His name is Jason. He's ten years old."

"Do you see him often?"

"Not as often as I'd like."

"Have you brought him out here? Does he like the ocean?"

"Maybe I'll do that. And you, no husband, no children?"

She met his gaze. That angular face, those seams and

creases, that thick cap of almost white hair; no wonder women threw themselves at him.

"I had a child," she said without expression. "A boy. He died."

He said nothing for a long time, but he held her hand. Then he released her and picked at his crabmeat salad. "We've both been around," he said.

"I've lived for thirty years. You can squeeze a lot into thirty years."

"We're not fighting, are we?"

"Don't you know?"

"Well, are we?"

"Questions," she said. "We talk in questions." She faced him directly before going on. "I know who you are, Danning. Once you had life by the tail, it all went your way. A big football star, the big bucks, all the women. It shows, you know."

She made him uneasy. Her seriousness, her refusal to act the compliant little girl, the insistence on holding him at a distance. She reminded him of those cheerleaders he was so used to, perky, bouncing happily as if glad to be freezing their sweet little butts off in the snow and rain of a football weekend.

"You ever been a cheerleader?"

"You're changing the subject. You avoid talking about yourself, your past. Oh, not football, you talk football easily enough. I mean, the other stuff, the stuff out of which a life is made."

"You want to know about the inner man, is that it? The real me?"

"You aren't prepared to acknowledge that you have an inner life, Danning. It's too threatening."

"Ask me anything, I'll talk." He did his best Bogart imitation. "Okay, baby, I'll talk."

She didn't smile. "Your past, your life, it's written on your face, Danning. The way your cheeks have hollowed, the cushions under your eyes, the cynical turn of your mouth. A depraved face, Danning, only slightly reformed depravity." She ended with an unexpected laugh, instantly youthful again, a bright teenager on a Saturday in early autumn.

He leaned her way. "You are beautiful."

"Unh uh," she admonished. "The deal was we'd keep our distance. Two people on a friendly lunch date, no heavy breathing."

"Let's cancel the deal."

"A deal's a deal."

"What would you say to a little fooling around?"

"No sneak plays, Danning. I know all about you football players."

He sat back in his chair, grinning. "Thrown for a loss."

On the beach, walking back to Ocean Beach, they scaled shells at the water and watched the terns scurrying up and down the hard-packed sand.

"Neil says you did some broadcasting," she said at one point.

"College games for a couple of years."

"But no more."

"I was hoping to do the pro games. It didn't work out."

"They didn't want you?"

She had a way of driving past evasions, past the easy deceptions of self. He wasn't sure he appreciated her honesty.

"Lots of ex-jocks are after those jobs."

"Sporting goods doesn't pay enough, the college game isn't prestigious enough, and the pros don't want you. Looks like you got a serious problem, Danning."

"Call me by my first name, dammit!"

"Don't shout at me, Danning."

"I'm not shouting."

"You raised your voice."

"You don't let up, do you? Constantly probing, digging around inside, trying to strip me bare. What's the point? It's beginning to get on my nerves."

She stopped in her tracks, and he pulled around to face her. "Why don't you go on without me?"

"Oh, damn, Cindy. I don't want to fight with you. What you see is what you get."

"Come on, Danning, you're too good for that. There's

more to you than the handsome ex-jock. That's the part I'm
interested in."

"So you can change me?"

"Any changes take place, you have to make them yourself. On your own, when you're ready. Back there"—she
waved an arm that encompassed the heavens—"you always got your own way. But here on earth life's a lot
tougher."

He agreed. "A lot tougher."

"And when the going gets tough, the tough get going."

"Smartass."

"You bet."

He reached for her, and she skipped past him down the
beach. He went after her, not quite catching up. "What
would happen if I kissed you?"

"That's not on my mind, Danning."

"It's on my mind. That and a lot more—"

"Stop complaining."

"I'm not complaining—" He broke off, laughing. "Just
trying to get your attention."

"You've got it."

He took her hand, she didn't object, and they walked on.
"Kolodny promised me a great summer, full of wine and
wild women. He never mentioned anybody like you."

"Kolodny never met anybody like me."

"I'll buy that."

She retrieved her hand and ran. "For that matter, neither have you!" she called over her shoulder.

"Damn right," he said to himself, and went after her.

Billy

Rain began to fall at midmorning, increasing in intensity as the day wore on. Winds whipped the island and
drove people indoors. It continued on through the night
and into the next day and into the day after that. Many
people went back to the city until the weather changed.
Those who remained planned parties or made their way to

the bars where they drank too much and looked for excitement, usually finding trouble along with it. Fights broke out between friends, within families, among housemates. Two couples swapped wives and later, when the weather improved, commenced divorce proceedings. A woman named Candace, who had been true to her husband during the eighteen years of their marriage, slept with four different men on the third day of the storm, finding pleasure in none of it. She used too much Valium that last night and drank too many vodka martinis and was transported back to Long Island by the Coast Guard where her stomach was pumped out. In Ocean Beach alone, four romances started earlier that summer were terminated; five others were begun. Mothers yelled at their children, and children fought repeatedly with their siblings. Tans faded and tempers rose in direct proportion to each other. A lot of books were read and a great deal of whiskey was drunk. In Cherry Grove, a group of gay men dressed up as Indians, complete with loincloths and feathers, did a dance on the beach to the Rain God, begging for mercy. At The Pines, a party aboard the biggest yacht in the marina turned into a brawl when the boat's owner discovered his wife in their stateroom bed with all four members of an English rock group.

The rain was beginning to get to Billy Grooms. He felt the time of his life slipping away, spent without profit, bringing him nothing. Certainly there were women willing to perform feats of sexual legerdemain on his body, but he wanted much more. Making a woman was a snap, making a fortune was hard work.

Maggie had led to Susan, and he'd gotten nowhere with either one. After them, in rapid order: Allison, who demanded his sexual attention twenty-four hours a day, wearing him out; Peggy was pleasant, dull and not nearly rich enough; Carolyn was rich but ugly, too ugly to pursue; Ruth Ann asked him to leave the minute he mentioned money.

What a bust.

And now this incessant rain. He became irritable, short-tempered, desperate to get on with his life and not knowing which way to go. New York was only a couple of hours away, top-heavy with rich, lonely women aching for the attention of someone like himself. Yet the city had failed him, all his efforts gone for naught. Henrietta was his best prospect, until that Cro-Magnon husband of hers had walked in on them and tried to separate Billy's handsome head from his body. Billy could never remember being as frightened. Thank God for Henrietta's pistol. If Caesar ever found him, Billy feared for his life. That decided it for him; he would wait out the rain, remain on the island for the rest of the summer, allow things to cool down.

But he could no longer tolerate this house. The walls were closing in. Danning was in his room reading or whatever the hell it was he did behind closed doors by himself. Kolodny was out trying to track down a woman who would go to bed with him. Neither of them understood where Billy was coming from, what a superior individual he was. He donned his slicker and headed downtown.

He propped himself up on the bar in Leo's and went to work on a dry Rob Roy on the rocks. The place was crowded, as if all the drinkers had been driven out of their houses and into the rain, seeking some slight contact with other beings. A young woman tried to engage him in conversation but he was brusque and disinterested, and she soon lost heart and departed. A man wanted to discuss the storms he had been caught in; Billy turned his back. He finished his drink and moved down to the other end of the bar and ordered another Rob Roy. Another woman appeared, making banal comments that drove him to another spot up the bar. Lost in his own thoughts, he jerked around as if to do combat when a soft hand touched his shoulder. It was Susan Morgan.

"You going to send me away, too?" she said.

"What do you want?" He spoke in a louder voice than he intended.

"It's the rain, it gets to everybody."

"Nothing bothers me, nothing. Least of all the weather."

"I guess I made a mistake. I'll leave you alone." She took a step away when he grabbed her wrist, yanking her back. "You're hurting me, Billy!"

"What turned you around?" he gritted out between

clenched teeth. "You decided you want some from Billy
Grooms after all? Can't you get it anyplace else, lady?" He
longed to pull the words back, to tell her he didn't mean it;
instead, he increased the pressure on her wrist, twisting
abruptly.

"You're hurting me, Billy!"

"Hey," a voice off to one side said, "take it easy, fella."

Billy shoved his face close to hers. "I'm tired of being
jerked around. I'm not standing here with my cock in my
hand waiting for you. So just fuck off, lady. Get away."
Without wanting to, he shoved her, sent her stumbling
backward to the floor, her drink spilling. Someone swore
and someone else screamed.

Billy felt himself being yanked around. "Watch yourself, fella," an ominous voice said. A pale blob loomed
close, issuing warnings, threats. Without thinking, Billy
threw a looping right hand at the center of the pale blob. It
never reached its target. A lumpy fist drove Billy against
the bar and he fought back mindlessly. He was hit several
times and fell to the floor. Rough hands hauled him erect
and dragged him toward the door, heaved him out into the
rain. He landed heavily on one shoulder and a sharp pain
burst through his lower back.

"Don't come back!"

He made it onto his feet and staggered down the nearest
walk. He stumbled and went down to his knees, the pain in
his back throbbing.

Behind him, he heard footsteps; they were after him. He
broke into a run, slipped on the wet pavement, and went
down again. Soft hands plucked at him, helped him up.
"Lean on me," a distantly familiar voice said. "I'll take
you home."

Through the rain and the shifting mist, he struggled to
identify the voice. Finally it came—Susan. He broke lose of
her and promptly fell on his chest. Once again she got him
onto his feet and on his way.

"Leave me alone," he muttered.

"Be quiet. You need help."

"Where are you taking me?"

"Where you'll be dry and warm. And safe. To my house."

He woke and was afraid. At the far end of the darkness, a dim light, blurred and flickering. He felt lost and abandoned, sinking into a sump of despair. A sense of something precious lost gripped him until a voice offered him something to swallow.

"Aspirin," the voice said. He accepted the two tablets and washed them down with water.

Soon he was asleep again. When he woke it was daylight, gray, oppressive, masked by bamboo blinds. He groaned and rolled over, and the agony returned to his back once more. A door opened, and footsteps brought someone to the edge of the bed. He worked one eye open: Susan.

"You must be starving," she said. "I've brought you a tray."

"No food. I'll upchuck everything."

"Try some orange juice. Freshly squeezed and cool. It will help."

He drank, and she sat on the edge of the bed until he was finished. "Better?" she said.

"Better. But not much. My head feels awful."

Two more aspirin taken with black coffee. He tried to straighten up, but the pain in his back was too acute. He collapsed on the pillows, moaning.

"Tell you what," she said. "Take a hot bath, it'll do wonders for your back. Afterward, I'll give you a rubdown, one of Susan's specials . . ."

"Why are you being so nice? If I recall, I wasn't very nice to you last night."

"No, you weren't. But you took a beating for your trouble. You were whipped, drunk, soaked through and through. Let's say I have a weakness for lost causes." She brought him towels and a terry-cloth robe. "I'll fill the tub."

"Is that what I am, a lost cause?"

"Take your bath," she answered. "When you're back in bed, I'll work on your back."

"Maybe I should leave."

"Your clothes were a mess. They're in the dryer now. You may as well have your bath."

He soaked for a long time, the wet heat reaching up into his back and softening the muscles in spasm. But when he started to dry himself, the pain returned, dull and insistent, but no less bothersome. Back in the bed, he lay on his stomach, drifting off into a shallow stupor. He heard Susan enter the bedroom but gave no signal that he was aware.

"I'm going to massage your back," she announced softly, as if from afar. "First, some warm oil . . ."

Her hands were firm and surprisingly strong, spreading oil across his shoulders, working her way along his spine. He felt the sheet being pulled away and knew that he was fully exposed, yet gave no special value to his nakedness, other than to note how peaceful he felt, comfortable, with her hands on his body. As she worked on his lower back, the tension lessened and the pain seemed to dissolve. His muscles went slack, the joints at rest, as she worked her way unhurriedly across his buttocks and along his legs. She massaged the soles of his feet, manipulating each toe separately, soon retracing the path.

"How do you feel?" she said, the words slowly penetrating the thick silence in which he existed.

"Nobody's ever done this for me before."

She spread clean towels alongside him on the bed. "Now," she said, "roll over."

"What?"

"Do as I tell you."

He obeyed and opened his eyes at the same time. Hovering above him, she was equally naked, her lean body shapely and glowing in the soft light of the candle. Without thinking, he reached for her. She slapped his hand away.

"Be still. Say nothing. Do nothing."

She poured warm oil on his chest and stomach and began the procedure again, beginning at the base of his neck and across his shoulders, onto his chest. At his sides, her hands were gentle and rhythmic; next, her fingers beat a tantalizing tattoo on his stomach. Then she was digging steadily into his thighs, finding the large, flat muscles, trailing them across his knees, attending the bunched calf muscles.

When she paused, he looked up at her. Very deliberately, she allowed a thin trickle of oil to fall into her cupped palm. "Close your eyes and give yourself over to the feelings. Nothing but pleasant sensations. No more fighting. No more pain. No more anger. Only pleasure and contentment . . ."

Her hands, warm and slippery with heated oil, came delicately down on his genitals, flexing and shifting with neither urgency nor tension, sending comforting waves through his middle. Almost at once he grew hard, swelling until he thought the outer skin would burst. Each movement she made extracted low sounds out of him, and his body rose steadily to meet her.

She directed him back onto the sheets as her fingers embraced him, slowly moving along the shining, hard length of his cock. A shudder passed along his torso, and he stiffened and cried out as the tips of the fingers on one hand tenderly caressed his balls. He writhed and reached for her.

"No," she cooed. "This is for you, baby. Relax, lie back, and enjoy. Clear your mind, give yourself over to your emotions. Feel, baby, feel, feel, feel . . ."

Words and movements blended, enriched by feelings never before known. Passion gathered up in one place, dark and boiling, all the withheld emotion of a lifetime focused, and began its certain, spasmodic journey forward until with loving hands and lips she drew all the pain and terror out of him, and he was able to rest at last without dreaming, no longer afraid. . . .

Twelve

Neil

It happened quickly, all parts falling into place. So quickly that Neil wasn't sure how it came about until much later. There wasn't time enough to consider his options or weigh all the possibilities or even to be afraid. Toward the end of the week he experienced a momentary twinge of conscience when he questioned the ethics of his action, but that passed swiftly, buried by his overwhelming ambition to transform what was only a dream into a finished motion picture. He knew he was right—and soon they would all have to acknowledge it.

It began with a breakfast meeting with Gus Bailey, president of a local trucker's union, whose members worked mainly in theater, television, and films.

"This is a fantastic project," Neil led off, having downed his orange juice.

Bailey dug into his grapefruit, taken without sugar. "The union don't put dough into pictures."

"Read the script, that's all I ask."

"I didn't know you had a script."

"A first draft. It may still need some polishing but that's

141

all right. We're talking about a very successful book. Ten weeks on the best-seller lists. Literary Guild selection . . ."

"Alternate selection," Bailey said.

Neil hid his surprise. "Yes, alternate. A big paperback sale."

The waitress brought their eggs. Sausage for Bailey, bacon well-done for Neil. He waited until she was gone. "This is a can't-miss deal, Gus."

"Ten million bucks, that's a lot of bread."

"I've revised the budget; make it thirteen."

"Thirteen million!"

"In today's market, that's peanuts. Especially if you mean to go with star names the way I do. I'm shooting for Lumet."

"Is it true Spielberg turned you down?"

"The man is incredibly busy. Contracts for four projects in a row. I told him I couldn't wait. This is perfect for Lumet. Gus, read the script, you'll jump on board."

"Thirteen million. The union don't put money into pictures."

"The money's laying in the union treasury collecting dust—"

"Collecting interest. You need money, go to a bank."

"I must admit, I haven't done too well with the banks."

"You hit them all?"

"Just about."

"Livingston-Manhattan?"

"I don't know that one."

"A private outfit. With some very important clients, I'm told."

"They invest in pictures?"

"They take risks, they like risks, the kind that produce big profits." Bailey scribbled a name and a number on the back of his business card. "Give me an hour to make contact, then call this guy. Use my name. You got everything to gain."

Marvin Livingston was a well-fed man, sallow, under carefully groomed hair. He wore banker's gray, and his black shoes were highly polished. His handshake was soft

and withdrawn quickly, as if he were fearful of being con-
taminated. He motioned Neil into a leather chair and sat
opposite him in its twin.

"Now, Mr. Morgan, our friend, Gus Bailey, tells me you
are in search of funds for a new motion picture. I know
your record, of course, and it's a pleasure to meet you. I
would've thought that a producer with your background
could have made his deal with the studios."

"You know how it is on the Coast, the people running
things aren't movie people in the true sense of the word.
They're afraid of their jobs, afraid to take chances. Say yes
and you may make a mistake. Say no and you can't be
blamed for anything going wrong."

"I've never heard it put more succinctly. However, Gus
is misinformed; the bank never puts money into show business projects."

Neil rose at once. "Sorry to waste your time, and my
own."

"Not at all," Livingston said mildly. "Have you ever
met Smiley Shapiro?"

Neil had never heard the name before. "Is he a potential
investor?"

"Not exactly. Smiley does business with the bank from
time to time. You might say Smiley is one of our primary
customers. He makes large deposits that play a vital role
in our continuing success."

"You think he'd be interested?"

"He might be able to help you. I'll call Smiley, if you
like."

Three hours later, Neil faced Smiley Shapiro across a
plastic-topped table in a dairy restaurant in the West
Thirties. Smiley ate cheese blintzes with strawberry jam
and sour cream, never looking up from his plate. He was a
slightly built man with a bony face and eyes that were
never still for very long.

"Thirteen million is the budget," Neil said, ending his
presentation.

Smiley drank some seltzer, sat back in his chair. "What
I do is I put money into banks."

"Does that mean you aren't interested in my picture?"

"It means my business is handling money, for which certain parties employ me for a fee. I am not a rich man."

"From what Livingston said—"

"I make deposits for people who are too busy to go to the bank. Such people have a great deal of money, in cash. The money comes from certain business interests that we will not discuss, but which are profitable."

"Dirty money?"

"Money can be washed, Mr. Morgan."

"I'm legitimate. My productions—"

Smiley Shapiro lifted his bony shoulders in a shrug. "Suit yourself. Sometimes my friends finance projects for people who find it impossible to get funds anywhere else. If you're picky, Mr. Morgan . . ."

Neil, half out of his seat, sat back down. "Livingston led me to believe—"

"Livingston is a banker. I bring him money, substantial amounts of money, all green. What do you know, he forgets to file the CTRs—the currency transaction reports—to the Treasury Department. Every deposit over ten grand is supposed to be reported. For services like this, and others, Livingston receives a very nice bonus."

"The money?"

"Banks are always traveling money in large amounts. To another bank, say in Switzerland or the Bahamas, Panama, places like that. Later on, when my clients decide they want their money returned, Livingston takes care of it."

"I see."

"You're looking for money, Mr. Morgan, and having trouble finding it. Otherwise you wouldn't be sitting with Smiley Shapiro. We are talking pure risk capital here, which no one else is gonna put up so quick. You got no production deal with a studio, Mr. Morgan. You got no big-name stars under contract. No important director. No distribution setup. What you got is a dream, a thirteen-million-buck dream. You want to make that dream come true or you want to talk about clean money and dirty money, Mr. Morgan? For some people in this world, thir-

teen million is nickels and dimes, you hear what I'm telling you?"

"I hear."

"So what's it going to be?"

Neil made up his mind. "I want to make my movie."

"In that case, you came to the right party."

"But you don't have the money?"

"But a friend of mine does."

"Who is he?"

"Never mind. I'll give him a jingle, see if he's interested."

"When should I call you?"

"Don't bother. Somebody'll call you."

They dined at Maxwell's Plum.

"I was surprised when you phoned," Julie said.

"*I* was surprised when I phoned," Neil said. "I was alone
in town and lonely. Three times I picked up the phone to
call and hung up each time."

"Four is a nice round number. I'm glad you called me.
You're a nice man, Mr. Morgan, nicer than you know."

"Neil," he said gently. "I thought, after the last time,
that you might not want to see me again."

"See, you were wrong," she said brightly.

Afterward, she invited him back to her apartment
where she smoked a joint and he sipped some orange juice.
They sat on pillows on the floor in front of her television
set watching *The Maltese Falcon*, which Neil had seen
eight or ten times and which Julie insisted was "the best
flick ever made." He resisted the urge to contradict her, to
instruct her in the finer points of cinematic appreciation;
he kissed her instead and felt her firm young breasts. She
pushed him away and scolded him mildly for interfering
with her pleasure and told him to wait until the movie had
ended. By then, he was asleep.

When she woke him, she had already removed all her
clothes. She led him over to the futon on the floor in the far
corner of the room and helped him undress. They began to
make love. She was a careful, skilled partner without inhi-

bitions; against his will, he wondered if she were the same
with someone who paid for the use of her body.

"In," she urged finally. "I want you inside of me." She
situated herself strategically under him, moving up to accept him, urging him on.

He went limp.

"Damn," she said with more force than she intended.

"I'm sorry."

"We shouldn't be doing this."

"Just give me a little time."

"That night on the beach, it happened then. Does it happen often?"

He was on his knees between her legs, gazing with dis-
may and disgust at his shrunken penis, glistening use-
lessly in the candlelight.

"Well?" she said.

"Well, what?"

"Does it happen often?"

"Once in a while." It had been happening each time he
was with a woman for almost a year. He couldn't remember when he had last been able to finish what he started,
last came to climax. He felt useless and used up, in the
throes of physical and emotional disintegration, old before
his time. "I'm sorry."

"Don't you want me?"

"It's not that."

"Then why aren't you hard? This never happened to me
before, not with anybody. The men I know, they're ready,
willing, and able."

He felt himself flinch. When he was Julie's age, sex had
not been discussed so openly and glibly, no matter the cir-
cumstances. And when it was talked about, it was in terms
discreet, veiled, in the abstract. Women never admitted to
having a lover—or lovers—and never boasted of their con-
quests, never were willing to rate a man's prowess in bed.
That sort of crudity was left to men in their clubs and bars
where they bragged and lied for each other's entertain-
ment. Appearance counted back then, reputation, the
opinions of other people; a little hypocrisy went a long

way, and he yearned for those simpler, more innocent times.

"Spare me the details of your love life," he said brusquely.

Her face grew taut, mouth drawn down. "BB has no trouble getting it up."

His face clenched in anguish. "Maybe that's what I get for trying to have sex with my son's girl friend."

"I'm not his girl friend. I'm not anybody's girl friend. You feel guilty, is that it?"

"I don't know, maybe."

"Is it something I did?"

"Of course not."

"Something I didn't do?"

"Don't be ridiculous."

"You want me to talk dirty to you? I can do it, if you want, I'm good at it."

"These things happen. I'm not a young boy anymore. I've had a long day, I've got a lot on my mind."

She fondled him. "You think he's dead forever?"

"Let's call it a temporary setback."

"I hope so. I was getting involved. Is there anything I can do?" she said as he lay back on his elbows.

"About what?"

"About that cute little thing of yours?"

"Oh. You think of something."

"I've been told I give great head."

"Don't talk about it."

"You are a very funny guy." She adjusted herself above him. "But you're kinda cute at that." Her head went down to him. "Hey!" she cried happily after a moment, "there's life in the old boy yet!" When he was completely hard, she lowered herself with surprising delicacy into place, moving with increasing speed and force until her buttocks slapped against his thighs with unfettered enthusiasm. He found himself listening with some distaste, and without warning his passion dissolved, and his penis came to rest once again. "Oh, shit," she said, her displeasure plain. She went after another joint.

"Don't swear."

"You're not my father."

"That's a fact."

"I'll tell you what I told my old man—"

"What's that?"

"Fuck you."

He began to dress himself.

Seated on the floor in the lotus position, sucking on a joint, she watched with considerable interest.

"What do you think you're doing?"

"I'm leaving."

"Not on my account. I mean, just because you're impotent. I don't mind if you're impotent. Not much, I don't."

"One experience doesn't make a man impotent."

"Two," she corrected. "And you said it happened before."

"You're too young to understand."

"But not to bang. I'm not too young to bang."

"I'm sure I'll see you out on the island, Julie."

"Hey, Neil!" He turned back. "If BB's free, you think he might want to finish what you started?"

"Sweet child," he said before he left.

He was asleep and dreaming when the phone rang. The incessant clanging was somehow incorporated into the dream, which was transformed into another dream in which he was very much afraid and alone in a dark place, gleaming green eyes advancing to the sound of disembodied screeching. His eyes opened, and he saw the green numerals on the electric clock on the night table and heard the phone. He answered.

"Lemme talk to Morgan," a muffled, gravelly voice demanded.

"Who is this?"

"You Morgan? Put him on the phone."

"This is Neil Morgan."

"Why'n't you say so? How soon can you get over here?"

"Who is this?"

"Smiley said you got a deal is worth taking a look at, maybe. What, was he shitting me?"

Neil sat up. "Would you mind telling me who you are?"

"Sure not. Regginato is who, Reggie Regginato. Who else you expecting to call this time of the night. You coming or not?"

According to the green numerals, it was just past two in the morning. "Where are you?"

"Antonelli's, in the Village. On Bleecker. You got that?"

"I'm on my way."

Antonelli's was on a shabby block between a candy store and a shop selling antique Victorian furniture. Inside, a long room of red-and-white checkered tablecloths on square tables and a handful of customers. Along the rear wall, three men huddled together. When Neil appeared, they broke off talking and stared his way. Two of the men went to another table, and the remaining man beckoned. Neil joined him.

"You Morgan? Sit down. You hungry? They make a great veal in this joint."

"You're Mr. Regginato?"

"Who else? Call me Reggie, like everybody else. How about the veal?"

"I'm not hungry."

"A little pepperoni, maybe, some peppers. How about a glass of vino?"

"I don't drink."

"What'sa matter with you, you got some kind of condition?"

"I never eat this late, that's all."

Regginato shrugged. He was a tightly strung man, swarthy, with hard black eyes that never left Neil's face. "Tell me about this deal of yours Smiley told me about."

"He said you were interested in investing."

"What's Smiley know about what I'm interested in? He's a messenger boy is all. He goes to a place I tell him and picks up some bags full of cash and carries them to another place, is what he does. He don't know a lot about anything I do. You making a movie?"

"I've got to raise thirteen million dollars." The hard eyes never blinked. "Maybe a little overage."

"You done it before, make a movie?"

"Pictures, television, TV commericals. I can send you a résumé."

"What's there about this picture I should know about?"

Neil told him everything, omitting the rejections from the studios, networks, and other sources of support. When he was finished, Regginato sipped some red wine.

"You run dry, that right, Morgan? No more suppliers. Otherwise, what are you sitting here for with a guy like me? Don't say nothing, it don't matter, I got you figured. But that's all right. If those guys in the movie business knew what they were doing, how come they make so many crummy pictures? How come they're always getting themselves canned? It's a crapshoot, the way I figure it." Another sip of wine.

"Smiley's right about one thing. I got lots of cash. Certain businesses I'm in produce a lot of cash flow, you understand? More cash than I can spend. Which don't mean I like to piss it away. Thirteen million, that's the number?"

"Approximately. Pictures sometimes go over budget. A twenty-percent override would—"

"Fifteen is all I'll go in for. Is there a script?"

"A first draft. Rough, in need of changes. I plan on—"

"Get it to me. Tomorrow, first thing." He wrote an address on a paper napkin. "When I decide, I'll be in touch."

At seven minutes after three the following afternoon, a call came in, a voice Neil didn't recognize. "Mr. Regginato wants you to see Miss Rita Boniface."

"Who?"

"Never mind who. Just take down this address and go there now. Miss Boniface is waiting."

Neil did as he'd been told. He found her in an apartment that was decorated like the lobby of the old Capitol Theatre on Broadway, a willowy blond in her early twenties. She had the look of a photographer's model with great round empty blue eyes and a fixed smile that revealed the work of an expert orthodontist.

"How good of you to come," she said.

"Reggie wanted me to see you."

She performed a pirouette, arms extended. "Well, here I am, Mr. Morgan. You're seeing me. What do you think?"

"You're a very lovely young woman."

"I act, too."

"Oh," he said, not surprised. "You're an actress."

"Didn't Reggie tell you? I take lessons every day."

"And you want a part in my picture?"

"Didn't Reggie tell you anything? I'm prepared to audition for you right now."

"That won't be necessary. I imagine I'll be hearing from Regginato soon enough."

"Oh, I'm to call him while you're here."

Neil sighed. "That figures."

"Would you rather I didn't?" She seemed puzzled, a naive inability to understand Neil's reaction.

"That's okay, call him. Sooner or later, we have got to talk."

She dialed, said a few words into the phone, and handed it over.

"Okay, Morgan," came the gravelly voice, "level with me."

"Miss Boniface is a very attractive young woman."

"You kidding me! She's damned beautiful is what she is. She goes with the thirteen million, you got the picture?"

"There might be a small part."

"Hey, don't you understanding nothing? I want to make Miss Boniface a star. Y'know, like Pia Zadora."

Neil groaned inwardly. "What if I say no?" he said, knowing the answer. He could hardly believe he'd gotten himself into such a situation.

"Don't be dumb. You say no, I say no."

Neil engaged himself in a serious moral battle and came out the other side with his mind made up; he did what he had done most of his life: he won and lost at the same time. He wanted to make the picture—no matter what.

"When do I get the money, Reggie?"

"Smiley'll be around to see you with a couple of duffel bags one of these days."

"You mean, you're going to send me thirteen million in cash?"

"Sure, cash, whataya think?"

An unsteady laugh slipped out of Neil's mouth. "What if I take off with the dough?"

"What kind of a thing is that to joke about, I ask you. Do a dumb thing like that you'll wake up some morning with the top of your head blown away. Okay, my friend, from now on you got a partner. Put Miss Boniface on the telephone."

Neil handed her the phone and left, not sure whether to laugh or cry.

On the ferry, he went over all of it in his mind. A mix of elation and shock scored by an undercurrent of fear ran through him. There was so much to do, so many details to attend to, so much to worry about.

"You look much better."

A woman was sliding into the seat alongside. He didn't know her.

"You've forgotten me," she said. "Well, that's all right. Debra Spangler. In Leo's that night, I helped you."

"Oh, God, yes. That was very kind of you. I made a fool of myself."

"Don't be silly. I haven't seen you since. I guess you keep to yourself pretty much."

"I'm not much for the bars or partying. When I do it, it's under duress."

"Your wife?"

"More or less."

"Well, I don't get over to Ocean Beach that much. I'm renting a small place in Robin's Rest. A pink house. I spend most of my time on the beach or reading at night. I've become a bit of a recluse in my old age." He stared at her, and she laughed nervously. "I'm nearly forty."

"From my vantage point, that's young."

"You're very kind."

"You were very kind to me. And it's true."

She was on her feet as the ferry began its smooth slide

into the slip. "Here we are! I can't wait to get into that warm sun. See you around."

He waved as she disembarked. It was not till later that he realized a broad smile had sliced its way across his face. She had that kind of effect on him.

Thirteen

Cindy

She had been working on the article for nearly two weeks. Under Alex Stainback's byline, it was to stress the importance of inexpensive art for the greatest number of people. "Art for the Masses," was the title Stainback had put on it.

"Rough it out for me in your spare time," he'd instructed her. "Later, I'll refine it."

For some reason, she agreed, even though she reminded him, "I wasn't hired to be a writer."

He thought that was amusing and said so. "A job like this," he told her, "no telling where it might lead, my sweet. Schlock galleries are only a small part of my interests. I have big plans for the future."

"The carrot and the stick?" she said.

He smiled a mirthless smile. "Have I brandished even a small stick? Do what you can with the article for me. I want to shoot for *Art & Muse Monthly.*"

Except for that exchange, he left her pretty much alone. She managed the gallery, serviced customers, attended to custom orders and dealt with painters who

155

turned out to be more temperamental than most of their artistic betters.

Twice she had written the article and submitted it to Stainback for his approval, and each time he had suggested major changes. She sat now in front of his desk in his private office while he read the third version, watching his face for telltale signs. Twice he looked up at her, but his expression revealed nothing. Finished, he put it aside and pushed himself erect. Those quick eyes fixed on her as he circled his desk. He brushed at the fall of dark hair and an enigmatic smile came onto his long face. He took her face in his hands and, without warning, kissed her on the mouth. Firm. Steady. Dispassionate.

"You are," he said, peering deep into her eyes, "perfect."

"Does that mean you like the article?"

"Also perfect," he replied, and kissed her again.

Her joints locked, and she was unable to move, to protest, or to respond. It was as if she'd lost some essential element of self-control, as if she'd surrendered a long-held authority over herself.

His tongue played lightly at the corners of her mouth, without desire, yet signaling his intentions. He released her and stepped back, resting on the edge of the desk.

"You're angry with me?"

"No, not angry."

"Disappointed?"

"You're my boss—business and pleasure, that sort of thing."

He laughed. "They mix very well, you know. All it takes is a modicum of good sense, a compartmentalization of one's life." He laughed again. "What else?"

He was mocking her, challenging her. "You're a married man."

"My sources tell me that has never stopped you before." There was a hard edge to his voice, a cruel note she'd never heard before.

"My good friend, Rafe," she said softly. "Never did know when to stop talking."

"Don't blame Rafe. I read people very well. It's a gift.

You reek of sexuality. Nothing you do, actually, but the way you are. Not so much the way you look, as the expression in your eyes, the pitch of your voice. And your body, not so much the way you're put together, but the way you hold yourself, the way you move. Waves of sexuality rise out of you, my sweet, and no matter how sedately you dress, no matter how demurely you act, I am not deceived."

"What if I told you you're seeing what you choose to see, nothing more?"

"That wouldn't cut it. I've had my eye on you from the first day. You've been in my thoughts. My fantasies."

"Maybe I don't share your fantasies."

"Mine are powerful enough for us both. I think we can be friends."

"Friends? You mean lovers."

"You find me unattractive?"

"The world is filled with attractive men."

"I should do as well as any of them, then."

"I keep thinking about your wife." There was an undercurrent of excitement attached to his approach, the directness of it, the coarse dismissal of the objections she voiced, the cool insistence. Plainly, this was to be for him an arrangement of convenience, her presence in his bed bought and paid for with the job. She would belong to him the way she had once belonged to BB, expected to perform on command. To respond, to obey, to subordinate all her instincts to his needs. There was a certain excitement connected to that as well.

"My wife," he was saying, "is no problem. We have an arrangement. She goes her way, I go mine. But no divorce, no scandal, nothing to embarrass either one of us."

Not much different from her mother, she thought, without judgment. For Maggie, promiscuity was a way of life, whether she was married or not. Four husbands and uncounted lovers. Not so much different from herself, excepting the husbands.

"Convenient," she said to Stainback.

"Listen to me, Cindy. I'm going to open a gallery uptown. Madison Avenue. I'm talking about the genuine ar-

ticle, none of this supermarket crud. I've been looking for
the right space for six months, and I may have found it. I'm
talking about *real* artists, a class operation." He swung an
encompassing arm. "All of this, just stepping-stones to the
top. You can come along with me. How would you like to
run my Madison Avenue place? Does that get to you, my
sweet?"

"I come across, you come across, is that it?"

"You pay a price for everything in this world."

"I've been there."

His grin was thin, malicious. "So I've been told. Try to
understand. I'm not after a quickie in the sack, Cindy. My
life is hectic, I'm constantly on the run, I don't have time to
fool around, to run after women. There is no one else in my
life."

"Except your wife."

"I want you."

"And if I say no?"

The lean face grew hard, and the quick eyes leaped
about, unable to focus anywhere. "I'm going a long way in
this business. Come with me or not, it's your decision."

There it was, take it or leave it. Put out or get out. She
had hoped she'd gone beyond that, able to rule her own
body, her own emotions, no longer compelled to make herself available on demand.

"I keep a little apartment on Beekman Place, here's the
address. I'll be there by nine this evening. If you don't
show up—let's say by ten—I'll understand you are not interested in me. Or in working for me."

She stood up and made ready to leave. "Rafe was wrong
about you."

"In what way?"

"He said you were a nice guy."

Like a bad dream, fragmented and painful, it came rushing back at her. Beekman Place, a dozen years ago.

Beekman Place was one of the more prestigious ad-
dresses on the East Side of Manhattan. A row of town
houses backing on the East River, chic and slick and very
expensive. She planted herself in front of Adam Gilbert's

town house, examining the facade with more than casual interest. Nothing had changed; the same red brick, the same painted black door and black shutters, the same solid look of wealth and power.

Old images came at her like meteorites out of the blackness of deep space. Invited for ten o'clock years before, she'd been there one minute before the hour. Unfashionably on time, her need to see him all-consuming. Adam Gilbert, a man so hyper, so exciting, so very much alive. She had avoided going in, taking a long walk so as not to appear too anxious, until she could no longer stay away.

Adam had been auditioning a girl singer. A zonked-out chick fated to a flashy career and a young, abrupt death. Adam had known it back then, had recognized all the signs, and had cared not at all. When the girl left, someone said, "She'll be finished or dead before she's thirty. Or both."

Adam's response: "That gives me ten years to cash in."

That was the world she had walked into on Beekman Place, a world of rock music, of dopers, of venal men and women lacking concern for anyone but themselves. She had wanted it, wanted Adam Gilbert, and when she got what she wanted, she discovered it was too much, more than she was able to deal with. And now she was back in Beekman Place, on her way to visit another man.

Alex Stainback lived in one of the apartment buildings across the street. A doorman announced her, and a swift, silent elevator delivered her to the tenth floor. He greeted her with a smug expression on that long face.

"Right on time," he said.

"That's me, Miss Punctual, never a surprise, never a disappointment."

Inside, the scene was set for seduction—complete with an intimate supper on a small table with wine and tall black candles. Soft music throbbed on the stereo, the lighting was dim, a hint of incense in the air. She was reminded of those sleek model rooms at Bloomingdale's, all shadowed glass and polished steel, rooms nobody lived in.

"I'm glad you came, Cindy."

"It looks as if you knew I would."

Again that taunting smile. "I've got Thai sticks, Colombian grass, or some fantastic coke, you name it."

"A little wine will do."

He brought out two glasses of white wine. Delicate, aromatic, not too tart. An expensive wine.

"Your taste is good, in wine, Alex."

"And in women." He maneuvered her onto the couch, kissed her lightly on the lips.

"If I hadn't come, would you really fire me?"

"We don't have to discuss that, do we? You're here, that's all that matters." He kissed her again, lingering this time, his tongue exploring her mouth. He paused long enough to put his wineglass aside. She took a long, slow drink, allowed him to take her glass. When he kissed her again, his hand went to her breast. At once all tenderness was gone, all pretense of affection; his fingers squeezed and his lips were hard, demanding, and when he thrust his hand between her legs it was rough and aggressive. She pushed him away and stood up.

"What's the matter?" he said with considerable annoyance.

"So much that I don't know where to begin." In a single motion, she took off her dress, stood there wearing only panties made of delicate blue lace. He gasped at the sight of her, reaching out. She avoided his grasp. Then, very quickly, expertly, she stepped out of her panties, cast them aside.

"Jesus," he muttered thickly. "You're unbelievable. Absolutely the best I've ever seen."

He went to his knees in front of her, pushing his face against her, breathing harshly now, working her legs apart, going down on her.

For a long, bitter interval, she experienced only revulsion for him and for herself. She had traveled so far for so long, only to return to this, allowing herself to be used, allowing herself to become some man's whore again. Was it ever going to end? Or was this her natural condition, surrendering too easily to the carnal needs of a comparative stranger?

She felt him tugging at her, bringing her to the floor, po-

sitioning himself between her thighs. His insistence, his
intensity, the sound of his passion aroused her, and she began to respond. Her hand went to his head, and she stroked
his hair. "Poor baby," she murmured. "Poor baby." He
wanted so much to go back to where it was warm and safe,
and she knew that he would never make it. None of them
would.

Susan

The room was small. A single bunk built out of the wall,
a Victorian chest painted white and in need of repainting,
and a shallow closet covered by a dropcloth. The door
wouldn't close all the way. Not that it mattered, since
there was no one else in the house. From the living room,
the harsh sound of Judas Priest's "Breaking the Law"
blared out of the tape deck, the driving beat intrusive,
unsettling. Susan would have preferred the soft love melo-
dies Sinatra used to sing or the show tunes of Gershwin or
Cole Porter. But there was a certain rightness to the insistent rhythm and the unintelligible lyrics that suited the
rough and impersonal way they had made love, each self-
involved, with neither romance nor tenderness, bodies
one, yet separated by an unbridgeable void with no honest
contact.

"Danning's out on the beach and so is Kolodny. Out
hunting for a girl, it's all he does, but without any success."

"Unlike you."

"I've got you, that's all I need," Billy said. "What about
your husband?"

"Neil went back on the death boat this morning. I saw
him off."

"Every Monday morning?"

"Like clockwork, along with all the other commuters."

"With my blessings," he said, looking up at the ceiling.
"Not my scene at all."

"What is your scene?" It was asked idly, without real

concern, without anticipation of a serious reply. He surprised her.

"I started asking myself the same question recently. I've been drifting for so long, calling myself an actor and not being much of one. All these years, the most I've done is a couple of weeks in stock now and then. A tour for six months a long time ago. Two commercials with no lines. I've never been very good, I'm afraid."

"I'm not going to believe that."

"I never let myself say that before, but it's true. I've got the looks, and that should've been enough, or at least I thought so. Looks like I was wrong. Just another blond beach-boy type is what I am, and they seem to be worth a dime a dozen. Besides, I'm getting too old to play those parts anymore."

"You're still a young man."

He shot a quick glance her way. "What number did I tell you—thirty? Thirty-five? Well, I'm forty, Susan. Forty years old. Christ almighty, the thing I can't figure out is where all the time went."

She came up on one elbow, smiling warmly. "You're ten years younger than I am. Forty seems so—so distant to me now."

"It's real enough to me. I've turned the corner. What's going to happen to me? I've done nothing, I've got nothing. I'm going nowhere." He swore and reached for a cigarette. "What the hell am I doing, I never talked this way before. Does it bother you?"

"That you're not a young boy, that you're forty, that you're not much of an actor? Which?"

"All of the above. And the fact that I hustle women, women like you."

"Is that what you're doing now, hustling me?"

"I'm not sure. I've lied so much, faked so much, I'm never sure what I mean and what I don't."

She almost laughed aloud. He seemed to believe he was the first liar she had encountered, the first faker, the first man trying to get something for nothing. So many men had lied to her, so many had used her, even as she had used them, so many had cheated. Even as she had cheated; on Neil, on BB, on herself.

What remained? Some sordid memories and a catalogue of psychic hurts, vacuums where good feelings might have been stored, emotional rashes where tenderness and gentle thoughts might reside. She loathed the life she'd led, the life she was still leading. Billy was not so very different from all the other men she had known, and sooner or later he would fade from view, having obtained what profits were to be had in the relationship, leaving her empty and in pain.

Pain, in short, was what she had come to expect of such encounters. Pain and punishment, her just deserts. Guilt and regret were the rewards for a lifetime of sin and degradation. Her marriage was a farce, an amalgam of shadow and no substance; she was alientated from her son, neither liking the other very much; and there was Turk.

In her more reflective moments, she wondered why she tolerated Turk, his insults and beatings, his considerable abuse. The answer was always the same: Turk delivered what she deserved: punishment, the punishment she deserved.

He made her remember how, years ago, she had defied her parents, how she had broken every vow she ever made: to church, to husband, to child. Failure was the pervasive element of her life, failure and cowardice, the fear of failing and the even stronger fear of succeeding, with its attendant obligations.

Should Turk Christie walk out of her life today, she would have to find his equal and thus make her life complete once more. Someone to make her remember her mistakes, someone to make her cry and feel cleansed, until the next time. . . . But for now, there was Billy Grooms.

"Don't fret about it. Mine hasn't exactly been an exemplary life, either." She traced the outline of his rib cage. "You have the body of a teenager."

"Well, I'm not," he said with a burst of resentment. "Not anymore."

"You're the most beautiful man I've ever known, Billy, beautiful enough to be a movie star."

"Fat chance of that happening anymore."

She took the cigarette out of his fingers, dragged deeply. Neil loathed it when she smoked, always had. What an awful history they had written together; the deceit, the repeated hurts, the willful betrayals. And the good times, as well. Mostly in the beginning, when they were young and in love, full of hope. In some still unfathomable way it had all been turned inside out. She felt as though she'd lived much of her life on the wrong side of a cracked mirror.

Regret over what might have been streaked her memory. So many misunderstandings, so many battles, so much time spent apart, alone, each going a separate way. Why was it so much easier to be tender and intimate with strangers, men she hardly knew, than with her own husband? She had failed Neil in so many ways. And he had matched her, step for anguished step.

"Maybe I can help you," she said to Billy. "Get your movie career started."

"What are you talking about?"

"Neil is going to make his picture. He has the financing. I've read the script, I read all his scripts, there's a part in it made to order for you, Billy."

"You're not putting me on?"

"Say the word and I'll talk to Neil."

His heart began to race, and a familiar dryness lined his mouth and throat. There had been so many promises and so many lost opportunities, all the dreams that had crashed in the harsh light of reality. He had had enough of disappointment and rejection, of failure. Enough of a life that teased and taunted him and never brought the rewards he so craved. Enough, enough . . .

"Sure, go ahead," he bit off. "Tell him I'm screwing his wife."

"Billy," she said soothingly. "I'm trying to help you."

He climbed out of the bed and stood near the window. In the soft, filtered light of the bamboo blinds, the lean, sculpted body seemed slender and youthful, the shadowed look of innocence and eternal youth.

"Nobody does anything for nothing," he rasped. "I'm a

whore," he said, swinging around to face her. "I fuck women for money."

"Please, Billy, don't do this to yourself or to me."

"It's true. I do it for money. For gifts. For a place to sleep or for a cruise on some fat lady's yacht. I've fucked my way around the world. I put a year in in Paris, servicing some wrinkled old countess. I skied the Alps with the wife of an Italian industrialist. I gambled in Monte Carlo with an English movie star. For me, the payoff is everything. And now this, you get me into your husband's movie. Don't you get it?"

"There are no guarantees," she said in a low, still voice. "I'll plant the idea in Neil's mind. Despite our differences, despite the kind of lives we've led, he listens to me. He respects my judgment about books, about scripts, about acting. It's a small gift, Billy. All I can do is open the door, if you let me." She motioned for him to come nearer, and he sat on the edge of the bed. "Will you accept my gift, Billy?"

"Are you sure?"

She nodded once.

"I want it so much," he said, voice breaking. His eyes grew moist. "You'll never know how much I want something that's mine, that belongs only to me, that I can do. Just me."

"I know, Billy, I know." She took him in her arms and held him and rocked him, crooning wordlessly against his soft, golden hair.

Nick

Sweat poured off Danning. Mind and body, he was involved in the game, concentrating and responsive. Playing with abandon, he swung from side to side, tracking the ball, making every shot within his range. He set up shots for his teammates, he dived for apparent kills, making spectacular returns, spiking ferociously when it was his turn at the net. Caught up in the play, his level of proficiency rose with each successive match. His team had won six straight times and he was within one point of winning again.

From his position at the net, Nick worked the ball over to the player in the middle, accepted a return pass at the apex of his vertical leap, slamming it with a short, powerful stroke. A clean spike and the game was over.

Congratulations all around and, as if by common, unspoken consent, serious play ended for the afternoon. Danning took a quick swim and came out of the ocean feeling invigorated. He threw himself down on his beach towel, letting the hot sun dry him off when one of the players approached. A man about his own age with a slight paunch, wearing sunglasses and a baseball hat. He held out his hand.

"You were superb on the court this afternoon, Mr. Danning." He held out his hand. "I'm Jim McMillan."

"You were pretty good yourself."

"Not in your league, anymore than the others were. Even those lifeguards. Half your age and in excellent condition, but none of them has what you have."

"I was on today."

"Yes, but it's more than that. You know *how* to play. You were always in the right place, you have a nose for the ball. I watched you, no wasted motion, always playing within yourself, getting to the ball before it got to you. Most of us, we let the ball play us, not you."

"Brains over brawn."

"Exactly what I mean."

"Those young guys, they work too hard. A little coaching and they'd run me into the ground."

"I like to think of coaching as another aspect of teaching. Needless to say, I'm an academic."

"What do you teach?"

"Used to be history, social studies, and a little baseball on the side."

"I made you out to be an old jock."

McMillan had an easy, pleasant laugh. He patted the paunch. "I thought this hid it."

"It's in the way you move. Nothing hides that. Where do you teach now?"

"A high school on Long Island. Not a very large student body, with limited facilities, but we do what we can. You're looking at the history teacher, principal, coach of the football team, and assistant on baseball, wrestling, and fencing. It gets to be a bit much."

Danning gave no sign he'd heard, his attention riveted on Cindy Ashe, spreading a blanket on the sand a hundred feet away. He watched as she applied suntan lotion to her face and shoulders, getting ready for the afternoon rays. Almost reflexively, he pushed himself erect.

"I'm sorry," he said to McMillan. "There's someone I've been looking for, someone I want to see."

"Can't say that I blame you. She's lovely. Go ahead, I'll be around. We can continue this another time."

Danning knelt alongside Cindy, said her name quietly. She sat up, startled, and made unexpectedly uncomfortable by his presence. "May I join you?" he said.

She hesitated. "I wanted to get some sun, maybe take a nap."

"I was hoping you'd show up before the weekend and all the people."

She lay back down, eyes closed. "I was busy. I work for a living, you know." There was a waspish edge to her voice he'd never before heard.

"I understand," he said, rising, not understanding at all. Had he said or done something to offend her? Nothing came to mind. "I'll let you alone. If you're not doing anything, maybe we can have a drink this evening. Or dinner?"

"I told my mother I'd spend some time with her."

"Of course. Some other time, then."

She spoke without opening her eyes. "I've brought some work along, an article I'm writing for Alex. That'll keep me occupied over the weekend."

He felt as he had the first time a general manager handed him his release. Fired, unwanted, no longer needed. The same dull hurt, the emptiness, the sudden surge of fear; he experienced it all again. He left without saying anything; there was nothing left to say.

Maggie

Naked in front of the full-length mirror on the back of her bedroom door, Maggie examined herself as a biologist might examine some alien object under his microscope, and with the same attention to detail. What she saw in the glass was foreign, no longer the shapely youthful body she had lived within for so long. Changes had taken place.

Not that she had ever been one of those bone-thin model types; she had always been rounded at the belly and butt, her breasts fashionably small.

No more.

All girlishness was gone. Gravity and time had exerted their inexorable pull. Not diet, nor exercise, nor clean living could reverse the process. Too much junk food, too much liquor, too many endless nights with too many men; the years were carved into her flesh forever.

She cupped her breasts and lifted them. Slightly, just enough so that she was able to imagine she was again the young college girl she had been on the day she met Roy Ashe. What a revelation he had been to her. Full of energy, full of fun, never still, never silent, an outpouring of ideas, information, tales of his adventures during the war. He made her laugh, he made her weep, he made her care about life as no one and nothing had ever done until then. Before that first meeting was ended, she knew that she had fallen in love. Passionately. Desperately. Crazily in love.

Two nights later, he sneaked her into his room in the men's dormitory, having bribed his roommates to vacate the premises. Four frenzied hours of lovemaking, an initiation into delectable mysteries she had always been too refined—and too afraid—to try. The raw satisfaction he took in her flesh aroused her as never before, and she responded in kind, doing things she'd never done, taking instruction, a fast learner. That's what he called her. "A fast learner. Smarts, that's what you've got, baby. Sexual smarts."

After that, she was always available to him. She cut classes when he called. Broke other engagements. Bypassed school activities. That first Christmas, she went off to Cuba with him instead of visiting her parents as she had always done before. They gambled and danced and drank, and one night they attended a private sex show, a man and two women; and afterward their lovemaking was wilder than ever, filled with exciting images and suggestions and promises of future delights.

How sweet it had all been. Their lovemaking in different places. Not caring if they were found out, the risk enhancing the excitement. Whenever and wherever Roy wanted to do it; whenever *they* wanted to do it.

All of that belonged to another life, to a different Maggie, to a young girl long dead even as Roy was dead. Once life had been so full of promise, all expectations within reach, all dreams possible. Until it all turned sour. Roy was gone, dead in a remote corner of a foreign land, and she was a lonely, frightened woman. An aging woman left alone in a world she no longer understood or cared to be part of.

Leaning closer to the glass, she examined her face. She brought her fingertips to the top of her cheekbones, tugging upward. Next she slid her hands back toward her ears, smoothing the skin. The face that looked back at her was vaguely familiar, reminiscent of the young woman she had once been.

She tilted her head, studied the lean jawline that resulted. Damn, why couldn't she make peace with what she was, what she was becoming? Nothing, nothing could turn back the clock. Did any of it matter, after all?

The harsh answer came swiftly. That afternoon she'd approached one of the lifeguards. How young he was, no more than nineteen, so callow, aglow with youth and beauty. She manufactured conversation, hinting at the pleasures that he would find in her company. But his eyes kept wandering along the beach, until at last he found what he was looking for.

"Excuse me, Maggie." How formal he had been, how polite; addressing her the way his parents had taught him to address his elders—with respect and courtesy. "I'm meeting a friend of mine. See you around."

He broke into a run, a healthy young animal, his movements powerful and natural, catching up with a girl who was certainly no more than seventeen, a tight-assed girl with firm thighs and luscious breasts. He looped an arm across her shoulders, and her arm went around his waist, hand falling without artifice onto his bottom. Seeing them together was so lovely and so painful to endure.

"Why?" she said aloud to the face in the mirror. Why couldn't she accept the facts of her life, her altered position in the natural scheme of things? "I just want to look better," she told herself, knowing that she meant *younger,* to make people believe she was younger, able to compete for the attention of nineteen-year-old boys so that she might convince herself they wanted her for herself, for the beauty of her body, for the loveliness of her face.

In the face reflected back at her she saw every man she'd ever had sex with. Every cigarette she'd ever smoked and every drink she'd ever had. The thousands of hours spent in the sun in an effort to preserve her fleeting youth, that was in her face. The pain, the anger, the disappointment, all etched in that face. The tears, the frowns, the lies, the prayers, the laughter . . . all of it had helped to carve out that monument to past folly and future hopelessness. How long could she go on this way?

She was afraid to come up with an answer.

Kolodny

Leo's was packed. Perfume mingled with the odor of alcohol and overheated flesh. The sound of the piano was lost in the babble of human voices. Kolodny struggled toward the bar, his crotch pressed tightly up against the cushiony behind of a tall, auburn-haired woman. He decided to stay where he was.

"Cut the funny stuff," the woman said over her shoulder.

"Just trying to be friendly."

"Don't push your luck. Or anything else."

He grinned salaciously. "Thirty seconds more and we'll have to get married."

"Anybody ever tell you you've got a way with women?"

"No."

"And nobody will."

Kolodny moved on.

Fourteen

Neil

Susan was already in the breakfast room, going over her list when Neil came down. He wore tennis whites, a sweater over his shoulders, and carried two rackets and a container of balls. She greeted him without looking up.

"What are you doing?" he said.

She gestured toward the fridge. "Orange juice, it's in there."

He carried the tall glass over to the table. "What are you working on?"

"The guest list for the party."

He groaned. "Is it that time again?"

"People always invite us, now it's our turn."

"The only thing I like less than going to parties is giving them."

"You always have a good time."

"I fake it."

She laughed and looked him over. "You look very handsome in white."

"I've got a match with Gerry Kingsley. He has no staying power. I always get him in the last set."

"Have you enjoyed the summer, Neil?"

"It's okay, and you?"

She avoided his eyes. "It's had its moments," she said, thinking of Billy Grooms. "Nothing to talk about."

"Tell you the truth, I've been a little bored. I'm getting tired of Fire Island. Do you ever think about trying something else, going somewhere else?"

The question surprised her. "Where would we go?"

"The Liebersons, they spent last summer touring Greece. Spider and Marilyn, they went on safari in Africa. I think I'd like that."

She examined him with renewed interest. "You've never talked this way before."

"There's so much to do, so much we've never seen."

"It's something to think about. But not today. I've got this party to plan. There are eighty-two names on the list. Which means a few hundred people will drift in and out of here."

"Drinking my booze, eating my food." He made a face. "Most of them I won't know and I won't like."

She laughed. "The love of your life will probably come traipsing through the door that night."

"You are the love of my life, Susan." He took her hand. "You always have been, you always will be."

She withdrew her hand. "And I love you, Neil, in my fashion." She rose abruptly, as if embarrassed. "Now, what would you like to eat? Nobody can play tennis on an empty stomach."

He lost three straight sets to Gerry Kingsley, the first time that had ever happened. Elated with his victory, Kingsley offered to spring for lunch at MacCurdy's. Neil declined.

"I'm completely depressed," he said. "The continued sight of you will only send me off into even lower regions. Next time, I'm going to run you off the court."

"For double the stakes!" Kingsley called after him.

Neil went back to the house, showered, and put on a pair of plaid swim trunks and a blue terry-cloth jacket before heading down to the beach. He spotted Nick Danning.

"We're having a party," he started out. "You'll come, of course."

"Sounds nice."

"Lots of people. My wife knows everybody on the island. Always plenty of single women. I assume that won't keep you away."

"I have a great fondness for women."

"Young, old, single, married. Whatever your taste, just reach out. If you want to bring a date, okay, but it's carrying coals to Newcastle."

Danning wondered if Cindy would be there. "Thanks for asking."

"The invitation's for nine, but no one gets there before ten and things don't start jumping until eleven. God knows when it will end."

"You're not mad at me?" Julie said.

"It wasn't your fault."

"It wasn't anybody's fault."

"I've got a lot on my mind these days. Business, a new picture, hiring a director, casting. All of that."

"Sounds exciting."

"A lot of hard work. So we'll see you at the party?"

"Next Saturday night, you said."

"That's it."

"Okay if I bring someone?"

"A man, you mean?"

"Woman does not live by grass alone."

He smiled to show he wasn't as square as he sometimes appeared to be. Not anymore, he reminded himself, not with the steady flow of young, hip women who'd passed through his life. "Bring anyone you want."

"I've got lots of friends."

"And we'll have lots of liquor for them."

By the middle of the day, he'd invited nearly fifty people. Some he knew only slightly, others were merely familiar and attractive faces he saw on the beach. Each summer he repeated the process, inviting strangers to Susan's annual party.

Why did he do it?

Partly to assure himself there would be a cadre of congenial people present, people Neil wanted to be around. It made it *his* party, too—not just Susan's. Partly to give the evening a festive, lively air, to create the illusion that Neil Morgan's party was the biggest, the noisiest, the best of the season. Partly in hope that some new and delightful presence would enter his life, stir up dormant passions, make him again into the vigorous and aggressive man he used to be.

He drifted away from Ocean Beach, strolling toward the setting sun. He was bored with all the empty chatter, the predictable jokes, the same pointless sexual thrust and parry. He increased his pace, walked faster, aware of the pull in his thighs. Was it his age or simply the lack of conditioning? Preoccupied with the picture, he had played very little tennis during the year. That was it, of course; he was out of shape. Otherwise, Kingsley would never have been able to beat him.

He vowed to work himself back into playing condition. Mean and lean, like Nick Danning. How he envied Danning. As an adolescent, Neil had yearned to play shortstop for the Yankees, but he'd always been awkward and uncoordinated, a mediocre athlete. Not until he began playing tennis was he able to shine at all. A lesson a day for two years, learning the rudiments of the game, then stringing the separate elements together. Until he became a first-rate club player.

Okay, not first-rate. But damn good. Solid and aggressive, willing to gamble, attacking at the net. Neil knew he lacked the fluidity of a natural athlete, but he made up for it with desire, he assured himself, with an overwhelming will to win. Not even Nick Danning wanted to win as much as Neil Morgan did.

You could bet on that.

He recognized her from the rear, which was absurd since he'd seen her only twice before and never on the beach, never in a bikini. He paused and watched. On her knees, she straightened her blanket, her body womanly and surprisingly full. Nothing girlish about her. With a softness to

her flesh, a comforting humanity, as if she had made peace
with her own mortality. She lay facedown and undid the
bra and settled in for some serious sunbathing. He came
up alongside her.

"Debra Spangler, isn't it?"

One eye opened reluctantly, squinting up at him. "Move
out of the sun," she said, "so I can see your face, whoever
you are." He positioned himself in front of her, sitting on
the sand, and she smiled in greeting. "Mr. Morgan. How
nice to see you again. Excuse me for not getting up but—"
She indicated the undone bra. "I may be liberated," she
said with a giggle, "but going topless is not my thing."

"That's reassuring. I find public nudity confusing."

She adjusted the bra. "Confusing?"

"I never know where to look."

Laughing, she sat up. "There, I'm correct and covered
now. I wouldn't want to confuse you."

He looked her over openly. "I don't think you'd confuse
me at all."

"I'll take that as a compliment."

"It's meant that way. You're a very handsome woman."

"And you're a very handsome man."

"Well," he said, "where do we go from here?"

"Where would you like to go?"

In the flimsy bra, her breasts were full and heavy. Hers
was a woman's body, the body of a woman who had experienced many things.

"Are you married?" he said.

"Divorced. But you have a wife?"

"Yes, and a son."

"I have two children. They live with their father."

"Isn't that difficult for you? I mean, you must miss
them."

"Once in a while. I was never designed to be a mother.
That sounds strange, I know, maybe perverted to a man
like you. The children are better off with their father. He's
remarried to a very fine woman who is good to them. You
can't understand that, can you?"

He sighed. "A few years ago, no. But now, well, I see life
differently lately. I guess I'm getting old."

"Or simply growing up."

"This son of mine—he shows up from time to time unannounced."

"And unwanted?"

"He's my only child. Still, there are moments when—" He broke off.

"You don't like him very much?"

"Is that perverted? Not liking your own child? I can't help it. He's not what I would have liked him to be."

"It happens. Those cute kids grow up to be adults who are not what we hoped for, not what we admire."

"I don't understand where I went wrong."

"Maybe you didn't. Put it down to genetics, over which none of us has any control." She smiled encouragingly. "At least you have a good marriage."

He chose his words with care. "Susan and I have been together a long time."

"I see. Your wife doesn't understand you."

He knew that he was being teased. "It may be she understands me too well."

"How refreshing! An honest man, a rare bird, Mr. Morgan."

"Honest. No one's ever accused me of that before. Maybe you're right, maybe I have grown up. And for crying out loud, will you please call me Neil?"

"I'm thirsty, Neil," she said. "I intend to go back to my little pink house for a long cool drink. Would that interest you?" She left him behind, watching her go. Until he leaped to his feet and hurried to catch up.

Susan

"I love you," he said.

The words ricocheted around the inside of her skull, faint, familiar, used-up words that lacked concrete meaning. Used too many times by men she had known. Used too many times by herself. Always empty and devious, intended to soothe the sayer, to deceive and distract, conveying nothing.

"I love you," he said again, a suggestion of surprise in his voice. "I truly do love you."

His head was on her breast, a leg across her thighs. She stroked his golden hair idly, thinking that it mattered not at all whether or not he loved her. What concerned her more were her own feelings, her own needs, the role he played in her life.

"You're sweet," she said to fill the silence.

He sat up, the handsome face twisted in rage. Or was it anguish? Not that she cared, not really.

"You don't believe me." He was challenging her.

"Don't push it, Billy." She was weary, oppressed by the day that lay in front of her, and the night. Weariness was the only constant in her life, weariness and boredom, a rising sense of the futility of everything she did.

"I want you to know," he said. "At first with you, it was all for me, what was in it for me. But it's different now. I have feelings, honest, powerful feelings for you. I love you, Susan."

"You seem so young . . ."

"Childish?"

"It's just that I've done so much."

"Haven't I? I've lived enough for two men. I can make you happy, Susan."

"I'm not sure I believe in happiness any longer. A few minutes of pleasure, that may be all we're entitled to. The pursuit of happiness, that's what the Constitution says. I've done a lot of pursuing and not much catching."

"You're so cynical. Leave Neil, come away with me. We'll make a new life for ourselves."

"That sounds like something out of one of my husband's movies. How romantic, how wonderful, how impractical."

"It could be wonderful."

"Where would we go, Billy?" The idea was titillating, an adult fairy tale.

"There's a little fishing village in Mexico that I've been to. North of Zihuatanejo. The mountains come right down to the edge of the beaches, all lush and green. Por-

poises play offshore, and you can catch your own dinner by
going out a little ways in a small boat. Pigs run wild in the
streets, and there are no telephones. The ocean is tranquil
and blue and the sky is clear. There are no tourists, only an
occasional fishing party. We can lie on the beach and make
love, and in the evening we'll dine at the cantina and
drink dark Mexican beer and—"

"It sounds like a Mexican version of Fire Island."

His mouth drew down. "You're making fun of me."

"Oh, no, my darling. The way you feel about your fishing village is the way I used to feel about this place when I
first came here. Idyllic. But nothing stays the same, Billy,
all utopias are finally corrupted. It's in the nature of
things." She propped herself up with a pillow, lit a cigarette. "What would we do there?"

"Do?" The question took him by surprise. "Eat, swim,
talk, make love."

"How would we live? Only the very poor and the very
rich can afford to do those things without concern about
money. I'm not rich, and I haven't been very poor since I
was a child."

"You are making fun of me."

"Not at all. What you see before you is a middle-aged
lady who has lived a certain kind of life, dependent all
these years on my husband, who has done very well by me.
You're saying I should change all that. Do you think Neil
would continue to support me if I went away with you?
Support me and you, Billy? You don't know Neil very well;
he is a man who takes rejection very badly and who won't
suffer defeat and embarrassment, if he can help it."

"I can work."

"Are there many jobs in Paradise?" She began to dress.

"We'll find a way, if you love me. Do you love me, that's
the point." He rushed on, not daring to await her answer.
"I love you and that's all that matters. You don't love your
husband, you never did. You hate him, you told me so. This
is our chance to start a new life. Come away with me."

Hate Neil, she repeated to herself. Had she told Billy
that? Certainly she despaired of Neil's ever transforming
himself into the man she believed him to be when first

they met. How strong he had appeared to her then, how in control, dedicated to carving out a good life for himself and for her.

She, a small-town girl transplanted to New York City, overwhelmed by the size and scope of the city, by the number of people, by the tall buildings, by the nervous tempo of the city. It seemed to her everyone was vastly more clever than she, quick and confident, so sure of themselves. And Neil was the quickest, the wisest, the strongest of them all. That had been a long time ago but no less vivid for being so. Yes, Neil had disappointed her, had turned out to be less than she expected him to be. Hate Neil? Oh, no . . .

"Don't leave," Billy said.

Perched on the bed, looking younger than ever. Too pretty to be part of this demanding world.

"Dorian Gray," she said softly.

He scowled and, rather than being fearsome, seemed even more boyish. Untouched somehow by the life he had led. "What's that supposed to mean?"

"Don't ever have your portrait done, Billy."

"I'm talking about love and you bring up painting. What are you thinking?"

She kissed the top of his golden head. "I think I do love you after all, Billy. Just a little bit."

"Does that mean you're coming to Mexico with me?"

"It means I'm going back to my house, shower, change my clothes, and get ready to go into the city."

"There's nothing for you in New York."

"Maybe you're right," she said, thinking about Turk Christie. "But I'm going, anyway."

His instincts took over. "It's a man, isn't it?"

"Don't be silly. Is that what you think, that I get out of your bed and go to another man?"

He refused to be diverted. "All this time, you've had another guy on the side. It's true, isn't it? How long have you been screwing him?"

She almost laughed. He, of all people, felt betrayed, even as she was betraying her husband with him. How many women had he slept with? Without concern for their husbands, lovers, families. Without a hint of remorse over vows broken, lies told, promises put aside. It wasn't as if she chose to go to Turk; she had no choice.

"There is no one else," she said with as much conviction as she could muster.

He brought the pistol out of the dresser drawer, even as Henrietta Caesar had brought it out. "I can't take this," he said.

"Put that thing away." She was afraid of guns, had been even as a child in South Dakota, frightened by her father's hunting rifles and shotguns.

He began to load it. "I'm going to kill you, Susan, and then kill myself." He snapped the cylinder back into place. "You're my only chance for a real life, my only chance to go straight. Neil's money, his movie, I don't care about them. I care only about us." He aimed the pistol at her breast.

"Billy, you're beginning to scare me."

"I mean what I say." And at once he began to believe himself. "I will kill you."

A shining glaze covered his eyes, and for the first time she believed him, too. "Please, put the gun away, Billy."

He worked the hammer back. Click, click, click. "Do you love him?"

The muzzle of the pistol loomed large and black, deeply ominous. "Billy, if you make a mistake—"

"Do you love him?"

"No," she said in a heavy, confessional voice, an admission of wrongdoing, an end to her life.

"Cunt," he bit off. "Is he better for you than I am?"

"No . . ."

"Is he better-looking?"

"Oh, no . . ."

"Does he love you as much as I do?"

"Oh, Billy, he doesn't even like me."

"Then why?" His eyes were moist, beginning to tear. "I love you so much."

"He—he frightens me."

"What do you mean?"

"He's hit me, he promises to do worse if I don't keep seeing him. He's mean, cruel—"

"He beat you, the bastard! The filthy bastard." He eased the hammer back into place, lowered the pistol. His shoulders slumped. "I'll kill him. . . ."

"Good-bye, Billy."

"Let me go with you. Or tell me where he lives. I'll go there myself, I'll shoot him. The bastard deserves to die."

"No, Billy. You stay out of this."

His chin was on his chest, his eyes downcast. "I don't want to lose you. Please don't leave me, please."

"I have to go now, Billy."

"When am I going to see you again?"

She answered on her way out of his room, "I don't know."

Billy

He made up his mind and dressed quickly, wearing a loose-fitting shirt outside his slacks. The pistol, under his belt at the small of his back, felt tight and cool, reassuring. He caught the next ferry for Bayshore and located his car, an ancient red Volkswagen. He got it started and let it warm up for ten minutes before switching off the ignition. He sat behind the wheel, eyes fixed on the ferry dock.

It was shortly after noon when Susan stepped off the ferry. She went through the parking lot, strikingly beautiful in a white linen pant suit, getting into a white Mercedes convertible with a black top. Seconds later she pulled out of the lot, Billy at a discreet distance behind.

The drive was uneventful, and they made it into Manhattan in less than ninety minutes. She maneuvered through city traffic with the almost arrogant skill of a taxi driver, parking in a no-parking zone in front of her apartment house on Park Avenue. She gave the doorman the car keys and he flagged down a taxi and off she went, Billy following. Through Central Park at Eighty-fourth Street and down Central Park West, onto Sixty-seventh Street, stopping in front of a solid, pale, granite building. She got

out and went inside. Billy double-parked and went in after
her. In the outer lobby, a doorman barred the way.

"May I help you, sir?"

"I'm with Mrs. Morgan. I was parking the car."

"Mrs. Morgan, sir?"

"The woman who just went in. I've forgotten the apartment number."

"That would be Mr. Christie, sir. I'll call up and an-
nounce you. May I have your name, sir?"

Billy thought fast. "The name's Bennett," he said, "but
I need some cigarettes. Is there a store nearby?"

"One block over on Columbus Avenue, a number of
places . . ."

"Be back in a couple of minutes."

Outside, Billy located the service entrance; a television
camera was in place above the door, traversing slowly
from left to right. When the camera began its swing, he
ducked out of range and went inside. On the wall, an
apartment directory hung along with another television
camera and an intercom system. Putting his back to the
camera, he located the name, Christie; apartment 5A.
Using the small blade on his Swiss army knife, he worked
the spring bolt back and opened the metal security door.

On the fifth floor, two plain brown doors facing each
other, garbage pails properly closed, standing alongside
each one. Billy felt safe; no one was likely to be using the
service elevator at this hour. He pressed the call bell. Seconds later, approaching footsteps, a lock released and the
door opened.

"Yeah?"

"Mr. Christie?"

"I'm Christie, whataya want?"

Offering his most disarming smile, Billy reached for the
pistol at his back, jamming it into Christie's considerable
middle.

"Inside, motherfucker."

"What the hell is this? This a stickup?"

"Where is she?" In the kitchen he located a swinging
door. "Let's go, through there."

The living room was a large chamber with a high,

carved ceiling decorated in surprisingly good taste. Susan
Morgan stood at the floor-to-ceiling windows, gazing down
at the street below. She turned as they entered, and her
eyes went round.

"Oh, Billy, you shouldn't be here."

"You know this creep?" Turk said.

"This will only make it worse," Susan said.

"Who is this guy?" Christie demanded. "What is he
doing here?"

"Billy," Susan said, taking a step toward them, "for
God's sake get out of here before you do something terribly
stupid." She could scarcely believe any of this was happening. It was incredible to her that she was in Turk's apartment again—but Billy?

"You heard her, fella," Turk said. "Take off while you
still can."

Billy shoved the pistol against Christie's back. "I'm
going to blow you away, scumbag. Then you'll be free,
Susan. We can be together, go wherever we want, do whatever we want."

Christie shifted his weight, sensitive to the pistol digging deeper into his lower back. He leaned slightly. "Take
my advice, fella, whatever you've got in mind, forget it."

"Shut up! Susan, you'd better leave. There's no need for
you to witness this. Wait for me downstairs. My car's
parked out front, a red Volkswagen. Once I take care of
this animal we'll head back to the island and—"

Christie moved with amazing speed for a man of his
bulk. His left arm swung out in front of his body as it spun,
his elbow driving the pistol off-line. In the same motion, he
sent his huge right fist into Billy's face, catapulting him to
the floor, the pistol clattering to one side. In swift se-
quence, Christie leaped in the air, landing on Billy with
both knees. The air whoosed out of the fallen man. Back on
his feet, Christie kicked him twice.

"Enough, Turk!" Susan screamed. "You'll kill him."

Christie's head came up, and the hot glow faded out of
his eyes. Susan held the pistol now, pointing at him. A
slow grin curled his fleshy mouth. "Okay, you want this
sucker alive, you got it." He prodded Billy with his toe.

"Get up, asshole, and get out of here. I see you again, I'll break your balls."

"Susan," Billy moaned. Blood seeped from his nose, and his mouth and eyes were dull and damp.

"Go away, Billy, while you still can."

When he was gone, Christie returned to the living room. He held out his hand. "Gimme the piece, I'll take care of it."

She shook her head. "I don't think so."

"Suit yourself; keep it, if you want. Only let's get on with the business at hand. I've had a hard-on for you all week."

"You touch me again, Turk, and I'll kill you."

"Jesus, first the asshole and now the cunt. I guess it ain't my day. Okay, so this is the finish for us, so be it. You think I'd try anything with a loaded piece pointed at my guts?"

She edged around him. At the door, she paused to put the weapon in her purse, and at that instant he charged, on her before she could react. His powerful arms encircling her, lifting her off her feet, carrying her into the bedroom. He heaved her on the bed, as if she were weightless, before he hit her. Only when she began to whimper, to plead for mercy, did he stop.

"Amateurs," he growled, taking off his pants. "Amateurs."

When Billy reached the street, the red Volkswagen was gone. He leaned against a parked panel truck and began to sob. Everything was going wrong for him today. Presently he wiped his eyes and blew his nose, and looked around. An elderly woman guarding three brown shopping bags watched from across the street, back against a building.

"Who took my car?" he yelled at her.

Her jaw worked soundlessly.

"You see who stole my car?"

Her head rolled from side to side.

"You didn't see him?"

Her mouth opened; some teeth were missing. "Wasn't stole," she said.

"It's gone, they took it."

"Was the cops," she said with considerable glee.

"The cops?"

"You was towed. Took you to the pound is what they did. Cost you plenty to get it back," she gloated. "Shouldn't've done it, shouldn't't've done it."

"What are you babbling about?"

"Double-parked. It's against the law, double-parking, it's against the law."

Fifteen

Cindy

It had been a productive day so far. Seven paintings sold off the walls to drop-in customers, and another thirty-five to Independent Manufacturing Corporation for its new headquarters building in White Plains. That was the bulk of Stainback's trade, selling art for the offices and corridors of big business. Most of the buyers knew next to nothing about art, making their purchases according to the recommendations of Stainback's salespeople. So many boats, so many flying geese, so many animal pictures. A dozen blues, a dozen reds, a dozen yellows. Waves breaking over rocks were always well received. Mountains did well, as did misty water scenes that resembled fishing villages in Maine. When a special order was received, one of a string of painters was employed to produce a masterpiece in his particular specialty. Earlier that morning, Cindy had ordered two clowns for a dentist in Queens and four pink nymphs with budding breasts for a negligee shop in the Village.

And then BB showed up.

The resemblance increased with each passing year, she

189

remarked to herself. More and more he looked like his father. The same pigeon-chest, the same intense expression,
the same swagger, moving as if he owned the space he
occupied. There was a scowl on his lean face that made him
less handsome than he would otherwise have been, and his
black hair hung limp and long to his shoulders, a remnant
of his long-departed youth. She was at her desk at the rear
of the gallery when he appeared, advancing without a
smile, jabbing a finger her way as if to mark his target.

"You," he began sullenly, "have been avoiding me."

"How nice of you to visit," she said with only a hint of
sarcasm.

"How come?" he insisted.

"Put it down to history, Boyd Benjamin, or have you forgotten?"

"I forget nothing. Anyway, that was all a long time ago.
No matter what, we've always been friends." He raked the
gallery walls with quick, cynical eyes. "Jesus, what garbage. How can you pass off such shit as art?"

"My customers know what they like, or so they tell me.
Yes," she went on in a softer voice, "we've always been
friends, we still are." She kissed him on one cheek and on
the other. "How in the world did you track me down?"

"Your mother."

"I should have known."

"Maggie thinks I'm hot stuff, always figured we'd end
up being married." He stared at an abstract expressionist
painting, compared it silently to the excellent O'Koren
hanging in his father's study. Say what you wanted about
Neil Morgan, his taste in art was impeccable. There was a
second, smaller O'Koren in his living room along with a
McGloughlin and a small Sokolov. This stuff, the stuff
Cindy was selling, nothing but cheap and worthless
frauds.

"A match made in heaven," Cindy said caustically.

"Make that Ocean Beach."

"Same thing to our parents."

The idea solidified in some crease of his midbrain, the
dark, stunning, titillating idea. He peered past it to where
Cindy stood. "You're looking good, Cindy."

"Is everything okay with you, BB?"

He spread his hands in answer, giving no answer at all.
"I heard about your father. I'm sorry."

"People used to laugh at him, that funny little man. But
he wasn't funny most of the time. I was with him at the
end, waiting for him to die, wanting him to die, wanting
him to say that he loved me. He never said it, not once.
Never said that he loved me. I waited while the life was
squeezed out of him for him to say those precious words, as
if they mattered, as if saying them would change all that
had gone before."

"I don't know," BB said. "Maybe saying them would
have turned everything around for you."

"I'll never know. He went out the way he lived, consistent to the end."

"Life sucks."

"Life"—she smiled wryly—"life is what life is. I've come
to understand that what I've been after all these years
is—"

"For your father to say he loved you," he injected.

"Not that simple, friend of mine. No, it's men like Roy
I've been chasing after. Men who won't tell me they love
me. Men who didn't love me. Men who don't care about me
and keep leaving me behind."

"Like me?"

"Like you, BB, and too many others."

"The world is a pisspot, we're all fucked up."

"Speak for yourself. I'm trying to stay straight, reasonably straight," she amended, remembering Alex Stainback. "It's hard." Two women wearing green sweaters and
plaid slacks entered the gallery. "Business beckons,"
Cindy said.

"Let's get together soon, there's so much to say."

"Anytime."

"I'll call you."

"I'm heading for Ocean Beach on Friday."

"If I can, I'll come out." He planted a quick, impersonal
kiss on her brow. "Talk to you soon."

She accompanied him to the door and then turned to the

two women, not getting too close, trying not to frighten them. "May I help you, ladies?"

BB

"Julie," he said into the telephone.

"Is that you, BB? I'm busy now."

"You once mentioned a john you serviced, the guy was a collector."

"Martin Callahan, you mean. What about him?"

"Can you put me next to him?"

"Forget it. That's private stock, BB. I won't have you cutting into my action."

"It's not what you think. I simply want to talk to the man."

"About what? I don't think I like this, BB."

"Didn't you say he buys art, legitimate and not so legitimate?"

"I might've said that."

"Good. All you have to do is put me together with this Callahan."

"And then what?"

"And then he and I will talk."

"About what?"

"About paintings, of course."

"What's in it for me?"

"A piece of the action, naturally."

"I'm not sure I trust you, BB."

"What have you got to lose? All it takes is a phone call."

"I better think about this."

"No, no time for that. Make the call now or the deal's dead."

"Okay, get back to me in an hour."

"Why so long?"

"Because I'm not alone, dummy, I'm with a client."

"An hour," he said, and hung up, pleased with himself. This could be big, bigger than anything he'd ever done before. And with no risk attached.

Nick

Danning presented himself for the audition at an advertising agency on Madison Avenue. A slender young man in a tweed jacket led him into an empty studio, got him seated at a table facing a TV monitor, and offered him a headset with a microphone attached.

"We'll run a game on the monitor for you. Last season's Giants–Bears game. Did you happen to see it? Not that it matters. Just ad-lib your way through, which is what we're concerned with here. Here's a list of the players and their numbers. Familiarize yourself with them. The thing we're after, the important thing, is your ability to explain to the listener what it is he just saw, why it was done, what to look for next. Inside stuff, Nick. I'll be in the control room. Give us a signal when you're ready to go."

It didn't go well at all. A nagging doubt that he was moving in the wrong direction persisted, shattered his concentration. He grew clumsy, his brain operating sluggishly, and halfway through he knew he wasn't going to get the job. His broadcasting career had been brief, unremarkable, and likely to remain so, he reminded himself on the way out.

If not broadcasting, was he doomed to a lifetime selling sporting goods? The prospect depressed him, and for the first time he was made fully conscious of how unprepared he was to face a life away from the gridiron. A grown man with worn-out skills for a boy's game.

Going crosstown, he passed the Punt 'n' Pass, an old hangout. Almost every night after a game, some of the players would wind up here to drink, to rehash the afternoon's exploits, to zero in on some of the football groupies who were positioned along the bar.

He paused at the entrance. One drink, he promised himself, the craving spreading down into his guts. But he knew that one drink would not be enough, was never enough for him or any other serious drinker.

Serious drinker. The phrase amused him. All euphemisms had become laugh lines for Danning; he was an old-fashioned drunk, an alcoholic, and euphemisms only disguised the truth. He continued on his way toward Pennsylvania Station and the train back to Bayshore. He was suddenly desperate to remove himself from the rising pressures of the city, to leave behind the pervasive sense of competition that existed in Manhattan, the always powerful need to *win.* He didn't feel that pressure on Fire Island.

The ferry was halfway across Great South Bay before he noticed Cindy Ashe, head bent over a book. He approached her tentatively, not sure he was presently equipped to endure another rejection. Instead, she greeted him with a huge smile and invited him to sit next to her.

"It's been a week since I saw you," she complained brightly.

"More like ten days. I didn't think you'd noticed."

"Do you always give up so easily?"

"You confuse me," he admitted. "There's a quicksilver quality about you. I don't know how to react."

"Any way you like."

"I guess I'm not that sure of myself anymore. When I was younger, I was a great deal more daring. Getting older, I guess."

"Premature senility," she joked.

"Too many forearm shivers, I guess."

"What's a forearm shiver?"

He explained. "In football, a forearm to the chest delivered with considerable velocity has a tendency to inhibit an opposing player."

"What a pleasant way to spend a Sunday afternoon."

"It discourages aggressiveness."

"Is that what happened to you?"

"In a manner of speaking. This has not been one of my better days."

"Want to talk about it?"

"Another time, maybe."

"Whatever you say." She made a concentrated effort to lighten the mood. "Are you coming to the party tomorrow night?"

"Neil Morgan's party? Yeah, he invited me."

"That's the one. Half the island puts in an appearance at the Morgans'."

"Will you be there?"

"Yes. If you'd like, we can have a drink together."

"I would like. Very much."

She made no reply, returning to her book, leaving Danning to wonder what was going on.

The night was long and difficult for Danning. He longed to be with people, to hear human voices, to make physical contact. He craved a woman with a rising urgency and tried to remember when he had last made love.

Nevertheless, when Kolodny went bar-hopping after dinner, Danning decided not to go with him. He was afraid he might see Cindy again, make a fool of himself over her. He was even more afraid that she might be with another man, afraid of how that would make him feel. Instead, he remained alone in the house, waiting for Neil Morgan's party, waiting to find out what her invitation actually meant.

BB

"I don't like it," Laura Lee said.

"Don't be dumb," BB snapped back. "There's real dough in this and no risks."

Jill dissented. "There are always risks."

BB glared her way, voice dripping with disdain. "I've worked it all out, gone over it a dozen times. This is a can't-miss job."

"I still don't like it."

"Trust me."

"You're doing all right at the Snap Shop. Why take chances?"

Jill said, "Laura Lee's right. We run a hustle on a john a couple of times a week. It's safe, it's clean, and the cops never get into it."

"The cops won't get into this," BB said. He jabbed his finger in Jill's direction. "Even if they did, there's no way to track it down to me or to you. You in or not? I can always get a couple of other girls to take your place."

Laura Lee looked at Jill. She shrugged. "In," she said without expression. "But it's not going to work."

"You trust him?" Laura Lee said later, when they were alone.

"Do you?"

"No way."

"Neither do I. Not for a second."

"Then why are we doing this?"

"For the dough, that's why."

"Ah, I almost forgot."

Sixteen

Neil

Purple Jesuses, a tradition at Neil Morgan's parties. Yet he had never tasted one, had never so much as tasted a beer or a sip of wine, convinced since adolescence of the subversive qualities of alcohol.

Purple Jesuses, served by the Morgans ever since that first party at Neurotics Anonymous, that first house during that first season on the dunes in Ocean Beach. The recipe had been Roy Ashe's, brought by him out of his college fraternity. "A festive concoction," he liked to say, "for a festive occasion." Gin, grape juice, and lemon, stirred into a huge punch bowl with lots of ice and ladled out into champagne glasses. This time the punch was prepared by servants, hired for the evening. In addition, there were kegs of cold beer and a full bar with two bartenders at one end of the large living room.

Guests began drifting in early, and before long the house was crowded, people making places for themselves in every room, on the two sun decks, adding to Neil's discomfort.

"Too many people," he complained to Susan, which he did every time they entertained.

"It's just one night," she answered, as if by rote.

"As far as I'm concerned, they can all leave now. I'm ready to hit the sack."

She touched his cheek with the back of her fingers. "That's not going to happen, my dear, so relax and enjoy yourself. There are dozens of pretty young things floating around who would be happy to make you happy."

He saw his chance. "Susan, there's something I want to discuss with you."

Her eyes spotted Maggie. "Later, my dear. Keep the thought, we'll talk later," and she was gone, lost in the ebb and flow of bodies. He retreated to the deck nearest the ocean, and for the first time that evening saw his son.

"Good evening, Father," BB said with a stiff, formal bow, a mocking bow, from Neil's perspective.

"What are you doing here?"

"It's nice to be made welcome."

"I didn't know you were on the island. When did you arrive?"

"A few minutes ago, on the last ferry. I'd never miss one of Mother's parties if I could help it. I'm staying for the weekend if that's all right with you."

Neil felt a surge of emotion for his only child. "I'm glad you're here, BB. You don't remember it, of course, but you were at the first party we had years ago. All those strange people, all that noise. It was our first house, right on the beach—"

"I've heard about that house. The way you people talk about it makes it sound like a church, a revered and sacred place."

"I guess it is revered by those of us who shared it. That was a special summer, a change in all our lives. You were very young, still sleeping in a crib and sharing a room with Cindy. I went in to check on you, make sure you were all right. You were awake, you said the noise had awakened you, and I explained that we were having a party, and what a party was. I always tried to explain things to you, BB. I said it was people having fun."

"You still sure of that, Father?"

"I'm not sure of anything anymore."

"A good sign, I'd say."

Neil tried to ignore the condescension in his son's tone. "Maybe so. Once I believed a man could do whatever he wanted to do, if he tried hard enough, if he were daring and inventive enough. Accomplish great things, shape his own destiny."

"Is that what you did?"

"Things haven't turned out exactly the way I expected them to."

"Not for any of us."

Neil exhaled, listening to his heart racing. Much too fast, he thought wryly, as if he'd been playing a hard three-set match of singles. A pulse along his arm vibrated and that frightened him. Until as abruptly as it had begun, the fibrillation was gone, out of mind. "Have you talked to your mother yet?"

"I'm sure we'll meet before the night's over." BB made little effort to disguise the hostility he felt toward his parents. He knew too much about each of them, more than a son was entitled to know, more than he had ever wanted to know. "If you don't mind, I'll wander a bit . . ."

"You do that."

What went wrong? Neil asked of himself. A massive barrier had been erected between himself and BB, an emotional combat zone, impenetrable, dangerous to them both. BB had become the enemy, in moral judgment of his father, barely able to conceal the loathing he felt. Neil found that increasingly difficult to endure; he had attempted to raise his son intelligently, with discipline and affection, with consistency. Where had he gone wrong? Perhaps he had not. Perhaps some bad seed caused BB to be angry and resentful, as if Neil had deliberately set out to damage him. Had his son's hostility in fact been conceived in Susan's belly, forming a deviant personality that none of them had ever been able to deal with? Neil shrugged it all away as he had shrugged away so many other family problems and went looking for someone attractive and pleasant to talk to.

* * *

BB

He wandered with a purpose. Talking to people who knew him. Three times he checked his watch against someone else's, fixing the time of night should the question arise later.

He introduced himself by name to the bartenders and flirted with the young woman serving hors d'oeuvres. Later, he joined Maggie and Cindy, at his most charming.

"You two could be sisters."

Maggie raised her glass in a mock toast. "I'll drink to that, BB, no matter how false."

"True is true," BB said.

"Listen to the boy," Maggie said to Cindy. "What a sweet child he was, and he's grown up into one of the world's greatest liars. I think I'll leave you two to your own interests."

Alone with Cindy, he positioned himself closer to her. "Still the sexiest lady on the beach."

"Save it, pal. Snow my mother if you want to, not me."

"I mean it. What do you say we go off someplace?"

"Why?"

"Let's say, for old times' sake."

"I think I'll pass."

"Give it some thought."

"I already have, BB. I remember the old times, and they weren't much. Anyway, I'm here as an observer of the social scene. A drink or two, a little party talk, and then it's bedtime for me. By myself. But don't worry, I'm sure you'll do just fine without me."

His eyes shifted past her and she laughed.

"Still those roaming eyes, BB. Go on, go after her. I'll catch up with you on the sand tomorrow."

He took her advice and sought out Julie. "I'm splitting now," he said.

"You sure this is going to work?"

"Do your part, I'll do mine. The boat's ready?"

"Ready and waiting."

"Okay. I'm ready to make my move. I've talked to a couple of dozen people, and half of them are so juiced they'll end up swearing I never left their side. I should be back before the party's half over. I know my mother's bashes, they go on all night. You stay in there and stick to the cover story."

"You can depend on me. Good luck."

"Yeah," he said on his way out. "Later . . ."

Nick

Danning drifted. Shortly after they arrived at the party, he and Kolodny had been separated. When last seen, Kolodny was at the bar, arm-in-arm with a pretty woman in green. Intimidated by the heaving crowd, Danning retreated to a spot along one wall where he could safely observe. He saw a number of people he had seen on the beach, but no one he cared to talk to. After a while, he went looking for the bathroom; it was locked. He waited patiently and soon the door opened, and a man and a woman exited together and went their separate ways without a word.

When he returned to the living room, the level of sound seemed to have increased. A few couples were trying to dance near the center of the room, their movements constricted, but determinedly bouncing up and down. Danning worked his way to the bar for a glass of tonic with a wedge of lime. Turning, he came face-to-face with a woman in a black sleeveless tank top and white shorts. Very clearly, she was wearing nothing underneath. The same woman he had seen earlier coming out of the bathroom.

She smiled up into his face, a glass in one hand, a joint in the other. "Why are you alone?" she asked, swaying closer. "Poor baby, as pretty as you are. Want a drag?" She offered the joint.

"I'm okay."

"You certainly are." She assessed him openly. "You sure are big."

"Not as big as some."

She examined his hand. "You know what they say?"

"What do they say?"

"Big hands, big cock."

The woman in the tank top was so like the women who populated team parties when he was still playing ball. Hero fuckers; after a world record, trying to bed down every player in sight. For a while he had allowed himself to be part of the scene, until he began to have bad feelings about himself and the way he was living. He stopped going to parties—long before he met Tiffany—stopped sleeping around. He became known as a bit of a flake, a loner, a man with an attitude.

"What do you say?" the woman in the tank top was saying.

"What?"

"I know a place we can be alone. Come on, I give the best head this side of Cherry Grove."

He left her standing with her glass and her joint and went out on the deck, forcing cool night air into his lungs.

"Nick!" Neil Morgan came forward, hand outstretched. "I'm so glad you came. Great party, isn't it?"

"Certainly more people in one place than I've ever seen before."

Neil's face hardened, and his eyes raked the deck, searching back through the French doors. "We do it once a year; my wife insists on it."

"You'd rather she wouldn't?"

"I could live without it."

"Then why do it?"

"I told you," Neil said with a flash of annoyance. "My wife. You're not married, you don't know what it's like. If I said no party, Susan would go into a snit for a month."

Was that what had destroyed his own marriage? Danning wondered. Had he been too indulgent of Tiffany's whims and impulses, too soft? Hardly. Looking back, he could see that he lacked flexibility, had been unable to adjust to living with another human being. At the same time, as a parent, he functioned on his own, making decisions

about Jason without consulting his wife, deciding important questions as if Tiffany played no role in the family.

"I was," he said aloud. "Married, I mean. I'm divorced."

"I never believed in divorce."

No one does, he wanted to say, but swallowed the words
instead. No one believes in divorce or murder or cruelty or
war or abortion. Which never stopped one murder from
being committed out of greed or jealousy or prevented one
uterus from being scraped; two thousand years of *believing*
in the Prince of Peace hadn't prevented Christians from
marching off to battle in His name. Believe in divorce? No
way.

"My wife and I," Danning said in a low, faintly ironic
voice, "found it impossible to live together. Divorce was
the only way out."

For an extended beat, Neil made no response. "I haven't
had a perfect marriage or a perfect life. But I was never
able to let go. It was as if I couldn't tolerate the shame of
divorce, of admitting my marriage was a failure. Not that
it's been idyllic, I don't mind telling you. Susan and I,
we've had our rocky moments. Adjustments had to be
made, compensations, concessions. I did whatever was required to keep the marriage intact, the family together.
Maybe I was wrong. Maybe all of us would have been
happier if I'd let go. Maybe my son would have turned out
differently. Maybe—" He broke off. "Sorry, I didn't mean
to run off at the mouth. Actually, I've had a good life, better than most. I'm got a beautiful wife, a handsome son,
my work. Do you have any children, Nick?"

"A boy."

"That's nice, a man needs a son to carry on for him, provide for his place in the continuum of life. You see him
often?"

Danning hadn't seen Jason since summer began. Always there had been some reason, some excuse, flimsy and
shallow, on Tiffany's part or his own. Why hadn't he insisted? Told her straight out: "The boy is my child, too. I
want him with me this weekend. We'll take walks on the
beach, run together, play ball, and go swimming." Instead,

he'd accepted every delay, every prior engagement, anything that allowed him to be free of responsibility.

"Not as often as I'd like," he said.

Neil stared at him without blinking. "I know what you mean," he said at last.

Danning wanted to believe otherwise.

Billy

Billy Grooms and Susan Morgan. He sought her out as soon as he arrived. What a pair they made! He so golden, she so sensually dark and full of mystery. Two spectacular people. She offered her cheek and he licked her ear.

"Stop it, Billy."

"I can't stop thinking about you."

"You must. This thing between us, it isn't going to work."

"Of course it will. I love you. I'd do anything for you, you know that."

"You almost got us both killed."

"I wanted to help."

"That damn gun of yours."

"Where is it?"

"Turk took it away from me."

"Damn. Did he hurt you?"

"Yes, Turk hurt me. My husband hurts me, my son hurts me. And you'll hurt me, Billy, if I give you the chance."

He took hold of her arm. "Let's go somewhere and talk. I want to hold you, tell you how I feel."

"That's not a good idea."

"I'm sorry about what happened. I'm sorry I didn't shoot that bastard. I love you, Susan, I want you for myself. You belong to me, Susan."

"No more of that!" she said sharply. "I've had enough of belonging to men. That's how it used to be with Neil and the others. That's how it is with Turk. I'm a piece of property, and Turk holds title. No, thank you. I'm through with all that. It's over between us, Billy, accept that."

"No. I won't accept it. You love me. We love each other."

"You have no choice. Oh, don't worry, I told Neil about you."

"You told him about me?"

"That you were an actor. There might be something for you in his picture. There he is now. Come along."

He considered letting her go without him. To hell with Neil's movie. Once she understood the dimensions of his willingness to sacrifice, she'd understand how much he truly cared for her, that he meant what he said. But he'd waited too long for this chance; Neil Morgan was his big opportunity, and he was unable to turn away from it. He went after her.

"Susan mentioned you," Neil began when they were alone.

"I don't want to impose."

Neil cocked his head, assessing the younger man professionally. "In all the years, this is the first time Susan ever recommended anyone to me. She has impeccable judgment, my wife, she's a very special person. I let her read all my scripts, you know, and her critiques are incisive and to the point, very perceptive. Still, all professional decisions are mine alone to make. Why don't you tell me a little about your acting background, Billy?"

"Now?"

"No time like the present."

Billy agreed and began talking in his most sincere, his most ingratiating manner. It was one of the best performances he'd ever given.

Maggie

Having finished her fourth Purple Jesus, Maggie viewed the heaving, noisy collection of bodies in Susan's house through a blurred lens. Nothing was clear, not the look of them surely, nor the continuous cacophony of jumbled sounds. Faces came and went, she laughed with them, talked with them, remembering nothing of what was said or done. Without knowing how she got there, she found herself against the wall of an upstairs corridor, sandwiched between two young men, slender and pretty, each one vying for her attention. They pressed themselves against her, hard young bodies, nervous young hands, eager eyes and bulging trousers. How sweet they both were, how insistent, how silly. She giggled.

"You're laughing."

"Why are you laughing?"

"Sweet boys," was her reply.

"Let's get out of here," one said.

"Let's see," she said, "you must be Tweedledee."

"What?"

"And if he's Tweedledee, you are Tweedledum."

"Let's go. I can make you happy."

"No way," Tweedledum protested. "Maggie and me, we're going for a walk on the beach." He kissed her cheek, licked her throat, sucked her earlobe.

The other one raised Maggie's hand to his lips. "I'm what you want, I'll be the best you ever had. See, feel this."

She brought her hand away. "It seems to me I've heard that song before," she crooned.

A mouth came down on hers, a warm tongue probing deeply. A hand stroked her breast and another hand squeezed her bottom. She made a feeble attempt to brush away the offending hands. No use.

"Get out of here!" a voice cried, angry and determined. Certainly not her own voice, Maggie reflected lazily, watching Tweedledee and Tweedledum withdraw, strewing insults left and right as they departed.

"Are you all right, Mother?"

"Is that my Cindy? Dear daughter, what have I done to you?" She began to weep.

"I think you can use some black coffee."

"I need us to become friends again. Have we ever been friends, Cindy? A mother needs a daughter to look after her in her foolish years. Did I do something awful? Have I made you ashamed of me, dear daughter? My apologies.

It's the way I've lived, alternating embarrassments and apologies. Where are you taking me?"

Twenty minutes and two cups of coffee later, they were in the powder room near the kitchen, Cindy holding her mother's head while she threw up. Then out the back door onto the small patch of sand that served as a backyard. Cindy went after aspirin and tomato juice, and they sat silently in the darkness until Maggie began to feel better.

"Once again," she said with considerable self-loathing coloring her voice, "into the garbage pit."

"Too much to drink, no big deal."

"Do I disgust you as much as I disgust myself? I doubt it. But then you don't have to spend as much time with me as I do. Lucky you."

Cindy chose her words carefully. "We all blow it once in a while."

"Not you, my darling daughter."

"We both know better than that."

"I know very little about you. Where have you been all these years? How long has it been between visits? Five years, six? Always on the move, my Cindy, putting distance between us. Keeping away from me. When you were eighteen, you went to Europe on your own. God knows what you did."

"I lived."

"We all live, some with more pain than others. Did you find what you were looking for while you were doing all that living? I hope so; I certainly did not. Or if I did, I have forgotten. There's so much I've forgotten, so much more I'd like to forget." She studied Cindy in profile, the delicate lines flowing into each other, the jaw surprisingly aggressive, angled stubbornly. "You look a little like Roy just now. The same determined set to your mouth, a willful look. Whatever he was, Roy was always true to his own miserable self, always consistent in his inconstancy. You don't look anything like the baby you were. What a beautiful child you used to be.

"It hurt when you went away. You can't know what it's like for a mother to lose her child."

"You forget, I, too, lost a child."

"Oh, my God! Sometimes I do forget."

"I never loved anyone the way I loved that sweet little boy. At night I would watch him sleep, and one night, when I fell asleep in the chair next to his crib, he died. I was right next to him and I didn't know my baby was dying. I didn't do anything to help him, to save him."

"I know," Maggie whispered. "I know."

"Nobody knows."

"I used to go into your room at night," Maggie said, ancient emotions stirring within, "to see if you were all right. I'd sit with you for hours until Roy led me back to bed. Sometimes I would sing to you, songs my mother taught me . . ."

"You sang to me?"

"To you, and sometimes to Roy." Her eyes fluttered shut. "On nights when he drank too much, he'd wake up from bad dreams covered with sweat and sobbing. I would hold him as if he were a child and sing to him until he was able to sleep again."

"Why didn't you go to Mexico?" Cindy cried.

"I wanted to, but he told me to stay away."

"You spoke to him?"

"Francesca told me."

"The man was dying in a strange place among strangers."

"Francesca was with him."

"He yearned for the past, Mother, for a supporting hand stretched out of his past. When he was brave and strong and unafraid."

"Unafraid? Roy? Roy was always afraid and always worked so hard to hide it. All that bravado, fast-talking his way through friendships and jobs and marriages and lovers. Light on his feet, that was Roy. 'Never stay in one place too long,' he liked to say, 'they may throw things.' I should never have married your father, but then I have always fallen in love with inappropriate men . . . not that it matters anymore. What counts is that you were with him at the end."

"I wonder why I went. Was it to comfort him or to satisfy some need in me? I wanted something from him, even at the end. Is that how it is always with women and their inappropriate men? Can they never provide what we want? Why can't people satisfy each other?"

Maggie stared into the night. "The disease of our epoch, the common emotional cold of modern times. Personal relationships don't seem to work."

"Life is a bitch."

"Life is full of odd rhythms and quirky side trips to nowhere. The conventions I was brought up to believe in were out of style before I knew it, and I was never able to successfully reconcile the old with the new. I kept sliding past the opportunities life offered. Don't you make the same mistake," she ended on a hard note.

"We're not alike, Mother."

"Parent and child, which is more dependent on the other at any given moment? Answer that one, my darling daughter, if you can."

"Don't blame me for the mess you made of your life."

"And the same to you."

"Oh, I had a dandy childhood, full of happy memories. Divorce after divorce. Stepfathers came and went through swinging doors. Not to mention the parade of strangers in and out of your bedroom, Mother dear. More than one of them came into my room in the middle of the night—"

"Don't you dare say that to me!"

"Why not? Does it disgust you, Mother? Does it frighten you? It frightened the hell out of me. I was too scared to fight them off or scream or do anything but give in. Reminds me of that old joke by Groucho Marx—I could never love any man who loved me. When Roy was dying, I prayed that he would say he loved me. He didn't even have to mean it, just say it. All my life, that's all I wanted, for my father to love me. And that's what I'm still hunting for, a man to truly love me. If it happens, I'll probably run away, like always."

Maggie stood up, struggling to maintain her equilibrium. "That business upstairs—"

"Please, don't explain."

"It isn't merely inappropriate men anymore. I don't want love, I don't want commitment, I don't want to be

committed. It's numbness I need, the quick passage of
time. Whatever it takes to keep memories in the back of
my mind, out of sight. I long for lies and deceit, for strangers who make only small demands. Alcohol helps—and
young, selfish men with strong bodies who manage to hurt
me even when they try to be nice. Anything to forget, anything to make the days go rapidly away." She took a step
and staggered, regained her balance. Looking back, she
spoke with a fleeting, humorless smile. "A pleasure talking to you, daughter. But let's not do it again soon. It hurts
too damn much."

Cindy sat in the dark for a while, staring after her
mother. Would they ever understand one another? Or
would it always be like this—bitter litanies of accusation
instead of real conversation? Would they ever forgive each
other? Really forgive?

Nick

Jim McMillan materialized out of the partying mob, a
matronly woman with an intelligent, pretty face on his
arm.

"My wife, Natalie," he said to Danning.

She smiled up at Danning. "Jim has been telling me all
about you and I'm impressed."

"Bragging about your football accomplishments," Mc-
Millan said. "I don't get to meet many professionals."

"Former," Danning amended.

"Which reminds me, I've been meaning to ask you what
your plans are for the fall."

"Nebulous, to say the least. I've been turned down for a
couple of broadcasting jobs, so it looks like I'll just keep
peddling sporting goods unless . . ."

"Unless something better comes along?"

"You put it well," Danning said with a smile.

"Perhaps I can offer something better. Do you have your
degree?"

"A B.A. in journalism. Contemporary communications,

they used to call it. Unfortunately, the networks are not impressed."

"Any postgrad work?"

"I took a master's at Columbia when I played for the Giants. Also journalism. Took me four years to pull it off."

It was Natalie's turn to speak. "That fits right in, doesn't it, Jim?"

Danning's eyes went from McMillan to his wife and back again. "Fits in with what?"

"Ever thought about coaching, Nick?"

"What jock doesn't?"

"I mean at the high school level. At my school. I received word a few days ago: the fellow who coached football quit for a job at his alma mater. That puts me in a spot with school starting less than six weeks away. I need a coach, and my hunch is you could be the man for the job."

"I never gave much thought to it."

"It would be different from the pros. But we take our football seriously, along with our academic program. It would mean giving a course in journalism and advising the school newspaper. The pay is a lot less than you're used to, but if you like to teach, like to coach, enjoy working with kids . . ."

Danning hesitated.

"Maybe it's not for Nick," Natalie said. "It may be a step in the wrong direction."

"I could understand that," McMillan said.

"It's a brand-new idea."

"When the opening occurred, you were the first one I thought about. The kids would be thrilled to have someone of your caliber coaching the team. It may not be the big time, Nick, but who knows what it might lead to."

"I don't know what to say."

"Give it some thought."

"At my age—I'm not sure I can handle it."

"I'm sure. I'm prepared to offer you a three-year contract at the top of our pay scale. We've never had a winning team, Nick. Maybe you could help turn that around. When you reach a decision, let me know."

Danning was about to respond when he saw Cindy. "I'll

think about it," he said, excusing himself, putting himself
directly in her path.

"I've been looking for you," she began.

"Best news I've had all day."

She shook her head. "I'm worried. It's my mother. She
seems to have disappeared."

"What do you mean?"

"She's been drinking, she was sick, and now she's gone."

"She probably went back to her house."

"I checked. And I tried the bars downtown. Neil said he
saw her grab a bottle of whiskey and leave. I think she's
out on the beach."

"Maggie's a grown woman—"

"You don't understand, she's upset. We had a—a discus-
sion."

"You mean a fight?"

"Not so much a fight. A lot that was painful and threatening was dredged up. She was sick and unhappy, and I'm
afraid I wasn't very much help. If she drinks too much, de-
cides to go swimming—"

"Has she done that sort of thing before?"

"Yes."

"In that case, let's look for her. She can't have gone too
far."

Susan

Amidst the turmoil, Billy found an unoccupied corner in
one of the bedrooms and was getting very quietly, very pri-
vately smashed. He sipped steadily from a tall glass filled
with excellent Scotch, not that he noticed the quality,
charged as he was with self-pity. He sulked.

Somewhere in the crowd, Susan was enjoying herself,
oblivious to the anguish she was causing him. He *loved*
her; why wouldn't she understand the depth of his feeling?
For the first time he loved someone more than he loved
himself. For the first time he wanted to make another human being happy, to please her, to give to her. He yearned

to wipe away her fears, to comfort her. He would have done anything for her.

On the small wicker table next to the couch along the wall sat a green Princess phone. On the couch, three couples necking, telling jokes, smoking grass. The phone began to ring. One of the women answered.

"Susan!" she screeched, "it's for Susan."

"Who is Susan?" one of her companions said.

Billy shoved himself erect. "I'll find Susan," he declared with all the dignity he could muster and staggered off.

He located her in the kitchen, fending off the advances of a small man with a red face. Billy placed himself between Susan and the red-faced man.

"There's a call for you."

She went across the hallway into Neil's study, Billy at her heels. She picked up the phone. "Hello?"

It was Turk Christie. "Sounds like you're having a big bash."

"I don't want to talk to you."

"I figured you'd be over your mad by now."

"Go to hell."

"Monday, I'll be in the apartment on Monday. Around lunchtime."

"You don't own me, Turk. You can't order me around."

"You're forgetting something."

"I'm not afraid of you anymore. I won't be bullied anymore, not by you, not by anybody."

"Suit yourself, lady. But you'll see me again, along with a bottle of acid."

He hung up, a soft, controlled click that frightened her more than any show of temper would have. She turned to see Billy standing in the doorway.

"The bastard," he bit off. "Let me help you."

"The way you helped me in New York? I can live very well without that kind of help."

"I love you, Susan. Let me prove it."

"What are you talking about?"

"I'll plan it carefully. No mistakes this time. I'll get rid of him, once and for all."

"Billy, forget about Turk and forget about me. You talk

so glibly of love, but what you mean is proprietorship. Which is the same thing that Turk means. You want to own me, use me, the way Neil owned and used me. No more, thank you. I am finally my own person, and intend to remain so. Be a nice boy, Billy, and leave me alone."

He grabbed her arm and jerked her around. "You don't mean that."

Deliberately loosening his grip on her arm, she faced him. "Did Neil offer you a part in his picture, Billy?"

The question startled him, an oblique reminder of what was at stake here. "Neil said there might be something. He said I should call his office during the week."

"I'm glad for you, Billy. Something nice may come out of this for you after all. Now get out of my way, Billy, and don't press your luck."

Her voice was so cold that he didn't even hesitate before letting her go.

Neil

"I owe you an apology."

"Don't be silly. Those things happen."

"Running out that way, it was childish."

"You were embarrassed, I can understand that. Besides, it was probably my fault. I was too aggressive."

"Oh, no, not you, Debra. Truthfully, it's happened to me before. I guess I'm getting old."

"They say it's all in the mind."

"Maybe there's something wrong with me."

"Listen to your body, it may be trying to tell you something."

"What do you mean?"

"That afternoon we were together, Neil, you were very sweet, very gentle."

"You're a lovely woman."

"But you didn't want to make love to me, not really."

"That's nonsense."

"You kept telling me about your wife. She's a beautiful woman. Are you trying to lose her?"

"I lost her a long time ago."

"I see. In that case, I'd say you've never gotten over it. I think it's Susan you want; you still love her."

He rejected the notion with a dismissive shake of his head. "It's over between us, it has been for years. Susan and I, we just live in the same house, that's all."

"Oh," Debra said in a warming voice, "I'm sure it's a great deal more than that."

BB

The entrance to the building the Morgans lived in was about thirty feet south of a corner on Park Avenue. Jill and Laura Lee felt an immense appreciation for Park Avenue, for anyone who lived on the prestigious boulevard. Life here represented not only wealth but entrenched power as well. Neither of them felt particularly comfortable strolling uptown on the avenue, but it was a necessary part of BB's strategy.

George was the doorman, a compact man of medium height in a black uniform trimmed with gold. When the two women in their short skirts and low-cut satin blouses paused under the fringed canopy, *his* fringed canopy, he stepped forward, tipping his hat with a white-gloved hand. At age sixty, George was wise in the ways of the streets of the city and recognized these two as hookers, definitely out of place in this neighborhood. Over on Lexington, they might have been more at home, certainly on Eighth Avenue or lower Third Avenue. But not here, not in front of his building. He greeted them with his usual amiable smile, spoke in his most gracious manner.

"Evening, ladies."

"Why, hello there," Laura Lee purred.

"Quiet, isn't it?" Jill said.

"Summer's slow on Park, ladies. Too slow around here for you girls."

"Who says so?" Jill said challengingly.

"Just take yourselves elsewhere, ladies. Move on now."

Laura Lee stuck her tongue out at him. "It's a free country."

"Nothing you girls do is free," George said, pleased at his little joke.

"What kind of a crack is that?" Laura Lee said, positioning herself at George's left shoulder.

Jill stepped around to his other side, thrusting her face closer to his. "Fuck off, hotshot."

George flushed. "Now, girlie, no need to act nasty."

"You know what I think, old man?" Laura Lee said thinly. "I think you're dumb. You got a dumb face."

"And a dumb voice," Jill said.

"And a dumb uniform."

"A dumb asshole in a dumb job "

"Asshole," Laura Lee repeated.

George's lips flattened. "Go on, get out of here."

Jill put her hand on his chest and shoved. "Make us, asshole."

George recovered quickly, advancing on the two women, his back to the building. "I'm warning you, get out of here."

Laura Lee knocked the cap off his head. "Dumb cap."

He bent to retrieve it, and Jill brought her knee up fast, catching him on the shoulder, sending him sprawling on the sidewalk. They mocked him as he struggled to his feet.

"I've had enough," he sputtered. "The police know how to deal with sluts like you."

In answer, Laura Lee slapped him across the face, and he went staggering backward. She leaped after him, bearing him down to the concrete. She beat him around the face, and at the same time Jill pulled his cap over his eyes, holding him down.

Jill looked up in time to see BB, keeping to the edge of the building, enter the lobby, open the locked inside door with his key, and disappear behind the bank of mailboxes in the direction of the elevators. Only then did they release the doorman and run for the corner, out of sight before George made it up to his feet again.

* * *

BB had it all worked out in advance. Using the key supplied to him by his father—"I want you always to know that this is your home, son."—he turned off the external alarm system. This done, he went into the apartment. The control for the backup system was in the large hall closet. Push a button, and the red warning light went off, replaced by a white light; the system was neutralized.

He worked swiftly. The large O'Koren in Neil's study, the McGloughlin and the small Sokolov in the living room. He placed each painting facedown on the floor and, using a mat knife specially sharpened for the occasion, he cut each out of its frame. He placed the McGloughlin on top of the O'Koren, the Sokolov on top of the McGloughlin, and rolled them into a tight tube, careful not to damage either canvas or paint. He secured the tube with five quarter-inch rubber bands. Last, he returned the empty frames to their places on the walls, a small joke at his father's expense.

Carrying the paintings, he switched the internal alarm back on and went out the back door, locking it behind him. He reset the primary alarm and walked down the eleven flights to the basement, in no hurry to get there. Moments later, he was out in the street, striding toward Lexington Avenue where Jill and Laura Lee waited in a rented car.

"Move it," he commanded.

In minutes they were on the East Side Drive, heading toward the Triborough Bridge and the highways leading out to Long Island where the boat was waiting.

"With any luck," BB said, checking his watch, "we'll be back at the party by two A.M. Early enough to have a nightcap with my old man, if he drank, that is," he ended, laughing.

Maggie

She sprinted up the beach until her lungs ached and her legs gave way, collapsing on the cool, damp sand. When her strength returned, she sat up and took a long pull on the bottle of Scotch. The moon hung low in the night sky, lighting the ocean below. She took another drink, remembering an earlier night like this one, after another party.

It had commenced in that old house, Neurotics Anonymous. No, much before that. Before she and Roy were married. Begun as fun and games, sparked by the promise of all the great things sure to follow.

Roy Ashe was unlike any man she had ever known. Vital and exciting, filled with drive and ambition, telling jokes, laughing, quicker than everyone else. Everything was enhanced by his presence, everything was better, charged with his energy day and night. In bed and out.

Inevitably, it went bad. Few things turned out as expected. Roy seemed to resent the baby—what a lovely child Cindy had been, beautiful to look at, agreeable, responsive—and his drinking increased. Both of them drank too much, she'd known it even then. And soon he began to stay away from home overnight. "On business," was the only explanation he ever gave. And she wanted to believe him.

Some mornings he would show up smelling of strange perfume, and eventually she stopped caring where he was or what he did or who he was doing it with. He had failed her too many times, failed her when she needed him most. And he beat her. Periodically, for no specific reason, as if he required a handy target for all the repressed rage he felt, all the guilt. Drunk or sober, it made no difference; he managed to blame her for each of the problems in their lives. One night in Neurotics Anonymous, he punched her until her ribs turned purple and sharp pains stabbed into her lungs with every breath she took.

That night she and Eddie Stander went out on the beach. A night like this, with the sea calm and the moon low, and nobody in sight. Eddie held her, comforted her, and made love to her. Slow and gentle, without much passion, a restorative commingling of needs.

Eddie was Roy's best friend—and her very good friend—and that night was the beginning of the end. Of her marriage. Of Eddie's friendship with Roy. Of her friendship with Eddie. Later, when she was able to think about it, she understood that it was the loss of friendship she missed most. But that was *much* later.

It went on that way until one night Roy showed up unexpectedly on the island and discovered them in bed. "Very nice," he drawled in that exaggeratedly cool way he sometimes had, the ultrasophisticate, a character raised whole out of an F. Scott Fitzgerald novel. "Best friend making it with best friend's wife. Gives a man something to think about." All said in that faintly ironic voice, his expression fixed and worldly. "You are my friend, Eddie," he had said, "and you fuck my wife. I would never have done that to you, Eddie," he ended with dramatic simplicity. "I would never." But of course he would have. Given the chance, he would have done precisely that.

Remembering that night brought back old feelings of regret and shame, and she staggered up to her feet and down the beach as if to leave the past behind. She drank out of the bottle, not stopping, not wanting to see what was behind her.

Tweedledee and Tweedledum were on the trail. They had seen Maggie leave the party alone, marked her path to the beach, followed after an appropriate interval.

"Finish up what we started."

"Beautiful."

They fell into step no more than thirty yards behind her, closing the gap steadily, watching her weave and stumble as she went. When she fell to her knees, they giggled behind their hands. Up again, she went on.

"Great body for an old hen," Tweedledee observed.

"The way her ass swings, a wild lady."

Tweedledee reached her first, bringing her around by the arm. Surprise shadowed her face but not fear. The beach was home to her, and even at night she anticipated no trouble, no danger.

"Who's there?" she cried gaily.

"Where you going, lady?"

"Oh, I remember you boys. Out for a stroll on the beach, are you? Well, all right, have a drink." She offered the bottle.

Tweedledum squeezed her buttocks with both hands.

"That hurts."

He pressed himself against her, rotating his hips.

"Hey, cut that out!"

Tweedledee unbuttoned her man-tailored shirt, taking hold of her breasts. "No bra," he said huskily. "Perfect little titties. Just the way I like 'em." His mouth came down on her nipple.

She spun away, arms swinging wide, the bottle slamming against the side of Tweedledum's head. Down he went, embarrassed more than damaged, and angry.

"Bitch! She hit me."

Tweedledee, laughing at his friend's discomfort, went after Maggie. Before he could get to her, Tweedledum pushed her onto her knees. Striking again, he sent her facedown on the sand.

"Easy," his friend said.

"The bitch hit me." He would have kicked her, but Tweedledee yanked him away, sending him onto his back.

"You're spoiling my fun, dummy."

Without a word, Tweedledum charged, head driving into the other man. Flailing at each other, they rolled around until Tweedledum got a handful of hair and yanked hard. His friend screamed, and as he did, Tweedledee swung a short, quick left hook. Tweedledum lay still.

Maggie, meanwhile, had tried to flee. But she was neither fast enough nor strong enough to escape. Tweedledee brought her down with a good tackle, rolling her onto her back. He ignored her pleas and pulled her slacks and panties off, forcing her legs apart.

"Beautiful," he muttered, and buried his face between her thighs. He never knew Tweedledum had come up alongside until he felt the broad toe of his heavy boot under his ribs. Spinning, convinced his ribs were fractured, he tried to avoid the other man's charge and failed. A blow he never saw put him down again.

Tweedledum went back to Maggie.

"Look what I've got for you." He was so intent on her that he never heard Danning's footfalls.

The first blow caught Tweedledum on the ear. Swearing, he rolled and scrambled, too late. A heavy combination battered his face, and he began to swallow blood until everything went black.

A few yards down the beach, Tweedledee, now upright, his legs planted wide, was swaying in the soft night air. Nick Danning approached him without haste and sent a long right hand into his face. Tweedledee went over backward, out cold.

Danning returned to Cindy, who was crouched over her mother. "Is she all right?"

"The bastards, they were going to rape my mother."

"Let's get her back to the house."

"What about them? I want them arrested."

"I don't think so. Your mother's had enough, and so have they. Why go public?" He lifted Maggie in his arms and began the slow trek back toward Ocean Beach.

"I owe you," Cindy said.

"No," he said firmly. "No debts between us. None."

Billy

"I'm an actor," Billy said.

"I knew it the minute I laid eyes on you. Your face is so perfect."

Billy gave her his most dynamic smile. She was ideal for his needs. About forty-five years old, she owned her own house in Seaview, an apartment in Sutton Place, and a condo in Palm Springs. She was a widow and lonely, she wasted no time telling him that. She qualified on all counts, Billy was certain, someone able to take care of his fiscal needs until his film career swung into high gear.

"There's a good chance I'll be playing an important role in a major picture this fall."

She looped an arm through his, breast flattening against him. "Now that we've found each other, I've had enough of this party. Shall we go back to my place?"

On Midway, in the darkness between street lamps, he kissed her. "Nice," she whispered.

"Very nice," he answered, reaching for her breast.

"Wait, lover, until we get home. You'll get it all."

Billy laughed triumphantly. At last he was going to get what he wanted—everything.

BB

As expected, the party was still going strong. A drink in hand, pretending to be drunk, BB made his presence known, speaking to everyone he knew, establishing the time. But that didn't seem sufficient to his needs somehow, as if he had to implant his presence firmly in everyone's mind. *They had to know he was here.* His eyes came to rest on a middle-aged couple, the woman stately and handsome, the man distinguished, composed. BB waited until the man went toward the bar for another drink before approaching the woman.

"I've had my eye on you all night," he started out, putting himself closer to her than convention dictated.

She took a backward step, alarm in her eyes. "Do I know you?"

"I'm BB, the Morgans' evil offspring." He laughed loudly and put his hand on the small of her back.

She stiffened. "Oh, yes, my husband knows your father."

"Your husband. That the creep you were with?"

She drew away. "If you intend to be nasty, I'd prefer not talking to you."

He leered. "I know what you'd prefer, and I've got it for you. Right here between my legs."

She gasped and started away. He embraced her from behind, hands sliding onto her breasts. "Don't!" she cried.

"Terrific tits!" he said in a loud voice, aware that people were watching him.

She struggled, but he held on until her husband appeared. One look and he reacted with speed and a force that startled BB, hurling him to the floor. BB bounced up and got a punch in before a couple of onlookers grabbed him, kept him from continuing his attack. Neil appeared out of the crowd.

"What is happening here?"

The woman, helping her husband, pointed at BB. "He molested me, put his hands all over me. When Jay objected, your son attacked him."

Neil confronted BB. "Is that true?"

BB, a lopsided grin on his fine, tawny face, said, "What the hell, all I did was cop a little feel. No damage done."

"Go to your room," Neil said grimly.

BB burst into laughter. "Past my bedtime, is it? No supper? Am I to be punished for my misdeeds, dear Father? What a joke, what a joke you are!" BB shook himself free of Neil's restraining hand. "This party's been a drag, anyway. In the morning, I'll be gone on the first ferry out of here." He spun away and went up to his room, leaving Neil behind to clean up the mess he'd made.

Susan

The last guests had straggled off into the waning night when Susan returned from Maggie's house. Neil, helping the servants clean up, broke off and took his wife aside.

"How is she?"

"Sleeping now. She had a bad time. There were two of them, they beat her and tried to rape her."

"God, I hate that. No one has the right to inflict himself on another human being."

She began to weep. "I'm so tired. Suddenly I am very tired."

"Go upstairs and go to bed. I'll dismiss the servants, they can finish tomorrow."

She was still awake when he entered their bedroom. "I thought you'd be asleep by now."

"All this, Neil. What happened to Maggie, the party, all those people we hardly know, why do we do it?"

"I'm not sure. I'm not sure about anything anymore."

A strange note in his voice alerted her, the dull ring of

melancholy, or was it the echo of discovery on his part, something recently learned? "The Neil I married was sure about everything."

"So sure," he said, as if chewing it over in his mind. "So often wrong. I had it all figured out, answers for every question, solutions for every problem. Except life doesn't seem to work that way. Sometimes I wonder how I got here, to this place in my life, how I became the man I am. All those twists and turns in the road, and I chose to believe that I could walk a straight line. What an arrogant fool I was."

"It takes a long time to grow up. You and me, Neil, and BB, I'm worn out just thinking about us."

He kissed her tenderly. "Go to sleep, rest; in the morning you'll feel better."

She grasped his hand. "Don't leave me. Not tonight. I'm so cold and afraid and so very, very lonely."

He embraced her and kissed the back of her neck. "Everything will work out. I'll take care of you, I'll fix everything."

"Yes," she said, meaning it. "You always were good at that, always."

Cindy

"Your mother's going to be all right."

Danning and Cindy sat on the sand, watching the horizon where the morning sky had turned to gray ahead of the rising sun.

"It's too late," Cindy said.

He wanted to touch her, hold her, comfort her. But he sensed that it would be a mistake. She would misunderstand, perceive any physical contact between them as sexual, an insensitive advance, an alteration in their relationship she would automatically reject.

"Maggie's not badly hurt," he said, aware that Maggie's physical condition was not the issue.

"Oh, yes, she is. We all are. We all bear terrible wounds.

Pain is the dominant trait in my family, it marks each of us, scars us for life. How said it was, growing up the way I did, living with Maggie and Roy, and living away from them. It was a mistake for them to have a child, they were never much more than children themselves. They played games with no sense of what their games did to other people.

"I remember how those early summers were. We—BB and me, the other kids who spent their vacations from school on the island—we were left to do as we liked. Freedom to grow, the adults used to say. It was safe on the island—no cars, no crime, no carnivorous beasts. But many of the people I met were meat-eaters. They devoured kids like us, they devoured each other. Safe? Fire Island was the most dangerous place I can think of, it still is. The ninth circle of hell, all decked out to make you think you've gone to heaven.

"Once I came back to our house to find a party in progress. Maggie, Susan, a few of the other women whose husbands left them alone during the week while they worked in New York. And men, none of whom I knew.

"I went up to my room and got into bed, but I couldn't sleep. After a while, the door opened, and a man came in. He began to make love to me. I was fourteen years old, and I didn't know how to react. I wanted to scream, to beat him, to call for my mother. But I had seen him kissing my mother earlier, so I said nothing. Then Maggie showed up. She saw what was happening and she laughed. She stood there and laughed. 'Oh, Ernie, what you need is a real woman. Come on, sweetie, I'll see that you get everything you want.'

"I didn't sleep at all that night. I loathed my mother after that, felt guilty because of it, and never could quite figure out why. But from that night on, it was as if Maggie had disappeared from sight, gone forever. I no longer had a mother. I hated myself for feeling that way, for being such a terrible person." She glanced sidelong at him. "You don't know what I'm talking about," she accused.

"Maybe I do. My mother was beautiful, intelligent, ambitious in her own right. She gave perfect dinner parties,

all very civilized. She took extended European holidays:
skiing in Klosters, summering in St. Tropez, yachting in
the Aegean. Always by herself. My father had too many
important obligations to fulfill to accompany her, and I
simply would have been in the way.

"My father came to see me play football once in high
school," Danning began. "I dropped three passes that day
and fumbled twice and he never watched me play again.
My father couldn't waste his time on anything or anyone
who was less than excellent. I always longed for their approval, but it never came. Do you believe in happy endings, Cindy? Was it Fitzgerald who said, 'There are no
third acts in American life'? Well, there are no happy endings, either. Decay sets in early, as soon as reality replaces
fantasy and you discover you'll always be less than you
dreamed of being."

"Is it too late to win your parents' approval? Is it too late
for all of us?"

"It doesn't matter after a while. Accept them for what
they are, don't ask them to change—they can't—and take
them seriously as human beings."

"And what about yourself?"

He laughed softly as the sun poked up above the horizon,
white-hot and spreading its warmth one more time. "Oh,
most important, take yourself seriously, too."

She stood up and walked a few steps, waited for him to
catch up. "Seriously," she said, "but not too seriously?"

"Not too seriously," he agreed, and they continued
along the beach, hand in hand.

LABOR DAY

Seventeen

Nick

Danning and Jason were the first ones off the ferry on the mainland. Almost immediately, Jason spied his mother and ran to her. Danning trailed after him.

"Hello, Tiffany."

She straighened up, arm looped protectively around Jason. "Hello, Nick, how are you?"

He had almost forgotten how lovely she was, a slender woman with classic features and flashing blue eyes that seemed to miss nothing. Her smile was controlled, displaying incredibly white teeth made whiter against her full crimson lips. She was wearing a summer dress in shades of green, and the skirt blew gently in the soft breeze that came off the bay.

"You're looking well."

"So are you. Tanned and handsomer than ever. Well," she said to Jason. "We must be going."

"I thought we might have some lunch," Danning offered. A jumble of emotions stirred him at the sight of his former wife, and he remembered some of the good times they had enjoyed together.

"I'm afraid that won't be possible, Nick. We've made other plans."

"Plans . . ."

"Gary's waiting with the car."

Danning followed her gesture. Gary Wells was a tall man with the confident expression of someone who'd known only the good things in life. He stood alongside a steelgray Mercedes, one hand resting possessively on it. Despite the distance that separated them, Danning felt that Gary's other hand touched his son and his wife. Former wife, he amended silently. He knelt in front of Jason.

"I enjoyed our days together, Jason. It was fun being with you."

"Me too," the boy said without emotion.

Danning held the boy by the shoulders. "I'm not the father I might be, maybe I never will be, Jason. We haven't seen each other as much as we might, and I'm sorry about that. I want you to know that I am your father, the only father you'll ever have, that I love you very much. I will always love you. More than that, you're a fine boy and I know you'll become a fine man."

"I love you, too," Jason said with a shy smile.

Danning clutched the boy to his chest. "Be kind to yourself, Jason, and to your mother." He stood up and faced Tiffany squarely. "You're doing a good job raising Jason, and I admire that."

For a moment, she seemed flustered. "He's got the genes, Nick, the best of us both."

"Have a good lunch," Danning said, and walked back along the dock to wait for the next ferry to carry him back to Fire Island.

Neil

Neil stood in front of the empty frame that had once held the O'Koren, as if willing the painting to magically appear. He squeezed his eyes shut and looked again. Nothing changed, the paintings were gone. Stolen. Taken from his apartment without a trace. He felt violated, some very tender, very private part of himself irrevocably damaged.

He sat behind his desk, staring at the empty frame, not knowing what to do next. Susan; she would tell him how to act in this strange and terrible moment. He dialed the Fire Island number and she answered. He told her about the robbery.

"Oh, no!"

"I'm so angry. I want to strike back and there's nothing I can do."

"I'm so sorry. I know how you loved those paintings. What else did they take?"

"I don't know. I haven't looked. I'll look now."

"Wait. How long have you been there?"

"I don't know. Half an hour, maybe more. I'm not sure."

"Are you all right?"

"I guess so." A numbness had settled in, and his words sounded slow, sluggish in his own ears. "Susan, what am I going to do?"

"Have you notified the police?"

"Not yet."

"Do that first. And then the insurance company."

"Yes. Susan, when I was a child, someone stole my bicycle. I cried then, I feel like crying now."

"Then cry, Neil, it's all right."

He blinked back the tears. "Oh, I could never do that. I'll get in touch with the police now."

"If you like, I'll come into town."

"That's not necessary. I can handle this." After he hung up, he considered calling back, asking her to come back to the apartment, to be with him during this bad period. But he wasn't able to do that, not yet.

"Insurance?"

Detective Second Grade Luis Corona was a slim man with a strong, tightly muscled body. His face was somber; under a thick black mustache his mouth was downturned, and his dark eyes were hooded, a man who had seen the underside of the human experience too many times and

232   BURT HIRSCHFELD

had come to expect nothing from any man other than his worst.

"Yes, they were insured."

"Full amount?"

"It's not the money, they can't be replaced."

"A new policy, Mr. Morgan?"

Neil saw where that line of questioning would lead. "I've owned the paintings for a long time. I bought the O'Koren more than a dozen years ago. The Sokolov and McGloughlin about ten years ago. I've had the same policy since."

"Any recent financial setbacks, Mr. Morgan?"

"You're not very subtle, Corona."

"It's my job to ask questions."

"Then ask questions that will lead to my paintings. To hell with the insurance money, I want those paintings."

Corona walked through the apartment again, occasionally writing something down in a small, leather-bound notebook. "Alarm systems?"

"Two of them."

"Show me."

Neil led the way. Corona examined the alarm systems with slow, professional curiosity. Satisfied, he headed back for the study, Neil behind him. Seating himself, Corona read over his notes. "The perpetrators were highly selective."

"So it seems."

"According to my forensic people, there were no fingerprints other than those of your family."

"They must have worn gloves."

"They?" Corona said.

"Yes, isn't that what you said, they?"

"Maybe so. A job like this, one man was all that was needed."

"I can't figure out how it was done. The backup alarm, everything in order. They bypassed both systems."

"Keys," Corona said. He put the notebook away. "Your wife have a set of keys?"

"Of course. And my son."

"Nobody else?"

"No one."

"Where were they when it happened? We're agreed it was Saturday night, aren't we?"

"How can you be so sure? I went out to the island on Friday and didn't get back until Monday. Plenty of time to rip me off."

"Saturday," Corona said firmly. "Two hookers worked over the doorman Saturday night, a fella named George. Put him down on the sidewalk and roughed him up a little, enough to keep him occupied for a while, enough to let somebody get into the building unobserved. Somebody with a key."

"Well, that clears Susan and me. My wife had her annual party that night, hundreds of people."

"And most of them would vouch for you and the missus being there, right?"

"Exactly right, detective."

"What about your son—Boyd Benjamin, isn't it?"

"Yes, BB, too. All night. Although I wish he hadn't been."

"What's that mean?"

"BB had a little too much to drink, put a move on a married woman and tried to punch out her husband. You know how young people can be."

"Kids," Corona said. "I'll nose around, Mr. Morgan."

"What are the chances of finding my paintings?"

"I don't know. Pictures like those, they can't be sold on the open market, too well known. That means a private collector somewhere. Maybe a job done to order, who can say? I'm having prints made of the slides you supplied us with, and once they're distributed, we'll see what we see. With a little luck, we'll find them soon enough."

"And if you don't?"

"In which case it'll take a little longer."

Cindy

Late August in New York was thick and slow, the concrete hoarding the day's heat, spreading it among the

pedestrians who sought relief in air-conditioned movie the-
atres or restaurants. Crowded buses stalled, causing monumental traffic jams, and brown-suited traffic officers blew
incessantly on their whistles in a futile attempt to stave off
gridlock.

Cindy approached Alex Stainback's apartment house
with mixed feelings. It would be cool and comfortable inside, relief from the oppressive heat, but Alex would be
there, and that was a considerable drawback. He greeted
her at the door with a tall glass.

"For you. On a day like this, a cooling drink is vital."

"What I need is to get back out to Fire Island and a long
swim in the ocean." She touched the frosted glass to her
brow. She sat in a straight-backed chair, legs outstretched,
letting the air conditioning soothe her fevered skin.

He sat opposite, clad in a striped cotton robe, certainly
naked underneath. He looked smug, too sure of himself
and of her, king of all he surveyed. Her employer, her
lover. No, hardly a lover. Simply another man she serviced.

"Why am I here, Alex?"

There was nothing subtle in his response. "For some
very energetic, very imaginative screwing."

Is that the way Nick would see it, she asked herself, another easy lay, another piece of ass? Funny to think of him
in those terms when holding hands was the most intimate
act they'd shared, and yet—

"That's what we've been doing, screwing? Each other
and the people who buy paintings in that art supermarket
I run for you."

He seemed bored by the conversation. "Bring your
drink. We'll be more comfortable in the bedroom."

"I need a shower."

"I'll take you the way you are. Everything turns me
on."

"A hen in a barnyard would turn you on."

"Only if it were good to look at. Let's go."

She took a long pull on the drink and made up her mind.
"You know I don't want you, Alex. I never have."

"I never asked you for love, only some good old-fashioned humping."

"I don't even like you, Alex."

"Save it, I'm not interested. Now get your ass in there."

"You're not concerned about what I feel, about what I want?"

He brought his penis out from under the robe. "Here, this is what you want."

"I'm not impressed."

"How many of these have you had inside you?"

"Enough to know you're no bargain."

His cheeks turned pink. "Don't give me any shit. Get your clothes off and do what you're supposed to do."

"You're the last of the romantics, Alex."

He gestured to his crotch. "This is all the romance you need."

"You're wrong about that. I need a great deal more."

"When you're finished here, you can look for whatever else you want. Now get down on your knees and work on this."

She wet her lips. "You're very raunchy, Alex."

"Better believe it."

"You need it bad?"

"The worst, baby."

She rose quickly. "I'll tell you what to do."

"What?"

"Go fuck yourself."

"Cunt!" he shot back. "There's plenty more like you around, plenty. I don't need you, not here, not at the gallery. You're fired. You hear me, you're fired!"

She left feeling better about herself than she had in a very long time.

Maggie

"Never again."

Susan and Maggie were sunning themselves on the deck of Maggie's house. Behind a tall redwood fence that

shielded them from prying eyes, the women had removed
their bikini tops, and their bodies glistened with tanning
oil. They lay on their backs on cushioned white-pipe
lounges, faces turned upward, limbs spread in order to ex-
pose a maximum amount of skin to the tanning rays. Next
to each lounge was a small iron-and-glass table holding
cigarettes and tall drinks.

"You've never said that before," Maggie replied. She
altered her position slightly, setting herself against the
painful reminders of the recent abuse she had suffered.
Her voice was flat, lifeless, her usual animation ab-
sent.

"I don't like what's happening. Those animals who attacked you. BB drunk and fighting. All those people I don't
know and don't want to know. The friends I have around
here—my real friends—there aren't more than half a dozen
people I truly care about."

"That business on the beach—"

"Try to forget about it."

"I don't want to forget it. It's made me realize clearly for
the first time what kind of person I've become. What I allowed myself to become. I'm just this side of being an alcoholic. I smoke too much. I use dope too much and end up in
the sack with men I don't even know, too damn many of
them."

"You're being too hard on yourself."

Maggie came up on her elbows. Beads of sweat rolled
down between her breasts. She drank from the glass and
lit a cigarette. "That's just it, I haven't been hard enough.
Tell me this, Susan, why do I abuse myself this way?
That's what I do, you know, what I've been doing for so
long. What do I get out of it? All those men inside my body,
strangers who care nothing about me, who aren't concerned with what I want or what I think or what I feel, as
long as I get them off. To hell with that, Susan, I'm tired of
being the world's girl."

"Those two—that wasn't sex. Raw anger, an exercise in
brutality. It had nothing to do with you."

"I think it did. And it might have happened to you, to
any number of women we know. Those men sensed that I

was vulnerable—available, they would say—they sniffed me out, Susan, they knew all about me. Half of Fire Island must know about Maggie Ashe, the easiest lay on the beach." She laughed without mirth. "Ashe, that's not my name anymore, hasn't been for years. But I still think of myself that way, as Roy's wife. Four husbands, sometimes I forget, get confused. Who am I? What am I? Looking back, it's all such a blur, so painful. Why did I do it? Why am I doing it still? Mrs. Roy Ashe, that's who I always wanted to be."

"Poor Roy."

"Poor Roy, poor me, poor every one of us. Impoverished in so many ways. Roy was the love of my youth, and I miss him so."

"You're forgetting how badly he treated you."

"We treated each other badly and never had the strength or the courage to see it through, to work out our differences. You and Neil, you kept on with each other, maintained your marriage . . ."

"That was Neil's doing. He was willing to endure, to ignore so much."

"Funny about Neil. Of all of us, I used to think Neil was the most likely to crack and break. He was the most rigid, the one least flexible. I was wrong. Looks like he was the strongest of us. He survived, intact, which is no small feat. You worked it out, Susan, you and Neil, you still have each other."

The words hammered at Susan, shaking loose fragments of memory, memories best left dormant. She sat up and put on her bra.

"Are you going?" Maggie said, a hint of panic in her voice. "Don't go yet."

"I want to take a nap."

"I'm afraid to be alone. I've always loathed being by myself, but these days it's worse than ever."

"Why don't you get out of the sun? Take a nap, too."

"Perhaps I will. A long rest will refresh me, exorcise all these morbid images." She embraced the other woman. "Oh, Susan, we've been friends for such a long time, a very long time, such good friends. I love you so."

"And I love you, Maggie."

Maggie stepped back, smiled sheepishly. "I don't know what to do anymore."

"Do? You'll do what you've always done, live your life, enjoy it. Get some rest, clean up, and we'll have dinner later."

"At Leo's?"

"At Leo's. A drink or two, some good food and, who knows, maybe we'll run into a couple of terrific guys and have a few laughs."

Maggie pulled back, face closing down.

"All right, no men. Just the two of us."

"Promise?"

"I promise."

Alone, Maggie mixed another gin and tonic and went back out on the deck to catch the last remaining rays of sunlight. So many husbands and so many lovers, so many people drifting in and out of her life, and yet here she was alone and so lonely. It was all a mistake, she told herself, a terrible mistake.

Or was it?

Billy

A disinterested voice told him to hold on, and he clung to the phone as if to a life raft. He checked his watch; almost five minutes had gone by. How long was he supposed to wait? Directors, what a bunch of bastards they were! Every one of them. Without regard for the feelings of actors. Didn't they realize that actors were human, too? With ambitions, fears, rent to pay. The trouble with show business was that nobody cared about anybody else. Not enough that you succeed; your friends had to fail. Shaft-your-buddy week. Get on the wire, Rickie Huber, he commanded silently, let's go.

"Yes?"

"Mr. Huber?"

"This is Rickie Huber. Who am I talking to?"

"Billy Grooms, Mr. Huber."

"Yes, well, what can I do for you, Grooms?"

Motherfucker! He didn't even remember. Billy spoke in a carefully controlled voice. "I read for you, the part of Bruce in Neil Morgan's picture. It's been a couple of weeks so I thought I'd inquire."

An ominous silence followed.

"Right, Bruce the young stranger. Well, I have my notes on your reading in front of me, Grooms. You did okay, a pretty good reading. But we decided to go with Helene Michaels as the Secretary of Labor, and that means you're too young to play against her."

"I'm not as young as you think."

"Maybe so, but you look too boyish, Grooms. What I had in mind was someone less clean-cut, a little more depraved, if you get my meaning. But thanks anyway for reading. Try again next time around."

Billy swallowed an angry retort. "Mr. Morgan arranged the reading personally. Neil Morgan, the producer."

"Yes," Huber said. "Morgan is the producer and I am the director." He hung up.

In front of the mirror, Billy examined himself. A fan of tiny creases had set in at the corners of his eyes, not visible to the casual observer but there nevertheless. And lately he'd noticed a certain slackness under his chin, along his throat. His body was changing, time was marking him, stealing his most precious asset, leaving him with an uncertain future.

"Damn," he said aloud, moving away from the glass. He felt betrayed by his face and his body. Over the years they had served to pay his way, and now, even as those very qualities of youth and beauty were departing, they had cost him his big chance to become a movie star.

Something had to be done and done soon. Make a connection, get money. Summer was almost over, and he was down to his last two hundred dollars. That woman he'd met at Susan's party, right in so many ways but unwilling to see him a second time. A one-night stand. She'd used him and he hated her for it. Made him feel like a piece of meat. Well, to hell with her, no point in looking back. It

was the future that interested Billy Grooms. Either he
made a quick strike, someone rich and generous, or a
gloomy fate would be his.

He made his way down to the beach, ambling idly. People in groups everywhere, families, friends, lovers. Children playing games with other children. It seemed to him
that only he was alone.

The houses looming over the dunes were larger along
this stretch of beach, the homes of the very wealthy, homes
to which he'd never been invited. Here existed a stateli-
ness, a solidity, as if constructed to stand forever against
the storms of the Atlantic, to last. One sprawling structure
caught his eye. Weathered silver by the salt air, it was an
amalgam of tall doors and windows, of widow's walks and
wide decks, dramatic angles. On the deck, a woman in a
white bikini faced the setting sun. On impulse, Billy left
the beach and made his way up onto the deck. His footfalls
on the planking announced his coming, but the woman
gave no sign she'd heard.

He inspected her with a practiced eye. Good-looking
with thick blond hair cut short, a woman of years but one
who took care of herself. A woman used to the good life and
willing, he hoped, to pay to keep a certain share of it.

"Afternoon," he began.

Her eyes opened, and she assessed him gravely. "I don't
know you," she said in a voice throaty and assured.

He introduced himself, and when she made no immediate response, he grew uneasy. Was he losing his grip, some
essential element used up over the years? He produced his
best smile. "I saw you alone up here, and since I was alone,
too . . ."

Again that long, penetrating stare, as if looking into the
heart of him, trying to determine what he was all about.
"You are," she said at last, "a pretty, pretty creature." His
smile broadened, and he took a step forward. "And at the
same time very transparent."

"Does that mean you want me to leave?" He was weary
of rejection, of always ending up with the short end of the
stick. "I was just trying to be friendly."

"The bar," she said, "is inside. I'm drinking vodka and

orange juice, lots of ice. Be a dear and fetch me another, will you?"

"Glad to. Mind if I get one for myself?"

She lay back down, eyes closed under the sun. "No, I don't mind at all."

Eighteen

BB

There were three girls in the reception room of the Snap Shop when Corona walked in. They made him for a cop at once, and it was Laura Lee who took the lead.

"May I help you, sir?"

Corona had worked vice a dozen years before and recognized the girls for what they were. But vice had been a dirty, thankless, pointless job, and disabused him of the notion that the oldest profession could be wiped out by police work. Simply a matter of supply and demand.

Corona flashed his shield and said his name and grade. "I want to talk to the manager."

Laura Lee made a face and went into BB's office, closing the door behind her. "There's a cop outside."

"Vice?"

"Never saw him before. Name of Corona."

"What's he want?"

"To talk to the manager, he said. You think it's about those paintings?"

"I told you not to mention that around here. Just forget it, nothing ever happened."

"As long as me and Jill get our money."

"When I get paid, you'll get paid."

"What about the cop?"

"I'm clean, send him in. Let's see what he wants."

Laura Lee ushered Corona into the office and left. BB rose and offered his hand. "Detective Corona, what can I do for you? Take a few photos of the girls? We can rent you a camera, if you don't have your own. The girls are experienced models and—"

"I know what the girls are, BB." Corona seated himself. "Never run when you can walk," he said. "Never walk when you can stand. Never stand when you can sit. Never sit when you can lie down."

"Sounds like a good philosophy."

"Cops live by it. Somebody ripped off your father, BB. You mind if I call you BB? There's a family resemblance, you and your father."

"Ripped him off?"

"Some of his paintings."

"Is that a fact?"

"Three paintings. Worth a great deal of money. Less to whoever bought them. A lot less to the dude who made the score, after he splits with his people."

A cold knot lodged in BB's chest. "You seem to know a great deal about the robbery."

"I know a great deal about the way these things are done. Even when they break the pattern, there's a pattern, if you follow my logic."

"I'm afraid I don't."

"You didn't know about the robbery?"

"How would I know? I don't see my father often, I don't talk to him much."

"What about your mother?"

"She spends all her time on Fire Island."

"You been out to visit lately?"

BB smiled grandly. "Matter of fact, I have. Last Saturday. My mother gave a party. I didn't want to miss it."

"When did you come back to New York?"

"Let's see, I slept late and planned on catching the one

o'clock ferry. But I ran into some friends of mine in a local pub and we all had lunch together, a few drinks."

"Convenient," Corona said.

"What do you mean by that?"

"When did you get into New York?"

"I drove in with Willy Gerstel. You know Willy, a fine fellow. Very big in insurance. I'd say he dropped me off at my apartment about six o'clock."

Corona made a note. "Tell me about your father."

"What would you like to know? Produces movies, makes money, collects paintings. But you know all that, don't you, detective?"

"How do you get along?"

"Get along with Neil Morgan? He is a man who discovered the one true road to Rome and either you travel it with him or you don't get along. My father and I don't get along very well, detective."

"Fathers and sons, it can be rough."

"Very rough."

"Rough enough for you to want to hurt him?"

"Hurt my father?"

"Punish him. Get even. Revenge is a powerful motive that could lead to anything, including robbery."

"Are you accusing me of ripping off my own father?"

"Did you do it, BB?" Corona smiled.

BB smiled. "Of course not. When was the robbery?"

"Saturday night, I think."

"While I was on Fire Island. No, I couldn't have done it, detective."

"A lot of people saw you out there?"

"A lot."

"Figures. It was a pretty neat job. Whoever did it had to bypass a double alarm setup and a doorman."

"You seem to have figured it out."

"Sort of a perfect crime, you might say. Two alarms and neither one goes off. The doorman saw nothing. No locks jimmied, no doors forced, no other apparent way in or out. Which means somebody had the keys. Walked right in through the front lobby and pulled off the job."

"You said the doorman didn't see anybody."

"Did I say that? He saw a couple of hookers. Hookers working Park Avenue, imagine it! From what the door-man said, they could even have been a couple of those girls outside there."

"Are you accusing my girls of being involved?"

"A little defensive, aren't you? Just trying to bring you up to date on the case so far. No fingerprints, except yours, your mother's and your father's. And oh yes, the cleaning lady, Frances by name. Nobody saw anything, nobody knows anything. I'm left with only one conclusion. The street fight was a diversion which allowed the perpetrator to enter the building unobserved."

"Makes sense until you try to explain how the robber got into the apartment."

"Didn't I tell you—keys, that's how."

"How did he get them?"

"Good question. Three sets outstanding—yours, your fa-ther's, and your mother's." Corona leaned forward. "You didn't by any chance lose your set?"

BB brought his key chain out of his pocket. "Every-thing's right here."

"Were they missing at any time? Long enough for some-one to make duplicates?"

"If they were, I don't know about it."

"In which case you can't answer the question."

"Right, detective."

"But it's always possible one of your lady friends lifted them, had a duplicate set run off, and got them back into your pants before you knew the difference."

"I always know when somebody puts a hand in my pocket."

"Unless your pants are off." BB grinned with tight satis-faction. "You trust all your lady friends?"

"All the way."

"Hookers?"

"I never pay for it."

"Still, with a hooker, who can tell? A girl might be un-der pressure from her pimp. Does you good until you sleep and she passes the keys to her accomplice outside. He gets them run off pretty damn quick and like that, bang, bang, they're back in your pants. How's that grab you?"

"It's a theory."

"But not really sound?"

"Slightly strained."

"You're right, slightly strained. You're good at this, BB, damn good. Ever think about becoming a cop?" Corona shoved himself erect. "I thought I'd have a few words with the girls outside, if you don't mind. Never can tell what a hooker hears in the course of her workday."

"Help yourself, detective."

"Pleases me that you're so cooperative, BB. Nice talking to you."

When he was alone, BB began to tremble. Corona possessed no hard evidence, but if he came down hard on Jill or Laura Lee, the party might end abruptly. All of them would be flushed down the drain. What if George was able to identify the girls who assaulted him? Certainly they would crack under that kind of pressure and implicate him. He was dialing the phone when the door opened and Corona looked in.

"Think about it," he said, that wise smile back in place. "Whoever did the job had to know the paintings were in your father's apartment, had to know their market value, had to have a buyer since no legitimate dealer would touch them. All that and access, too. Can you think of anybody in a position to do all that, BB? No, I guess not. Grasping at straws is what I'm doing, just grasping."

It was thirty minutes later when BB's hands ceased trembling and he was able to complete that call.

Susan

Turk was waiting when Susan came back from visiting Maggie. She was halfway across the living room before she sensed his presence. He was seated in a white wicker chair in the far corner of the room. Just the sight of him sent her running for the door, but she stumbled and fell backward onto the floor.

"This morning," he said, standing astride her. "You were supposed to be at my place this morning."

"No more, Turk. No more. You're not going to abuse me again."

"Sure," he said. "Have it your way." He stepped back and watched her climb hesitantly to her feet. He smiled. "See? Anything you want."

She turned to face him. Still smiling, he slapped her across the face, then pushed her across the room and slammed her down onto the sofa.

She looked up at him, but there was no defiance in her gaze.

"I own you," he muttered. "But you're not even interesting anymore." He ran his hand across her cheek which was still red and burning. "You're just a beat-up old broad, Susan. Not worth it anymore."

He turned and walked out of the room.

Susan stared after him, still rubbing her face. She was relieved that he hadn't assaulted her any further, but wary that he was lurking somewhere nearby, waiting for her to feel safe, secure. She sat there for almost an hour, inert, unable to move, paralyzed with fear and self-loathing. When she finally moved, it was to collapse onto the floor, sobbing against the oriental carpet, never wanting to get up again.

Nick

Danning lengthened his stroke and stepped up his kick, swimming faster. Kolodny kept pace without difficulty. They swam parallel to the beach for nearly a mile before turning back.

"You're full of surprises," Danning said, drying off.

Kolodny, grinning, lay back on the still-warm sand. There was a bite in the air, and he marked it down as the start of the end of the summer. Labor Day Weekend was upon them, and that meant the lease on their house would expire. Back to the real world.

"Didn't think I had it in this cuddly little body of mine, did you?"

"Where'd you learn to swim like that?"

"My old man taught me at such fashionable spas as the Rockaways and Brighton Beach. Kept insisting the trick was to stay loose and breathe right. Promised me if I did it his way I'd never get tired."

"And?"

"Two things never tire me, Danning. Swimming's one of them."

Danning grinned. "And the other?"

"I'll never tell." Kolodny sat up, hugging his knees. "Whataya say, Nick, have you had the kind of summer I said it would be?"

"Very interesting."

"As bad as that, too bad."

"What about you?"

"I met a lot of fine foxy ladies."

"And?"

"And would you believe every one of them turned me down?"

"You're putting me on."

"I got off to a slow start, slumped a little in the middle, but lately matters have come to a screeching halt. Not like you. I bet it's been hot-and-cold running stuff for you."

"You lose."

"Mustn't lie to your pal. What about that perky one, the one with the curly hair and those marvelous—whatchama-callems?"

"Her name is Cindy."

"Cindy. Fits like a second skin. From the look of Cindy, she's enough for any man."

"She's on my mind."

"What's she think of that?"

"I haven't told her."

"For a guy with your looks, you certainly are a bust where the ladies are concerned."

"I'm serious."

"What makes you think I'm not? If I had your face and build I'd put a calendar on the outside of my bedroom door and let the chicks make appointments. This Cindy, maybe she doesn't like men."

"Don't get smarmy. She's a lovely woman, but she's got very little interest in me, I'm afraid."

"I'm beginning to wonder about you, Danning. What I'm saying is, any man who's better-looking than I am is probably gay, which puts you in a terrible bind, my friend. Have you got a severe sexual problem you'd like to confess? Are you in need of therapy? Confide in the good Doctor Kolodny."

"I think I'm in love with Cindy."

"Ridiculous. At once you must move on to more fertile fields. In a phrase, drop the chick."

"I can't do that."

"You can do anything you put your mind to. You were an all-American in college, you resemble a middle-aged Greek god, you were all-pro."

"I was never all-pro."

"Lie. Distort your accomplishments. Exaggerate, inflate, insinuate. If you really want the lady, press your case upon her as well as anything else that strikes your fancy."

"I have a feeling that this is a case of the lame leading the blind."

"Find her, tell her straight out how you feel. Love is a four-letter aphrodisiac that rivals ground rhino horn for potency."

"Kolodny, you are sick."

"You know where she is, don't you?"

"Her mother's house."

"Go to her at once."

"And say what?"

"Declare your undying devotion."

"I couldn't do that."

"Marriage, at least a proposal thereof, that is the answer to your dilemma."

"I've been married, it was a mess. The last time I saw Tiffany, all those old feelings came rushing back—the way it was to be with her, and the bad times, as well. I don't want to go through that again. I'm not prepared to endure another divorce."

"Everybody from Richmond, Virginia, to Boston has been married at least once, and divorced. Woody Allen movies, designer jeans and divorce; all de rigueur for our generation. Proceed accordingly."

"The thing is, we've never even—"

"You mean, never? Not even one teensy tiny little zetz?"

"Never."

"Danning, I retract any compliments I paid you. You are a certified one-hundred percent pure schmuck."

"I'm miserable, and you call me names in Yiddish."

"A schmuck with earlaps."

"What am I going to do?"

"Only one strategy remains. Throw yourself upon her mercy. Swear your unrelenting fealty and grope her mightily."

"Kolodny, you have the moral standards of a Times Square Flasher."

"Ain't it the truth?"

Cindy was not at her mother's house; neither was her mother. On impulse, Danning hurried down Cottage Walk to Midway and over to where the Morgans lived. No one responded to his knock, so he opened the screen door and went inside, calling, "Anybody home?"

A soft, plaintive sound drew him into the living room where he found Susan sprawled out on the Kirman rug, sobbing. Her bruised face was swollen.

"Go away," she moaned, "please just go away."

But Danning didn't go away. He held her gently and listened as she poured out the story of Turk and what he had done to her. He rocked her like a child when it was over, then put her into her own bed where she fell into an exhausted sleep.

Nineteen

Neil

The days weren't long enough. There was so much to do; the budget of the picture, for one. Twice it had to be revised, and each time the result was unsatisfactory; including the override, it fell short of what the film would eventually cost. Neil held off contacting Regginato for fear of what the moneyman might say, although in the end he would be forced to explain the situation, ask for additional funds.

Nor was the script right. Still soft in the middle and in the last few scenes, as if the author had lost interest. Structurally it was fine, but the dialogue too often lacked bite. This was a serious story of quirky, exaggerated characters, their overweening egos, and a succession of unlikely mishaps that befell them. The pathos of the script was, rightly so, cloaked in comedy, but the scriptwriter had managed to let most of the comedic values slip away. In an attempt to remedy this, Neil had brought in Lou and Fran Mailman, a husband-and-wife writing team with extensive Hollywood credits. So far their efforts had fallen short of what he was hoping for.

And now Rickie Huber was on his back. Huber, a young director in years and experience, was a wispy man with long, graceful hands. He had started out as a dancer in Broadway chorus lines, advanced to featured parts, become a choreographer, and managed eventually to make the leap to director. He had done four musicals and a dozen television dramas, had received accolades and awards, but this was his first feature film. It occurred to Neil that he might have made a mistake, the biggest mistake of his life.

"She's got to go!" Huber began in that thin dancer's screech as soon as he entered Neil's Manhattan office.

Neil put the budget out of his mind. He stopped worrying about the script. He made himself forget that he had yet to conclude a distribution deal. He gave his full attention to the slender man on the other side of his desk, always the solid producer, reliable, strong, and inevitably available in a crisis.

"Who has to go, Rickie?"

"Boniface, Neil. That girl is beyond belief, no talent, no intelligence. She can't act, she has a voice like a fishwife, she keeps bumping into the furniture. A stiff, Neil. She's a lemon. A rotten egg. A real turkey."

Neil tried to blunt the harsh edge of Huber's anger. "I don't want you to hold back, Rickie. Say exactly what you think about her."

Huber growled. "She stinks. Absolutely, positively without ability. Dump her now."

"That may not be a very good idea, Rickie."

"The part calls for a star name, anyway."

Neil leaned forward. "Boniface comes with the money, Rickie."

Huber waved the words away with a practiced, graceful gesture. "I'm an artist, not an accountant."

"Let me explain. Miss Boniface belongs to a Mr. Regginato, who is backing our picture to the tune of one hundred and fifteen percent, to be exact."

"So?"

"So, now I must go to Mr. Regginato and ask him for additional sums, another three million, to be precise."

"This has nothing to do with me."

"But it does, Rickie, with all of us. Mr. Regginato will certainly take a dim view of things if his protégée is canned four weeks before shooting commences."

"She's a stiff."

"Work with her."

"It's no go. She can't remember her lines. She— Neil, either Boniface is out or I am."

Neil sat back in his chair, made a steeple with his hands, arranged a pleasant expression on his craggy face. "Let me explain about Mr. Regginato. He is a person with a great many business interests, none of which are considered legitimate by Internal Revenue or the NYPD, if you grasp my meaning. Do I make myself clear?"

"You mean he's a gangster?"

"I mean he's a man I don't wish to annoy, anger, or have as an enemy. Nor do you, Rickie."

Huber grew calmer. He became quite reasonable. "If Boniface does the lead, we'll never get an important male star to go opposite her."

"You've got a point. Let me give it some thought. Meanwhile, you help her as much as you can."

Alone in his office, Neil performed a series of isometric exercises designed to relieve tension. The tingling in his fingers diminished, the ringing in his ears faded away, his heartbeat slowed. Why, he asked himself, go through all this? So much work, so much conflict, so many disappointments. Retire to a farmhouse in Bucks County, a well-insulated farmhouse with a backup heating system; Pennsylvania winters could be fierce. Or maybe a villa on the French Riviera. Or a round-the-world trip on the *QE 2*. He sighed; none of it would ever happen, it was just not his way to go. He made the call, identified himself.

"Yeah?" a gravelly voice answered.

"I'd like to set up a meeting with Mr. Regginato."

"Hang in there, champ."

A moment later Regginato was on the line. "You got a problem, kid?"

"You could say that."

"That's what I do best, solve problems. Be here in an hour. I can give you fifteen minutes."

Regginato was immersed in a huge, square, pink plastic tub when Neil arrived. The tub had been set up at one end of his bedroom, a chamber of kingly proportions. The hot water swirled around in a constant rise of bubbles and steam. Sweat poured off Regginato's chin, and he was talking on the telephone.

A burly aide placed a chair at the foot of the tub, indicated that Neil was to sit. A female secretary passed a note to her soaking employer. A valet polished a pair of wingtip shoes. A tailor displayed fabric samples for Regginato's inspection. Finally, Regginato put the phone aside, waved his secretary away, dismissed the tailor. The valet continued his labors, and the aide took up a defensive stance against one wall.

"Okay, Morgan, what's on your mind?"

"Two things."

"When a man's got two things on his mind, one of them is always money." Regginato grinned mirthlessly. "Am I right?"

"We've had problems with the script."

"Hire a writer."

"I've hired two."

"If that's not enough, get some more. Get as many as you need. How much dough you want?"

"Three million."

Regginato never flinched. "What's problem number two?"

Neil felt the tension return to his body. He began to blink. "I had a conference with Rickie Huber."

"Oh, yeah, the fag dancer. Long as he knows his business, it don't matter how he gets his jollies. The word is he's a pretty good director, is that so, Morgan?"

"He's very gifted."

"Sure, that's why he's working for us. Get to it, Morgan."

"It's about Miss Boniface."

Regginato stood up, a taut, muscular man with two long scars on his torso. The valet brought him a towel. "Out,"

Regginato said to the man, who obeyed at once. The burly aide remained in place.

Regginato put on a blue silk robe and lit a long cigar, clouds of blue smoke rising around his head. "What about Miss Boniface?"

"Well, you have to admit she's relatively inexperienced."

Regginato glared through the cigar smoke. "What the fuck you talking about? I mean, okay, she's pretty young, but the dame has been around, if you know what I am saying to you."

"Her acting."

"I seen her act. Off-off Broadway, she said it was. Best thing in the whole cockamamie show."

"I'm sure she was. But this is her first motion picture, and that's a big responsibility. It requires a great deal of skill and experience in front of the camera, in accepting direction, in reading lines."

"Huber's so good, let him teach her."

Neil had a premonition that his film, his project, his dream, was about to unravel before his eyes, and nothing he could do would prevent it from happening. "Rickie can't give her experience or presence before the camera."

Regginato paced and blew smoke. "That little girl, I promised I'd get her into pictures. The money I'm putting up, I ought to be able to get her into pictures without some fag dancer making insulting remarks."

Neil tried again. "Huber feels that Miss Boniface isn't ready for the part."

"This Huber, is he reliable? I mean, he says a thing like that, is it true?"

Neil sighed. "I'm afraid it is, Mr. Regginato. There's something else; we need a couple of box-office names. Without a star in the female role, we'll have trouble getting an important male actor for the picture."

"Miss Boniface is bad for business, is that what you're telling me?"

"I'm afraid I am." Suddenly, Neil perceived relief in sight and pressed his case. "I don't intend to drop Miss Boniface from the project. There's another female part that she'd be perfect in. Remember Marilyn Monroe in *All About Eve?* Little more than a walk-on, but everybody noticed her. She made her presence felt."

"You think this other part can do the same for Miss Boniface?"

"I hope so."

Regginato swore softly. "I'm a businessman, first thing. People got to understand that about me. I make an investment, I expect a return. A bad picture, what happens to my dough? Into the toilet is what happens. Okay, Miss Boniface takes the other part."

"I suppose you'd prefer to tell her yourself."

"You crazy? The broad'll blow her top. You tell her. You're the pro, you can convince her. Leave me out of it. And about the three million, somebody'll pay you a visit in a day or two with a satchel."

"I appreciate that."

"What else?"

"I can't think of anything."

"Okay, you do, you call. It's what I do best, solving problems."

Twenty

Cindy

A fine mist began falling about the time Cindy woke up that morning, and it continued to fall during the train ride to Bayshore. But by the time she boarded the ferry, the rain had stopped, and halfway across the bay the sun broke through the clouds promising a fine, final weekend of the summer.

Labor Day Weekend was a wild, noisy time up and down the length of the island. One extended party, the tempo increasing as the weekend wore on. More liquor would be consumed, more dope smoked and sniffed, more casual sex engaged in, more lies told, more promises made, all designed to squeeze an extra dollop of pleasure from the fading hours of the summer.

By noon on Friday, the bars were overflowing with drinkers and the partying had begun. Those who could arrange it had arrived the day before in order to avoid the traffic that would turn Long Island's highways into long parking lots. The beach was a nearly unbroken carpet of near naked bodies soaking up sunlight as if to hoard it through the winter. Two volleyball games were in progress, and a six-man touch football game was being played on the hard-packed sand.

Maggie had written all of it off. She paid a last visit to Susan. "I'm leaving," she said.

"Stay for the weekend," Susan implored over a cup of coffee.

"I can't trust myself out here. That night with those two boys, the worst of it, the part that has lingered and still hurts so much was that a part of me wanted it to happen. While they hurt me and used me and treated me as if I weren't human, all that time I wanted it to continue. A warped part of me enjoyed what they were doing, some sick, secret part, as if I deserved to be treated so badly, deserved to be punished for my sins."

"You're a good person, Maggie."

"What I am is weak. I've wasted so much of my life. Look at us, Susan, what in God's name have we been doing with our time on earth? All the years, the men, the booze, and nothing to show for it."

"You're having a bad time, that's all. We've had bad times before, you and I, Maggie, and they passed. This will pass also."

"Not unless I make it happen. My life—for so long, it's been the same damn mistakes. No more."

"You make it sound so permanent."

"I mean it to be."

Maggie arrived at the dock just as a ferry began disgorging its passengers. People hurried past, a blur of unrecognizable faces, strangers every one, already fueled by the excitement of being back on Fire Island. It was a feeling she was familiar with; the anticipation of unreality, someone had called it. Who had said that? Maybe Eddie Stander, or was it Mike Birns? Mike had been a man of words. No matter who had coined the phrase, it was accurate; unreality hung over Fire Island like a low, dark cloud. They chased after unreality as if it were the Holy Grail, and found only cheap thrills and transient pleasures, mistaking them for lasting satisfaction. For so many years, Maggie had been one with them. But no more.

"Mother!"

The word brought her eyes into focus, and she saw Cindy coming toward her.

"Your timing is exquisite, my dear."

"Are you expecting someone?"

"On the contrary—I'm about to depart."

"You're leaving before Labor Day? I don't believe that."

A wan smile lifted the corners of Maggie's mouth. "Believe it or not, I am going." She picked up her suitcase.

"When will you be back?"

"Don't plan on it. I've put the house up for sale. Until it's sold, you use it whenever you like."

"It's so sudden—"

"Not really. It's been on my mind for some time now."

"Where will you go?"

"I'll stay in town until the apartment is sold."

"You're getting rid of that, too?"

"I'm getting rid of all excess baggage, my dear. As to where I'll go, I don't know. The necessary change has to take place in me. Now, I'd better get aboard the ferry."

Cindy touched Maggie's arm. "Not yet. There's always another ferry. Let's go somewhere and talk."

"Why not? But out of doors, near the water."

They found a place at the marina that looked out past the boats to the Great South Bay where some gulls were lazily circling. Beneath them, two boys and a man were digging for clams in the shallows. Maggie breathed in the damp salt air as if experiencing it for the last time, a vital piece of the island to carry along when she departed.

"What brought this on, Mother, that business with the two boys?"

"That, and a lot more. That wasn't my first experience on the beach with a young man. More than once I brushed night sand off my backside in the name of sexual immediacy. Oh, no, life isn't that simple."

"What then?"

"You know about Susan?"

"What about her?"

Maggie told her what had taken place. "Your friend, Nick, found Susan."

"Nick? What was he doing there?"

"Looking for you, apparently. Odd, isn't it, first he res-
cues me and then Susan. I'll say this for him, he certainly
manages to be around when he's needed."

"So it seems."

"I haven't known many men who were there when you
needed them. It's a rare quality."

On impulse, Cindy embraced her mother and they sat
without moving for a long interval, neither speaking. Finally Cindy broke the silence. "I can't remember the last
time we bothered to touch each other."

"You left me a long time ago, my dear."

"I never felt I belonged."

"When my marriage to Roy fell apart, it was as if something vital went out of my life. Nothing held, if that makes
sense to you."

"I think I understand."

"But I never stopped loving you, Cindy. Oh, I might
have resented certain qualities in you that I lacked, the
strength you possessed, for example."

"Strength! Me?"

"Oh, yes. You were always so involved in life in so many
ways, so much a part of the world you lived in. When you
were in Paris during the student uprising—"

"I was so afraid."

"But you were part of it. I was afraid for you and very
proud of you, too."

"I wish you had told me."

"It was never easy for me to talk to you, to express my
feelings." She swung around and examined Cindy closely.
"You look almost the same as you did when you were an
infant."

"Slightly more shopworn."

"One night, in that first house, I was asleep, and Mike
Birns woke me up." She smiled fondly, reliving the memory. "He was reluctant to come into my room because he
knew I slept nude and he was worried about seeing me naked, offending me."

"And?"

"But you were crying, and he had tried to quiet you
without any luck."

"And?" Cindy said again, remembering how Mike Birns had looked on another day, a day she had gone to his apartment in New York uninvited, on some pretext or other, her aim to seduce this writer friend of her parents. But he had made her feel like the adolescent girl she was, made her ashamed and resentful, bitter that she couldn't have what she wanted when she wanted it.

"And," Maggie said, "I went to you and soothed you until you went back to sleep. That was a lovely night for me. Mike's modesty, his concern for a crying infant, the quiet, intimate time I spent with you. An important night in my life . . ."

"But it all went wrong— why?"

"There's blame enough to go around, I suppose. Roy and I—we were little more than children ourselves, always playing, as if having good old times was what life was all about."

"I lived the same way for so long. If it feels good, it must be good. That was our rallying cry, a license to smoke dope or have sex or plant a bomb. We all were so sure we were part of a moral and historical imperative that permitted any action.'"

"I loved you when you were a child, Cindy, I still love you."

"People used to say that love was enough, love could cover every problem, provide the ultimate answer. Not true. Love is not nearly enough."

After a while, as if by common consent, they strolled through Ocean Beach. "You were right, you know."

"About what?"

"When you said we were sisters under the skin. With a slight change here and there, we might have been friends."

"Can't we still be, Mother?"

"One day, maybe. When the wounds are not so raw and the memories are less acute."

"Stay for the weekend. We'll spend the time together, the two of us. There's so much to talk about, so much I want to say to you, so much I want to know about."

"Better if I go now. I need to put distance between myself and my past. Time to think, and space to do it in. Have

to get my head straight, as they used to say." Out on the
Great South Bay, another ferry was angling in toward the
dock, looming larger. "That's my boat," she said. "Use
the house as much as you want to, it's beautiful out here in
the fall. Not many people and if the weather is kind, it can
be the best time of the year."

"Take care of yourself, Mother."

"I will, and you do the same."

"I love you, Mother."

"And I love you, daughter."

The ferry had long since disappeared into the mist of the
bay before Cindy left the dock, wondering what kind of a
weekend it was going to be.

Twenty-one

BB

"Take it easy," Martin Callahan said. "Things may not be as bad as you think." His voice on the phone was lyrical, seductive, the voice of a man for whom words were weapons.

"The hell you say," BB burst out. "That cop, that Corona, he knows I lifted the paintings."

"Not necessarily. Policemen are devious creatures by nature and by training. They enjoy stirring up the waters so that they can watch the fish scurry for safety."

"I tell you he suspects me."

"Of course he does. You and your father, your mother, the maid, the boy who delivers groceries, even the doorman. All of you had the opportunity, had access to the apartment."

"But what about the keys?"

"Your parents and you have them, that makes you inevitably suspect. However, Corona is no fool. He has quite a reputation when it comes to solving art thefts. He knows how efficient thieves can be. Like himself, they are professionals. He knows how they work. They plan, they plot, they arrange disposal, even as you did. A team of experienced professionals would know how to have duplicate keys made. They would enter and leave as you did without leaving fingerprints and would make sure no attention was drawn to their work for as long as patience endures."

"Meaning what?"

"Such pros would be careful to nurture the monies they received for their efforts. They would refrain from altering their ways of life; they would spend frugally or not at all for a long time, years even. They would keep a man like Corona at bay."

"I haven't seen a penny of that dough yet."

"I intend to move two of the paintings to other collectors. That doesn't happen overnight. When I get my money, you'll get yours."

"I thought you were loaded."

"Dear boy, I never use my own funds in such affairs. Now practice patience, and all will turn out as planned."

"I'm worried about the girls."

"That could be a problem. Of course, he doesn't know who they are."

"He's smart, Callahan. He has to figure out they were a couple of girls from the Snap Shop."

"Perhaps. Still, you do have a turnover in personnel."

"If those girls talk, they'd turn us all over."

"Just you, my young friend. I've never met the ladies."

BB didn't like the sound of that. He could envision Jill and Laura Lee cutting a deal with Corona that would incriminate him and leave Callahan free to sell the paintings. As for Julie and the boatman, they too were beyond the law. Only Boyd Benjamin Morgan would end up in jail.

"If Corona tracks down the paintings . . . ?" BB said.

Callahan was amused. "Do you believe they're hanging on my wall, dear boy? Try not to be stupid about this. All three paintings are securely concealed where no one can possibly find them, where no one can possibly see them—except myself, naturally. Beauty and genius must be viewed by those equipped to appreciate them."

"What am I supposed to do meanwhile?"

"Solve the problem that is most immediate."

"Meaning what?"

"The girls."

"What about them?"

"They're your only link to the job. If the doorman identifies them, they'll give you up, and farewell to your future, dear boy."

"What am I supposed to do?"

"In your own words, the girls who work at that little photographic studio of yours come and go. Make sure this pair goes."

"They could leave town for a while."

"Not exactly what I had in mind."

"What then?" BB said, anxious for a solution to his troubles.

"If it were me . . ." Callahan let it hang.

BB slammed the phone down. He decided he'd do a little coke while he thought about his problem.

He called Laura Lee at her apartment.

"The cop was here," she began, her voice rising.

"Corona?" he said, cautioning himself to stay cool. "Well, it figures."

"I'm scared, BB, and Jill is, too. That Corona, he's smart and he's tough. We better talk."

BB smiled into the phone. It was all falling into place, as if they were privy to his plan. "That makes sense."

"You want to come over here?"

"No, Corona may have you under surveillance. Tell you what, pick me up. We'll go for a drive and talk it over. I've got some ideas to share with you girls. How about Seventy-second Street and First in about an hour?"

"Sure," Laura Lee said, and hung up.

Jill drove. A sleek white Cadillac with red leather seats. BB climbed in next to her and turned to Laura Lee in the backseat.

"You're late."

"Sorry, heavy traffic.

Jill turned onto Seventy-ninth Street, heading west. "Only twenty minutes."

"Where you going?" he said. "I thought we'd head up to Connecticut."

"New Jersey," Jill said. "I like New Jersey."

That made BB uneasy. Why New Jersey? What in hell did New Jersey hold for any of them? On the other hand, why Connecticut? He knew no one who lived there, had no specific destination in mind. Just a country road, a deserted field, someplace still and empty.

"Fill me in on Corona," he said.

Laura Lee answered. "He asked about the paintings."

BB stared at her. In the darkness of the backseat, with her hair pulled straight back off her forehead, she looked very young.

"Told us is more like it," Jill said.

"Yes, told us," Laura Lee said. "He told us about the business with the doorman. Made it sound like he was hot on the trail."

BB shuddered. In profile, Jill looked like what he knew her to be, a very tough, very determined lady. Her lips were set, her jaw angled forward, eyes fixed on the road. He wondered what she was thinking. He answered Laura Lee. "The way you girls were made up that night, the doorman could never ID you."

"That's what we've been telling ourselves," Laura Lee said.

"Except we can't be sure," Jill put in.

BB was insistent. "It was night, dark, you beat up on him, an old guy like George would never remember your faces."

"He might," Jill said. She gave BB a swift glance. "Corona is on to us."

"Cops are like that, they sniff around. The trick is to make people nervous, cause them to panic. If we all stay cool, nothing will happen."

"I don't mind telling you," Laura Lee said, "I'm scared."

"Corona is too sharp," Jill added.

On the New Jersey side of the George Washington Bridge, they continued on Route 80. Jill drove fast, in control of the big car, putting miles between them and the city. A half-hour later, she left the Interstate for a local road.

"Where are we?" BB said.

"I'm tired of big highways," Jill said. "It's hard on the nerves."

They passed onto a quiet street lined with maple trees swollen with the late summer burden of leaves. A sudden left put them onto a country lane.

"Where is this place?" BB said. He felt for the .38 caliber police special in his belt for reassurance, not yet ready to make his move.

"I was brought up around here," Jill said easily. "This road, a place a little bit along, is where I did it for the first time. In the backseat of an old Buick while my girl friend was giving head in the front seat. Up ahead, not far from the lake."

She pulled off to one side, letting the Cadillac roll under the trees and come to a stop. She shifted around to face BB.

"Laura Lee and me, we don't like what's going down, BB."

"That cop is bugging us," Laura Lee said. "I'm scared."

Jill broke in. "What we got for our trouble is more trouble, nothing else. Where's the money, BB?"

"I get it, you get it. Callahan has to make his deal first."

"Nobody said a word about Callahan making a deal. Just do a job and get paid, that was *our* deal with you, BB. We deserve better treatment than you been handing out."

"Deserve! What is it with you girls? If it wasn't for me, you'd be peddling your asses on the street. I brought you into the Snap Shop. You make damn good dough posing for pictures and picking up extras on the hustle."

"We want our money, BB."

"It's only fair," Laura Lee drawled, a strange, hard note in her voice. "You should've given us our share."

"There's been no payoff yet, I told you."

Jill snapped out the words. "The cop is after us and what do we do about that?"

BB made up his mind. He had hoped for a familiar area, but this place would have to do. Once they were dead, no one but Callahan could connect him with the theft. He braced himself and reached for the pistol in his belt, eyes on Jill all the time. But it was Laura Lee who brought a .22 target pistol out of her purse, jamming the muzzle against his temple.

"Don't do it, BB?" she said with unaccustomed toughness.

"What the fuck is this!" he screamed.

Jill made a sucking sound. "Oh, wow! How dumb do you think we are, BB?" She located the .38 and removed it, pointing it at his navel. "Awful dumb, I guess."

"Listen," he said.

"Shut up," Jill said.

"You were right, Jill," Laura Lee said.

"You got it all wrong," BB said shakily.

"Out," Jill said.

"Listen to me," he pleaded.

"Out," Laura Lee said.

Jill slid out from under the wheel, went around to the other side of the Cadillac, and opened the door. "Out."

One on each side of him, they walked him deeper into the woods. They would take him far enough so that his body couldn't be seen from the dirt road, then kill him. Time was running out.

"Girls, listen to me. You're wrong, I'd never do anything to hurt you. The gun was just insurance, that's all. Protection. The money's coming, I promise you. Callahan promised it to me. Jill, you can trust me, I'll double your share."

Anger caused her to make her first mistake, and she swung the police special at him, using it as a club. Reacting instinctively, he deflected the blow, driving his fist into her face in one motion. Allowing his momentum to carry him, he went charging straight ahead, stumbling, bouncing off unseen trees but moving forward at the same time, fading into the night.

Jill cried out, "Shoot him! Shoot him!"

Laura Lee fired, but the slugs went wild and high. He threw himself to the ground and waited, listened for following footsteps. He heard nothing. They were not coming after him, not in those dark woods. Soon, the sound of the Cadillac's engine turning over. He saw the headlights switch on, backing away, disappearing down the road in the direction from which they'd come. More than an hour passed before he could bring himself to move, to make his way back out onto the road, trying to plot his next move.

An unhurried return to New York. He needed time to consider what he'd done, almost done, almost had done to himself. How strange that at the moment he was closest to taking the lives of two other people, it had all seemed unreal, an unsettling dream; what had transported him to this place in his own life where he could even consider committing an ultimate act of violence? What insane impulses drove him, unloosing the dark spirits he harbored?

In the morning, after he had failed to kill and barely escaped being killed, he met the widow. Dappled sunlight sprinkled the country lane as he strolled, still chilled from the long, terrifying night, when he happened upon her. A plump, friendly woman throwing sticks for her dog to chase down, a game both of them enjoyed. She was surprised at the sight of him but not startled, not afraid.

She invited him back to her house for breakfast, supplied him with a razor, clean towels, and the run of the house. When he was fed and spotless, she led him to her bed and, except for meals, kept him productively engaged for two days. Only at his insistence did she drive him to the local bus stop, so that he might conclude his journey.

"You'll call me?" she said.

"Absolutely."

"Promise?"

"You've got my word."

"I don't trust you," she said with regret.

"I'm not a man who lies," he told her before he climbed on the waiting bus. Five minutes later, he tore up the piece of paper on which were written her name and phone number.

From the Port Authority Terminal, he went directly to the apartment on Park Avenue. The doorman, George, was on duty. BB greeted him cheerfully, and George responded in kind.

"Sorry about the troubles you had, George."

"Hard to believe, women acting in so savage a manner." George seemed to relish the telling. "Ladies of the night, they were, without a spark of decency in them, believe me."

"What's the world coming to? I'm sure the police will find them, with your description, that is."

"Oh, dear, that is a problem. My eyes are not good, you see. Poor vision has always been my curse. Knocked my glasses off first thing, they did, almost as if by plan, you might say."

"Then you weren't able to provide a description for the police?"

"I wish I could have."

"What a shame." BB swore to himself; none of it had been necessary, not his plans for Laura Lee and Jill, nor their vicious reaction. They would have murdered him in cold blood if he hadn't been too smart for them. Quicker. Braver. Bitches is what they were, total bitches. "As long as you're all right, George."

"Too bad about your father's paintings."

"Crime is rampant."

"City's getting worse all the time."

"Disintegrating right before our eyes."

"Not safe anywhere for decent people."

"Not anywhere."

In his parent's apartment, BB showered and shaved and changed his clothes. He looked at the empty frames that still hung in place, a reminder of what once had been and never would be again. It was all over, he assured himself; the girls were gone and he was safe. Nothing, no one, could connect him to the theft.

In the kitchen, he had just brought a glass of milk and a package of Oreos to the table when the phone rang. Corona, he was sure, and decided not to answer. On the thirteenth ring, he picked up.

"Yeah?"

"Good afternoon, BB. Hope I'm not interrupting anything."

He recognized Corona's voice. "Who is this?"

"Detective Second Grade Corona, BB. How have you been?"

"What do you want, Corona?"

"I've been trying to locate you since yesterday. Been away?"

"I'm busy, Corona, I can't talk."

"Next time you decide to leave town, keep me informed, will you? In case I want to get in touch, you know what I mean?"

"Is that why you called, to tell me that?"

"Police work can be extremely frustrating at times, BB. You follow leads, they go nowhere. You have a witness, she disappears. You ask a question, the answers tell you nothing."

BB lifted his left hand; it was trembling. "Try another line of work, Corona."

"Oh, don't get me wrong, I love my job. But a number of human qualities are vital to its pursuit. Patience, for example. Persistence. And luck. That's what makes me a good cop, you know; I am a very lucky man."

"That's great, Corona, you should play the horses."

"Oh, no. I never win. Horses and cards, before I got wise, that's where all my salary went. Horses and cards. Would you believe I got a call from a certain anonymous informer? Happens all the time, people know something, but they'd rather not become involved."

"Is that a fact?"

"Oh, yes. Every cop would vouch for it. But this caller— one of the two women who put on that phony fight over the doorman the night your father was ripped off."

BB's hands turned cold. "You are lucky."

"Wait'll you hear what she told me."

"I can't wait."

"The lady wants revenge. Wants to shaft the dude who pulled the job. Said he failed to pay off, the two ladies, that is."

"The plot thickens."

"No, BB," Corona said expansively. "Just the opposite. It's thinning out, opening up, letting me look inside. The lady said that while she and her pal were keeping George occupied, you slipped into the building, snatched the paintings, and went out the service door with the goods. Anything to that, BB?" A long silence ensued. "Anything you'd like to tell me?"

"An anonymous informer, you said?"

"That's right."

"Would that kind of an incredible accusation stand up in a court of law, Corona?"

"Oh, I would never want to go to trial on such a flimsy case."

BB filled his lungs with air. "Then you're just bullshitting, Corona. For all I know, you never even received such a call."

"Oh, there was a call, all right."

"So you have no evidence, no witnesses, nothing to link me with the crime, and still you're telling me you think I did it."

"Oh, you did it, all right, BB. I'm sure of it. That's another thing about being a cop, kid; you get hunches and learn to go with them. My hunch about you is strong, one of the strongest I've ever had."

"I think you're wasting my time, detective, and you're own."

"I'm going to get you, BB."

"Harassment, isn't that what they call this, harassment."

"Look for me, BB. I'll be around."

BB couldn't finish the milk and cookies. The Oreos tasted like sawdust, and the milk seemed to curdle in his stomach. There was only one thing he wanted to do, and that was to run for as long and as far as he could.

Twenty-two

Susan

The telephone woke her, and she came up into a sitting position, startled, afraid, unable to remember where she was. There'd been a dream, and now a layer of cold sweat clung to her skin. She shivered and answered the phone.

She heard Turk's voice. "I want you in here, today."

"Leave me alone."

"You're a slow learner."

"I'm sick."

"You're okay. By noon, that's your limit."

She wept and was unable to stop. Her isolation was complete, without anyone to go to for help. Downstairs, she poured gin into a tall glass and began to drink. Along one wall, on a low table, a collection of photographs. She examined them one by one. One was of her and Neil, taken before they were married. Neil was in his army uniform, tall and straight and proud. Neil . . .

She dialed the New York apartment, saying his name over and over again when he answered, crying pitifully.

"What is it?" he said.

"Neil, please . . ."

"What's wrong?"

"I need you," she managed to get out. "I need you so much."

Nick

He was alone in the house when Cindy arrived.

"You're a hero," she started out.

"Not me."

"In the army they give people medals for acting the way you do."

"In football, they paste stars on a player's helmet. Has about the same value."

"A long time ago I knew a man who insisted that he could never take violent action against another human being, no matter the provocation. Not even if his life was at stake. Not even if the lives of his children were threatened, he said. I thought he was marvelous, a real hero, a saint. I was wrong. He was a fool and a coward. A man like that invites the bad guys to take advantage, to give pain, to cause trouble. A man like that wouldn't have lifted a finger to help my mother."

"It was nothing."

"It was a hell of a lot, Danning. You saved her."

"No big deal."

"And when Susan needed help, you turned up again."

"I was looking for you."

"Well," she said simply, "here I am." She waited, hoping he would take her in his arms, kiss her, make love to her. Instead, he stood without moving, offering nothing. "Thank you for what you did," she said coldly, turning away. "I'll leave you alone now."

By the time he opened his mouth to speak, she was gone.

Twenty-three

Neil

She began to weep again when he arrived. He held her
on his lap the way one might hold a child, stroking her
hair, speaking in a soft, soothing voice.

"You're the most beautiful woman I've ever seen."

"You always say that."

"From the first moment I laid eyes on you—"

"So long ago."

"It was love at first sight."

"I was so intimidated by you. You were so sure of yourself, so forceful. That first night, you kissed me so hard, so
passionately."

"I wanted to make sure you'd never forget me."

"Oh, Neil, what kind of lives have we lived? So many
wrong turns, so many mistakes. And now this business
with Turk."

"I'll take care of Turk."

"I don't think you understand, he could kill you, kill us
both and never think twice about it."

"He's never going to hurt you again. That's a promise."

She wanted to believe him. "What's to become of us, Neil?"

The words stirred old memories in him. In the early days of their marriage, when they were so much in love and every day was a new adventure, she would put the same question to him: "What's to become of us, Neil?" seeking reassurance and support.

His reply was always the same: "Once upon a time always becomes They lived happily ever after." He said it now.

A chill worked its way down her spine. "I'm so afraid."

"I'll take care of us. I'll take care of Turk."

"He's too dangerous."

"I'll see him today, I'll go back to New York this afternoon."

"Don't go, please."

He shook his head. "This is something I have to do."

He presented himself at Turk Christie's apartment early that evening. The bulky gambler admitted him with a tight, mocking grin.

"No game tonight, baby. More important business on the fire."

"Stay away from my wife, Turk."

The gambler showed no surprise. "That it, that why you came? To say that? Okay, you got it off your chest, so take off, sucker."

Without hesitation, Neil threw a looping right hand. Turk slid underneath and sent his big fist into Neil's stomach. Neil doubled up, gasping, and Turk landed a second blow that put him on the floor.

"I'm pissed off," Turk growled, "the way Susan's acting. Look what she made me do to you. Tell her to get her act together. Now you get out of here and don't come back."

A taxi carried Neil back to his apartment, and a hot bath eased the pain in his middle. How stupid to confront Turk head-on; clearly he was outmatched. He sought some other approach, something practical, something possible. By the time he finished his bath, an idea had begun to form.

Wearing a long white terry-cloth robe, and carrying a

container of milk, a glass, and a bag of Famous Amos's
chocolate chip cookies, he settled behind the desk in his
study. The empty frame that once housed the O'Koren still
hung on the wall, a reminder of the great loss he had suffered. He had prized it beyond all his other possessions. Insurance would cover the financial loss, but nothing could
replace the sweet delicacy of the artist's vision and talent.

Footsteps on the Mexican tile floor in the entry hall
drew his attention, and he swung around just as his son appeared in the doorway.

"I figured you'd be here," BB said.

"I miss the O'Koren," Neil replied. "More than the
other two. There was magic in that painting. I never tired
of looking at it."

"I have to talk to you."

Neil cocked his head. "What's your best opinion; will I
ever get my painting back?"

BB commanded himself to remain calm, to show no response. His father, like Corona, was trying to provoke him.
He lifted his hands and let them fall. "Maybe the cops will
get lucky."

"I think I know how it was done."

"You and Corona. He's got a handful of theories. But I'll
tell you what I think. Some damn smart operators pulled
off a perfect job, that's all."

"That simple?"

"Guys who know their business. It makes sense. They
were pros, in and out in no time at all."

"What about the alarms?"

"Sure, a lock is just another lock to those guys."

"I don't think so. The girls who attacked George?"

"Coincidence."

"Part of the plan, so that someone was able to enter the
building unseen. It would have to be someone George
would know and recognize, someone with easy access to
the apartment. Your mother or me or you, BB."

"Are you accusing me of ripping off my own parents?"

"I suppose I am."

"Oh, boy! Why would I do that?"

"Out of meanness, orneriness, out of a desire to hurt a

father who failed you, at least in your mind. And for the money, of course."

"That's shit, Father, pure bullshit. You must be certifiable, accusing me of a thing like that. What kind of a son do you think I am? That's your style, betraying your family. I know the kind of a life you've been leading all these years, screwing young girls behind my mother's back and maintaining such a proper moral facade. You haven't fooled me, you haven't fooled Mother."

"I doubt if I've fooled anybody except myself."

"Well, let's leave off the moral superiority. You can't get off the hook by accusing me of stealing those paintings."

"It was you, BB. I've worked it all out in my head; it couldn't have been anyone else. Turning the alarms back on after you left, that was your signal to me—you wanted me to know you did it—but you didn't think I'd dare confront you."

"You never let go, do you? I read you like a book, Father. What a hypocrite you are. Let's talk about you and Julie, for example. Try to make something high-minded out of that, a father making it with his son's chick. Right out of the Old Testament."

"I want the O'Koren, BB. Can you arrange it?"

"Don't look at me. Go to Corona."

"I begin to understand. He's after you."

"Nobody's after me." BB hesitated, and the tension drained out of his face; his voice when he spoke was conciliatory, softer. "What you're saying is crazy. I had nothing to do with it. Corona, he means to make a score on my back. Well, I'm not about to stand still for that. I'm getting out of here. Tonight. Right now."

"I see."

"Maybe we don't always get along, but I am your son."

Neil leaned back in his chair. "What is it you want from me this time?"

BB slumped into a chair. "Corona is trying to frame me, set me up to take the fall. The police can do that to a person if they set their minds to it. I have to beat him to the punch, get out of town. I need money."

"What happened to the money from the paintings?"

"Don't say that!" BB shouted. Then in control again, "Somebody's got to help me."

Somehow BB's deal had fallen through, which meant the paintings were lost forever. A deep feeling of sadness settled over Neil, sadness for all the losses he had suffered during his lifetime, the loss of love, of treasure, of his faith in God and in other people. He questioned whether or not he possessed strength enough to go on.

"Where will you go?"

"Somewhere where they don't have an extradition treaty with the United States, somewhere safe."

Safety, Neil thought. It was what everyone ultimately wanted, safety and comfort, peace, an end to conflict and trouble. "Brazil," he said. He pushed himself erect. "Whenever I got into trouble when I was a child, my father would say he hoped I learned something from it. Learned my lesson. I don't suppose you've learned anything from all this."

"I didn't do it."

At the far end of the leather sofa, sat a square end table. The front of the table swung open, revealing a small safe. Neil spun the dial and brought forth a packet of bills, tossed them to BB. "Five thousand dollars. Part of me wants you to face the music, pay for what you've done. But I can't help send you to jail. You're my son, and in my own way I love you, so run for it, BB. Run for it, and if you're lucky, one day you might even find a place for yourself, a place to start all over, a safe place. But I doubt it."

He was asleep in his chair behind his desk when the telephone rang. "Mr. Morgan," the gravelly voice said, "Regginato here, returning your call."

Neil struggled to come fully awake. "There's something I want to discuss with you, something important to me, something personal."

"I understand. My car will be in front of your building in approximately ten minutes."

"I'll be downstairs."

Neil dressed rapidly. Gray slacks, a black cotton knit shirt from Brooks Brothers, and a tan rain jacket. When he reached the street, the limousine was parked in front, Regginato in the backseat.

"We'll drive around town for a while," he said as the car rolled into the stream of traffic. "In an age of advanced electronics, very few places are secure from eavesdroppers. Is it about the movie, Mr. Morgan? Do you intend to drop Miss Boniface out of the production altogether?"

"Oh, no. Miss Boniface was very understanding about the change."

"Miss Boniface recognizes her limitations in this cruel and demanding world. She is prepared to be patient in her quest for stardom in a tough line of work. I made her a promise, eventually she becomes a star, and she will." He glanced at Neil from his place in the corner of the seat. "What is your problem, Mr. Morgan? Got to be some problem or you would not have called."

Neil found it difficult to speak of Susan's sexual escapades, of her affair with Turk Christie, of his own ignoble encounter with the gambler. As if plumbing his brain, Regginato went on.

"In my line of work, accurate and detailed information is vital. I got lots of different sources of intelligence. Most of what I learn is garbage, but sometimes word reaches me that affects my business interests directly. I heard about your difficulties, Mr. Morgan. And your wife with a certain Mr. Turk Christie."

"I tried to settle it myself."

"That's not what you're good at. Certain guys are experts in that line of work. Among my business acquaintances, certain forms of behavior are not accepted. Beating a woman is high on the list. Are you asking for my help in settling this matter?"

Neil nodded.

"Okay. But you must say what you want done. Spell it out, Mr. Morgan, so that there can be no misunderstanding between us."

Neil spoke carefully. "I'm not sure I know what I want."

"Let me say it—Mr. Christie could be permanently removed from the scene. He would disappear, never to bother you or your wife again."

"Killed?"

"Is that what you want, Mr. Morgan?"

Neil stared out at the passing city sights. Parked cars, pedestrians, walls of buildings in which lives were lived out, never touching the lives of their neighbors. "I don't think I could live with that."

"Good. Too many people talk about killing like it's nothing. Want to hear what I would do?"

"Please."

"You and me, we're parnters, Mr. Morgan, and we can't let Mr. Christie go on terrorizing you and Mrs. Morgan. So—"

"Could someone talk to him?"

"Talk to him, yes. But such talk counts only when it is backed up. If you say so, a team of specialists in this work could visit Mr. Christie, impress on him the error of his ways. They will suggest that he leave the city at once, that he have no further contact with you or your wife. Being the sort of human being he is, this will be a painful lesson for Mr. Christie to learn. Very painful. But learn it he will, and he will remember it forever. With your approval, naturally."

A wide, pleased grin spread across Neil's face. "I certainly do approve. Without reservation."

Twenty-four

Susan

"I miss your mother already."

"You've known each other for a long time."

"Maggie has been closer to me than anyone else in my life. Closer than my husband, certainly closer than my son."

Susan and Cindy, side by side in the long, westering rays of the sun behind the Morgan house. They sipped tall gin and tonics with a wedge of lime, and ignored the cheese and crackers Susan had served.

"Poor BB," Cindy responded. "I loved him a long time ago."

"I love him still, but I don't like him very much. All the empty rebellion, the futile defiance. He never came through that stage, never grew up. Maybe it was my fault—I never was able to reach him."

"He told me once, 'I can never become the man my father is, I don't want to. But somehow I'm going to get square with them all.' Those were his exact words."

"Get square? All the anger, the hatred. I don't think he was ever able to forgive Neil and me for being less than perfect. He never allowed us to forget we were flawed, he never made peace with our fallibility."

"It's sad."

"You aren't that way."

A wild laugh broke out of Cindy. "I'm carrying my full load of resentment."

"Against your father?"

"Oh, Roy was easy to forgive, once I grew up a little. He was so transparent, the little boy playing at being a man. I meant Maggie."

"She loved you so much. I know, she told me."

"She hurt me a lot, Susan." She looked away, across the tall dune grass undulating gracefully in the late breeze. "There was always something, somebody, getting between Maggie and me. When I was hospitalized—" Susan showed surprise. "I was in Bellevue a very long time ago. Maggie was still married to Bob." When Susan made a face, Cindy laughed, a genuinely happy sound. "I never cared much for him, either. A dull man, bland, he must've been an antidote to my father's craziness, the frantic life she had led till then. They came to see me a few times with candy, books, flowers, the usual. Maggie knew all the right moves. But she never stayed for very long, and we never talked, not in any way that mattered. I can't remember us ever being alone. When I needed her most, Maggie was never available to me."

Cindy laughed again, without humor this time, a crisp, brittle sound. "Not that I blame her now. What a little bitch I was! I was zonked out on acid that time, and even the shrink decided I was an impossible case. Vernon Miller was his name. He wore horn-rimmed glasses, smoked a sweet-smelling pipe, and was an Episcopalian. An Episcopalian shrink is not to be depended on. Shrinks should be pudgy Jewish men with beards and, if possible, talk with a middle-European accent. Poor Vernon tried so hard. I shocked hell out of all his proper and righteous Episcopalian notions about how life should be lived."

Another laugh. "Once I complained that life in these good old United States of America was not all it was cracked up to be, and Vernon talked about the home of the brave and the land of the free. What was it I said? Oh, yes, 'I can't take off my clothes when I want to. I can't travel without a passport. I can't smoke pot. Balls to your freedom.' Poor Vernon, I'm sure he thought I was receiving my orders directly from the Kremlin."

Her face closed up again. "When they were ready to turn me out of Bellevue, Maggie didn't show up. When I got home, she said it was time for me to accept responsibility. By that she meant not to drop acid anymore. A few martinis were socially acceptable, even blowing grass—"

"She did her best, she loved you."

"Sometimes love is not enough."

"Without love there is only the void, a terrifying emptiness that can never be filled."

"Maggie and I, we made our peace before she left. At least I hope we did." A slow, sad smile curled her full mouth. "Treaties can always be broken, I'm afraid." She lifted her eyes to the older woman's face, that still-incredible face, looking in the soft light as if it had been chiseled out of stone, brought to a high sheen, each feature delicately made and perfected. "Still," Cindy went on, you and Neil managed to stay married."

Susan met her gaze. "And you, have you never met a man you wanted to marry?"

Cindy framed her answer carefully. "It's in my mind. More than marriage, I think about having a baby. Some nights I wake up and think about my baby, the baby I lost, and I weep for that little boy and for myself. You knew about my baby? Born and so soon dead. Dying in his sleep that way, an infant, so happy and healthy, with so much to live for. Maybe if I'd been a better mother, he'd still be alive. Maybe I should have sat up all night, next to his crib, watching him, protecting him.

"There are times when I don't think about my baby for weeks at a time. Until the awful emptiness returns. Losing him—oh, the life I've lived, the terrible ways I've treated people, the terrible ways I've treated myself. God didn't want me to have that beautiful child, and so he was taken away from me, the cruelest punishment. I wasn't married, you see, and that was part of my crime."

"You mustn't blame yourself."

"Who else is there to blame?"

Susan answered slowly. "I suppose you're right. There never is anyone else to blame, not for you, certainly not for me any longer. Such terrible things happen to human beings—"

"Not to you."

"Especially to me. But no more. I refuse to allow myself to be a target any longer for the rage of other people, for their frustration, for their sadism. No matter what I've done, no matter what any of us have done, there comes a moment when we're entitled to cry 'enough' to additional punishment and pain."

"When I think about that little boy, I long desperately to give him a little brother to play with. Until I remember that he's gone. Still, I long to have another child."

"The genetic clock is ticking."

"That frightens me most of all. I thought about becoming pregnant, finding a man who is physiologically and psychologically suitable, getting him to knock me up. But that won't cut it. My baby is entitled to a father, to know his father, to be loved by his father. Then I ask: What if I never meet a man I want to marry? A man who cares for me? Most men I meet are damaged goods. All those gaping emotional wounds. What the hell, I'm fresh out of Band-Aids. No, thanks."

Susan addressed her drink. "There's Nick Danning. He's attractive, he's single, he likes you."

"I've known him all summer and—nothing."

"He hasn't taken you to bed, is that what you mean? The way my life has gone, I'd consider that a plus."

Cindy laughed, a vision of Danning floating into view. Tall and strong with that faintly ironic cast to his angled face, those hooded eyes under the cap of silvery hair. "I'd make him crazy inside of a week. He's so correct, walking a narrow line."

"Don't be too sure. He has a lot of strength, a lot of courage, and he's gentle. They don't make many like that anymore." She shrugged. "Like the rest of us, there's a lot he hasn't worked out for himself—"

"He doesn't seem to be interested in me."

"He's a little shy."

"A former footballer? No way. I never knew a jock that wasn't world-class horny." She eyed Susan across her drink. "Did he put a move on you?"

"Very proper, all the time. It's you he's after."

"He knows where to find me."

"A little feminine encouragement never hurt."

"Is that your advice?"

"I speak from experience." She shivered and stood up. "It's getting chilly. Summer's almost over, and I simply despair of living through another winter before I can come out here again."

"With all that's happened, you still like Fire Island?"

"Like it? Why, I love it, dear girl, and I always will."

Kolodny

She was plump, pretty, and giggled a lot. She had a friend, she said, if Nick was interested, a really pretty, very pretty girl. Loads of laughs and lots of fun.

"I thought I'd spend some time by myself tonight," Danning said.

Kolodny groaned in mock despair. "Man, I have bought you books and shoes, sent you to school, taught you right, and you're going to turn down Bunny, who is an eighteen-carat committed sex machine."

"Later," Danning said, already on his way.

"What we have here," Kolodny shouted after him, "is Labor Day Weekend. Last chance to stock up on phone numbers for the long, cold months ahead."

Danning paid no attention.

Nick

She wasn't in MacCurdy's or Mom Stone's, so he made his way along Baywalk to Leo's. More people in that one

finite space than had made it all summer. At a table near
the door, Jim McMillan motioning to him.

"I'm looking for a friend of mine," Danning said over the
noise of the crowd.

McMillan leaned closer. "Glad I ran into you, Nick.
Have you considered my offer? School starts in less than
two weeks, and practice starts the week before that. We
could certainly use you, unless you've got something better."

Danning grew annoyed, as if McMillan were forcing him
into a corner, causing him to look at parts of himself best
left unexamined. "Better not depend on me."

McMillan wrote his name and phone number down,
gave it to Danning. "If you change your mind, call me. If
the job stays open, it's yours."

Outside, Danning cleared his lungs of smoke and de-
cided that he was not destined to locate Cindy this night.
When someone called his name, he turned to see Neil and
Susan heading his way.

"How are you feeling?" he asked her.

"I've been worse, Nick. I want to thank you again for
what you did."

"I want to thank you, too," Neil said. "If there's ever
some way I can help you. There might be—I have excellent
contacts in broadcasting. I know of an opening over at
NBC, just came on the market. The Director of Television
Sports is a friend. Radio play-by-play, if you're interested. I
might be able to swing it."

"Is this for real?"

"Absolutely."

"Well, I am very much interested."

"I'll make a phone call and let you know. You want my
opinion, the job's as good as yours."

Danning took his hand. "You have no idea how much
this means to me."

"A man like you, you belong in the big time. You'll become a star. I've got a gut feeling, and I trust my feelings."

"We're going to have a drink at MacCurdy's," Susan
said. "Won't you join us?"

"I'm looking for Cindy."

"Yes," Susan said. "Try her mother's house. She's there, all alone."

Billy

"You don't intend to keep him, surely?" There was disapproval in Christina's voice.

Diane smiled sweetly. "Of course I do. Isn't he a pretty thing?"

"He's a child, my dear. Certainly not more than twenty-five. Darling, that's half your age."

Diane smiled a sweet, tight smile. "How kind of you to remind me, darling. Billy claims to be thirty. Not that I believe a word he tells me. The man's an inveterate liar."

"I could never tolerate a man who lies."

"They all lie, darling, and you should know that better than most of us. Three husbands and each one a flagrant adulterer."

"Oh, let's not dredge up the awful past. I still think you're making a mistake. He lacks style and substance and class. Furthermore—"

"Furthermore, dear Christina, Billy is one of the three best lays in modern history and, believe me, I know. Where other men stop, Billy begins. He never seems to get enough, day after day after day."

"I am impressed."

"Besides, he needs me."

"Needs your money, you mean."

"Naturally. And the nice thing is he's willing to do just about anything to get his grubby little hands on some of it." She waved at Billy, talking to some people across the huge living room, and beckoned. He broke off at once and attended to her. She handed him her glass. "A refill, darling."

"You've hardly touched any of it."

"A fresh drink, Billy." She spoke with the slightest change of inflection.

He left for the bar.

Christina said, "You can hire all the servants you want, for a lot less money."

"Discipline," Diane said. "My first husband, the general, was a great believer in discipline. Start them off right, he used to say. Demand obedience and instill it by repetition until they react on command. The general was an ass, of course, but he was on target in that case."

"If it were me, I'd get rid of him."

"If it were you, darling, you'd hide him away in your closet, the way you did with the fisherman you brought back from Greece."

"Diane, you have a nasty streak."

"Part of my charm," she answered as Billy returned with her drink. She sipped it and made a face. "Another ice cube, darling. You know how I detest a warm drink."

"Nice party," he said, stripping off his shirt.

Diane lay on her back under the sheet. "My friends disapprove of you."

"They're not much, none of them. The men are eunuchs, and the women are jealous."

"Because I have you, is that what you mean?"

He stepped out of his pants, positioning himself at the end of the bed so she could get a good look at him. "Damn right. They know a good thing when they see it."

"They know you for what you are, Billy."

He watched her eyes flicker across his broad, hairless chest, along the ridges of his flat stomach, pausing where his cock lay heavily in the pouch of his bikini.

"And what's that?"

"You're a hustler, Billy."

"And you love it."

She wet her lips. "You're a whore, Billy."

"Go to hell," he said, reaching for his pants.

"The day you came up on the deck of the house, what you did to me that day you haven't done since. Why?"

"You'd like that again?"

She pulled the sheet aside, her knees falling apart. "Do it to me now."

"If I'm a whore, then pay for it."

"Yes, how much?"

"One thousand dollars."

"Yes, yes."

"I mean it."

"So do I. Do it now."

He arranged himself between her legs, tracing a path from knee to pubic area with the tip of his tongue. She shivered and cried out in anticipation. He went across her belly, along the inside of her other thigh.

"I don't know," he temporized.

She pleaded with him. "I'll give you anything you want."

"Remember that." His mouth came down, and she rose up to meet him, urging him on, pressing hard against his face as she felt his hot tongue exploring. Her thighs closed over his cheeks, and she reached for his golden hair, holding on lest they fall apart. And in the end, she begged him to stop, her body trembling and out of control, laughter mixed with sobs, afraid that he was going to destroy her.

"Billy," she said in the dark.

"Hmmm."

"I own a house in St. Tropez. New York in the fall, St. Tropez in the winter, maybe Paris in the spring. Would you like that?"

"Sounds good."

"Get me a cigarette, Billy."

It was clearly a command. "Get it yourself."

"Get me a cigarette or get out, Billy. You're a great lay, Billy, and I'd miss you for a little while. But soon enough somebody else would come along. Somebody young and strong and willing to please me. In the bedroom, we can play out our little games, whatever they may be. But out in the great big real world, Billy, I am in charge."

He got up and began to dress himself. When she failed to stop him, he swung around to face her. "You'd really let me walk?"

"There's a lot I'll do for a great fuck, Billy, and a lot I won't do. Take it or leave it."

"I like you a lot, Diane," he said slowly.

"And I like you, Billy."

"I don't want to go."

"Of course you don't, and I don't want you to. So why not take off your clothes and come back to bed."

He hurried to comply.

"Before you lie down, I'd still like that cigarette . . ."

He hesitated briefly. "Sure, why not?"

"And Billy."

"What?"

"Light it for me."

"Okay."

"And Billy."

"What?"

"A little Drambuie would be nice."

"Sure."

"Help yourself, if you like."

"I will."

"Then hurry over here and I'll tell you what I've planned for this winter, for the two of us. If you're interested, that is."

"Oh, I am."

Twenty-five

Cindy

They wanted to put distance between themselves and everyone they knew, with everything familiar, and they made their way up to Ocean Bay Park and Flynn's for dinner. The circular bar was alive with people, and they had to wait nearly thirty minutes for a table, but it was worth it. They dined on broiled bluefish and new potatoes. She had some Chablis, and he ordered ginger ale.

They made small talk until halfway through the meal when Danning dared meet her eyes. In jeans and a long-sleeved cotton sweater, she looked very young, very vulnerable, the most desirable woman he'd ever known. He wanted to tell her so.

"I thought you were angry with me," he said.

"I guess I was. I felt rejected."

"By me? Oh, God, no, that's not what it was. When I'm around you, I feel so inhibited, shackled. You make me feel as if I'm a shy, frightened boy again."

"You shy? I can't believe that about you."

"I've never been entirely comfortable around women."

"I guess I haven't been entirely comfortable with you,

295

either. Susan said I should be more aggressive, go after you."

"But you didn't."

"If you hadn't come around, I think I might have. Anyway, here we are."

He raised his glass. "To a good autumn."

They touched glasses. "Was it a good summer for you, Nick?"

"Meeting you, that was the best of it. And I had a lot of time alone."

"You enjoy being by yourself?"

"I needed the time to think. To consider what I wanted to do with the rest of my life. In the last few days, I've been given a choice."

"And?"

"Neil Morgan offered to help me get a job announcing football games. He made it sound like a sure thing."

"Neil knows a lot of people. Are you going to do it?"

"The money's good, it'll keep me at the center of things."

"The big time, you mean?"

"When I played ball, I had all the moves down pat, but I lacked the natural ability. I developed the look of a football star, but I never had the talent. Am I making sense? I knew what I was supposed to do, I knew how to do it, but I couldn't always pull it off. It's the same for me in broadcasting—I seemed always to be slightly off center, missing. Not by much, but enough to make people uneasy. To make myself uneasy. When I look back, I think that I might not belong behind a microphone."

"Maybe you don't."

A flash of resentment, tempered by the awareness that there was no hostility in her manner, no implied criticism.

"In that case, what do I do? Football's all I know, all I care about. Peddling athletic equipment, it's not the way I want to go."

"You spoke of a choice."

He shrugged it away. "A man I met out here—name of McMillan—he's principal of a high school on Long Island. He's looking for a football coach."

"That doesn't appeal?"

"It doesn't pay much, peanuts when compared to broadcasting or playing ball."

"You're not a player anymore." She said it plainly, without emphasis. It was a reminder—nothing more.

And again that flash of resentment, a building anger; it passed swiftly. "You think I ought to take McMillan up on his offer? Don't you understand? I was an All-American when I was in college. And in the pros, okay, I wasn't a star, but I was damn good. Damn good."

"And it's been downhill ever since. Maybe you're too good to bother with a bunch of high schoolers."

He stared at her for a long time, and her eyes never wavered. "Am I clinging too hard to the past?"

"Lots of us do. Maybe people have to hit bottom before they can bounce back."

"Is that what you did?"

She gave it to him straight. "Smack down on my fanny in the pits. If it can be done, I did it. All the stuff that looks so good and makes you feel so bad. I made a habit out of it, letting other people use me and abuse me, convinced it was all I deserved."

"And now?"

"I'm past it. I want to be past it. Not so long ago, I found myself sliding back into that same rotten scene. I caught on and pulled out."

"And now you're out for good?"

"I wish I could say that I am. I certainly want out, and I intend to try. But life's a day-to-day proposition, isn't it? Like football, you do your very best, and then some big strong linebacker takes you down and breaks your knee apart."

That made him grin. "What do you know about linebackers?"

"Only that they're obstacles to progress, whatever the game."

"I'm beginning to think you're a very wise lady."

"I'd like to be."

"What else would you like?"

She answered deliberately. "A friendly relationship

with a man who cares about me and whom I care about. A family."

"My wife . . . my ex-wife," he corrected. "Tiffany used to say I fell short in all those areas. She claimed I didn't give enough of myself."

"Is it true?"

"It was, then."

"And now?"

That slow, ironic grin faded across his face as he lifted her hand. "Who knows what ugly linebackers are lurking out there, waiting to blindside a man with two bad knees?" He kissed her hand lightly.

"As long as you're willing to give it your best shot . . ."

"My very best," he answered.

Halfway back to Ocean Beach, on the darkened path near the tennis courts in Seaview, they kissed, a lingering kiss that ended in a long, silent embrace. Neither of them spoke again until they reached her mother's house. Inside, they kissed again, a tentative exploration, as if about to enter an alien and ominous land. She was afraid, but through the fear she understood that she wanted to be with him in every possible way, to share his thoughts and his feelings, to experience his flesh at one with her own, to become part of him in every conceivable way.

She led him to her bedroom, undressing without a word, sliding quickly between the sheets to find him waiting for her. Under his hands, her flesh grew sensitized as never before. Every touch, every kiss, every stroke unloosed circles of warmth and spreading passion throughout her body. Locked against each other, they writhed and twisted, embracing with arm and leg, ending finally in a succession of inner explosions that gathered power, then diminished, only to grow again, dissolving at last in a series of weakening spasms.

"Never like this," she said, words muffled against his chest.

"No one made me feel so much."

"With you I'm replenished, made over, purified."

"There is so much feeling in me for you. To say I love you seems so mundane, inadequate."

"I love you, Nick," she whispered.

"I love you."

They made love again and slept and woke when first light seeped around the edges of the blinds, and made love once more. Huddled against each other, neither of them was willing to lose even a moment to sleep.

"It's over," he said. "The summer's over."

"What a beautiful way for it to end."

He paused, reluctant to put into words what he felt. He started to speak, broke off, and began again, coming from another angle. "What would you say if I were to take that coaching job?"

"Is it what you want?"

"I don't know. Oh, damn, I want something that belongs to me, something that's part of me, past and present, something I'm good at."

"You must know a great deal that you can give to those young boys."

"Yes, to give back. To share with them what I've already had, to prepare them—to teach them what it's like."

"You'd be a fine teacher, a fine coach."

After a moment, he said, "Will you come with me, live with me?"

She weighed her answer. "Not too fast, Nick. Time is what we need to find out how we feel about each other. A few months."

"Without you in my life, I'll expire on Long Island, never to be heard of again."

She laughed and rolled against him, kissing him affectionately. "There's always the Long Island Railroad. . . ."

"It never runs on time."

"And the parkways. I don't intend to let you get away from me."

"I was afraid—"

"Don't be. We'll see each other."

"Often?"

"Very often."

"How often is that?"

"Every weekend, if you want."

"And during the week—I'll come to New York."

"Or I'll come to you."

"I love you, Cindy."

"I love you, Nick."

He bore her back on the bed, locking her in place. "This," he gloated, "has been the best summer of my life."

"The very best?"

"The absolute cotton-pickin' ever-lovin' best summer, and I mean for it to go on for as long as I last."

"Me too," she said before he kissed her, and again afterward. "Me too . . ."

Twenty-six

Neil

At noon on the day after Labor Day, a biting wind began to blow in from the ocean, reshaping the beach, building up the dunes. Windows began to rattle, and Neil closed the shutters and later built a fire in the fireplace. By nightfall, rain began to fall, a cold slant that beat insistently against the seaward side of the house,

Neil made the evening meal: cheese omelet with chopped vegetables and pieces of bacon, toasted English muffins, coffee for Susan, milk for him. They sat on the floor in front of the fireplace with their backs against the sofa and ate off trays, wearing pajamas and bathrobes.

"You never stayed before," Susan said, "on the day after Labor Day. It was always back to the city for you, rushing to catch the death boat, back to work. I always stayed behind to close up the house by myself."

There was so much Neil had left behind in their relationship. For so long they'd lived separate lives, each of them proceeding separately, sharing very little. In some ways, Susan and he had remained strangers occupying the same spaces but seldom in contact with each other, seldom sharing anything of value. Even now, he had yet to tell her about his last encounter with BB, that her son, *their* son, had once again run away.

"Lately," he said, "I've been taking a long, hard look at myself, and I don't like what I see. I did a pretty good job of messing things up. Our lives, yours, mine, and BB's."

"You give yourself too much credit," she said, a tenderness in her voice he hadn't heard for years. "Your son and I, we certainly have made our very substantial contributions."

He put his tray aside and stared into the fire. "Changes," he said after a moment's contemplation. "Nothing is the same. My tennis game, it's been sliding downhill. Oh, it isn't the damn tennis I care about."

"You always loved to play."

"Yes, and I worked like a dog at it. Lessons, practice, staying in shape. But I was never any good, never loose and fluid enough, never really enjoying it, caring only about winning. I'll tell you something I never told anyone before. I would very carefully choose the people I played with. No one too good, no one who might make me look bad. Winning was so important. Even that doesn't help much anymore.

"My body no longer does what I tell it to do. It's changed, my body. A stranger's body, it belongs to someone else. Diet, exercise, massages; nothing helps. The changes are permanent, inside and out, and I don't like them." He stole a glance at Susan. "What I'm trying to say is that I'm not the man I used to be."

"When I met you," she said, speaking to the flickering flames, "you were a knight in shining armor. That man, Neil, didn't always live up to the image he presented. Now, a little dim of vision, not so sure of yourself, the armor, tarnished and dented, there's been a decided improvement."

He averted his eyes. "When you lose it in one area, you lose it in others as well."

She took his hand. "We've been through our share of bad times, my dear."

"There's more," he said, and told her about his meeting

with BB. "Was I wrong to give him the money, let him run away again?"

"I would've done the same, I suppose. He did steal the paintings, didn't he?"

"You figured it out, too? It was the only way he could find to strike back at me, to hurt me. I must've hurt him badly, failed him all along the line."

"He always wanted to surpass you, Neil."

"The way I wanted to outstrip my father."

"BB never found a way to do it."

"Sometimes I miss that old man. When he died . . ." Neil turned away.

Her arm went around him. "Are you crying?"

"I never cry."

"If you did cry, it would be all right."

He jerked around, anger on his face and tears in his eyes. He opened his mouth to speak, but no words came out. He wiped away the tears and drank some milk.

"I missed him, I said. That's enough."

"It's a beginning," she said, shifting closer to him, neither of them speaking or moving for a very long time.

"Tomorrow," he said. "Tomorrow I'll start working again. Streep and Paul Newman, how's that grab you for the leads? Both of them are interested. Newman says he'll do it if some script revisions are made. Huber won't like that, but I'm going ahead, anyway. This could be the best movie I ever made. Tomorrow's going to be a very busy day."

"Tomorrow," she said in dismissal. "There's still this night to be lived."

"What do you mean?" There was a quickening of his pulse, a growing tension in his limbs.

"I mean you and me, Neil. I want something more than we've had in our marriage for all these years. I've been so lonely for so long, and I've been looking for someone to be with, someone to fill the emptiness. I want my husband back, Neil."

"Oh, Susan, I want that, too. I never stopped wanting it. I never stopped loving you."

"There's a lot that happened, Neil, a lot to put aside, so much to forget."

"I'll make it just like it was in the beginning."

"Oh, no!" she protested. "That girl from the country no longer exists, and neither does that arrogant young man. Maybe we can make something different, something that's right for us as we are, if we both try hard enough. If you want that, too?"

"I do." He hesitated. "Is it all right if I kiss you?"

"Remember our first kiss?"

"You're right, I was arrogant. A kiss you'd never forget, I said."

"I never did forget it. Yes, it's all right if you kiss me. Kiss me the way you did then, Neil."

"Here on the floor? What if somebody walks in?"

"Let them," was her answer. "Let them all know what a fantastic lover my husband is. To hell with them!" She fell back, laughing, drawing him down with her, arms circling his neck.

"To hell with them!" he said aloud. "To hell with all of them!" And he kissed her, a kiss he was sure she'd never forget. Not ever.

A FAREWELL TO FRANCE
Noel Barber

"Exciting...suspenseful...Masterful Storytelling"
Washington Post

As war gathered to destroy their world, they
promised to love each other forever, though
their families were forced to become enemies.
He was the French-American heir to the famous
champagne vineyards of Chateau Douzy. She
was the breathtakingly sensuous daughter of
Italian aristocracy. Caught in the onslaught
of war's intrigues and horrors, they were
separated by the sacrifices demanded of them
by family and nation. Yet they were bound
across time and tragedy by a pledge sworn in
the passion of young love, when a beautiful
world seemed theirs forever.

"Involving and realistic...A journey to which
it's hard to say farewell...The backdrop of
World War II adds excitement and suspense."
Detroit News

Three Novels from the
New York Times Bestselling Author

NEAL TRAVIS

CASTLES 79913-8/$3.50
A woman reaches for her dream when she joins Castles, a prestigious international real estate firm, and follows her driving passion for life from the playgrounds of Bel Air to the boardrooms of New York. On her way to the top, there would be men who tried to keep her down, but one man would make her see the beautiful, extraordinary woman she was.

PALACES 84517-2/$3.95
The dazzling, sexy novel of a woman's struggle to the heights in Hollywood. Caught up in the fast international scene that burns up talent and dreams, fighting against power moguls who have the leverage to crush, she achieves fame and fortune at Palace Productions. Yet amid all the glamour and excitement in the celluloid world of illusions, she almost loses the one man whose love is real.

And now...

MANSIONS 88419-4/$3.95
Her first success—as Washington's top TV news personality—was ruined by a lover's betrayal. As wife to the young scion of the Mansion media empire, she was expected to sacrifice herself and her dreams. But if the world gave her a woman's choice between love and success, she gave the world a woman's triumph. And when real success was hers, she was ready for the man who offered her love.

AVON PAPERBACKS